ANIMAL SENSES

JODIE MANGOR

Rourke
Educational Media

rourkeeducationalmedia.com

Teaching Focus:

Have students locate the ending punctuation for sentences in the book. Count how many times a period, question mark, or exclamation point is used. Which one is used the most? What is the purpose for each ending punctuation mark? Practice reading these sentences with appropriate expression.

Before Reading:

Building Academic Vocabulary and Background Knowledge

Before reading a book, it is important to set the stage for your child or student by using pre-reading strategies. This will help them develop their vocabulary, increase their reading comprehension, and make connections across the curriculum.

1. Look at the cover of the book. What will this book be about?
2. What do you already know about the topic?
3. Let's study the Table of Contents. What will you learn about in the book's chapters?
4. What would you like to learn about this topic? Do you think you might learn about it from this book? Why or why not?
5. Use a reading journal to write about your knowledge of this topic. Record what you already know about the topic and what you hope to learn about the topic.
6. Read the book.
7. In your reading journal, record what you learned about the topic and your response to the book.
8. After reading the book complete the activities below.

Content Area Vocabulary

Read the list. What do these words mean?

cells
detect
echolocation
environment
interprets
mates
organs
prey
receptors
tentacles

After Reading:

Comprehension and Extension Activity

After reading the book, work on the following questions with your child or students to check their level of reading comprehension and content mastery.

1. What do animals use their senses for? (Summarize)
2. How does an animal's habitat affect its senses? (Infer)
3. What is an example of an animal sense that people don't have? (Asking Questions)
4. How do your senses compare to a bear's? (Text to Self Connection)
5. How can an animal's eyes and ears help us to figure out if they are a predator or prey? (Asking Questions)

Extension Activity

Pick an animal that you are interested in and research its senses. Which sense does it rely on the most? The least? How do its senses compare to yours? Draw a diagram of the animal, labeling each of its senses and what it uses them for.

TABLE OF CONTENTS

Sensing the World 4

Sight 8

Smell and Taste 12

Touch 18

Hearing 22

Special Senses 26

Glossary 30

Index 31

Show What You Know 31

Websites to Visit 31

About the Author 32

SENSING THE WORLD

Animals have senses to help them survive. Like humans, most animals can touch, taste, see, smell, and hear. Animals use their senses to find food, water, and shelter. They also use them to find each other, protect themselves, and escape danger.

Each sense is connected to one or more body parts called **organs**. Eyes, noses, tongues, skin, and ears are all sense organs. These organs collect information about an animal's **environment** and send it to the brain.

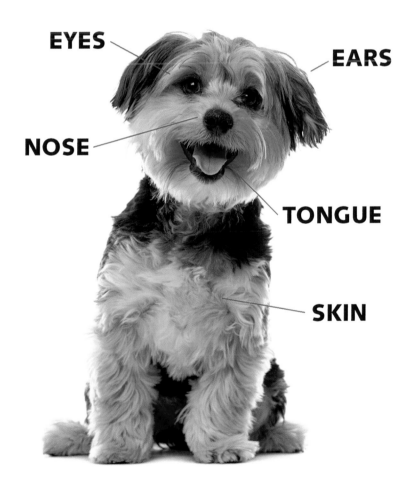

EYES

EARS

NOSE

TONGUE

SKIN

Animals live in a variety of habitats. Each type of animal has developed senses that help it survive in its particular habitat.

Get a Clue!
There are many types of ears, eyes, tongues, noses, whiskers and skin. These body parts give us clues about how an animal lives.

For example, a desert snake can sense its **prey,** a kangaroo rat, in the dark. But the kangaroo rat can hear the snake sliding toward it over the sand. Both are using their senses to help them survive.

Animals with large ears usually have excellent hearing.

SIGHT

Many animals rely on their sense of sight to get around. Some animals see fewer colors than humans. Some see more. Scientists think birds and butterflies might see 1,000 times more colors than humans!

Chameleons can move each of their eyes separately.

Scientists discovered that reindeer can see ultraviolet light. This makes some things, like the lichen they eat, look dark against the snow. It also helps the reindeer spot light-colored wolves from a long way off. Other Arctic mammals may also share this ability.

Human Vision

Bee Vision

Birds, butterflies, and bees can see patterns on flowers that human eyes cannot.

 **Invisible Light**

The colors we see come from waves of light. Ultraviolet (UV) light has wavelengths that are shorter than visible light. These waves are invisible to the human eye.

Birds of prey can see about three times better than people. A hawk can spot a rodent from 10,000 feet (3,048 meters) in the air. As the hawk dives down to catch it, it can reach speeds of 100 miles (160.93 kilometers) per hour and still keep the rodent in focus.

There's a saying: "Eyes on the side, born to hide; eyes on the front, born to hunt."

Eye See You

Hunters' eyes often face forward to target their prey. Prey animals usually have eyes on the sides of their head to see all around to watch for danger.

Animals that are active at night, such as cats, owls, and geckos, have eyes designed to see well in the dark. Their eyes are often large and have pupils that can get very wide. Inside their eyes, a special layer of **cells** acts like a mirror. These features help collect more light.

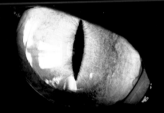 

Many nocturnal animals have pupils that close to form slits in the daylight.

SMELL AND TASTE

Smell and taste are important senses for finding food. Animals also use smell to locate **mates** and offspring, avoid enemies, and mark their territory. Taste can help an animal tell if something is poisonous.

A dog's sense of smell is 10,000 times more sensitive than a human's. A bear's sense of smell is even better. Black bears can smell food up to 18 miles (28.97 kilometers) away. Polar bears can smell a seal through 3 feet (1 meter) of snow.

Bears have much smaller brains than humans. But a much bigger area of a bear's brain is used for smell.

Smelling in Stereo

A rat's nostrils can work independently of each other. This allows the rat to figure out the direction a smell is coming from.

Most animals taste with their tongues. A tongue is covered with nerves, or taste buds. These send messages to the brain. The brain **interprets** the taste.

Tasty Toes
Butterflies taste with sense organs located on their feet. When they land, they immediately know if they're on something good to eat.

Humans have about 10,000 taste buds. Cats have about 500 taste buds. Chickens have just 24. Cows, on the other hand, have about 25,000. Their sense of taste helps them decide which plants are safe to eat.

Catfish can **detect** tiny amounts of food in dark, cloudy water. They have as many as 250,000 taste **receptors** spread over the surface of their bodies. Most are on the whiskers, also called barbels, around their mouth.

LET'S EXPERIMENT!

A dog needs to have a wet tongue to taste. Is this true for humans?

To find out, you'll need:

1. A pinch of salt and a pinch of sugar, mixed together
2. Optional: other dry foods (crackers, cereal, powdered milk, etc.)
3. A glass of water
4. Paper towel

What to do:

1. First, you'll need to dry off your tongue. You can do this by sticking your tongue out and panting or drying your tongue off with a paper towel.
2. Without putting your tongue back into your mouth, sprinkle the salt and sugar mixture onto your tongue.
3. Wait 5 seconds—can you taste anything?
4. Now bring your tongue back inside your mouth and let your saliva wash over it. How does this affect your ability to taste?
5. Sip some water to cleanse your mouth and repeat with other dry foods.

What's Happening?

Our taste buds convert some of the chemicals in food into electric signals that travel to the brain. They need liquid to do this.

TOUCH

An animal's sense of touch can help it find food and shelter. Touch can also help it move around in the dark.

Star-nosed moles spend almost all their time underground. Their nose **tentacles** have six times more touch receptors than a person's hand. These sensitive tentacles help them find their way.

Crocodiles have about 9,000 sensors around their heads, jaws, and bodies. The sensors can detect even the tiniest ripple in the water. They help crocodiles hunt prey.

Manatees have special hairs all over their bodies. These hairs can detect changes in water movement and temperature.

Wondrous Whiskers
Many mammals have whiskers. A cat's whiskers are very sensitive. They help it judge size and distance and feel slight shifts in the air.

LET'S EXPERIMENT!

How sensitive is your sense of touch? To find out, you'll need:

1. 5 different grades of sandpaper
2. Scissors
3. A marker
4. A blindfold

What to do:

1. Cut an index card-sized rectangle from the roughest grade of sandpaper. Using a marker, write "1" on the back.
2. Do the same for the second roughest grade, this time labeling the piece with a "2."
3. Do the same thing for the remaining three grades of sandpaper, labeling the pieces "3", "4", and "5", from rough to smooth.
4. Now put on a blindfold.
5. Mix up the pieces and turn them all rough side up.
6. Using your sense of touch, try to order the pieces from roughest to smoothest.
7. Take off your blindfold.
8. Flip over the pieces of sandpaper. Are their numbers ordered 1 to 5?
9. If this was easy, try a matching game: make a second set of sandpaper rectangles just like the first. Mix all 10 cards together, put on your blindfold and try to match up identical pairs.

Our fingertips have a strong sense of touch. But our sense of touch can become less sensitive when it is exposed to something for a long time. This is why we barely notice our clothes, glasses, or jewelry after wearing them for a while. Do you think this is an advantage or disadvantage?

HEARING

Animals use their hearing for many things: to sense danger, prey, and other animals. Humans only hear some of the sounds around us. Some animals, like mice, can hear in a higher range. Elephants and pigeons can detect sounds that are too low for people to hear.

Elephants use their ears, trunks, and feet to detect sounds 20 times lower than humans can hear. Elephants can send each other low-frequency messages. These can travel over long distances, as far as 3.7 miles (6 kilometers).

High Pitch

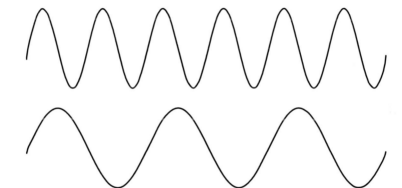

Low Pitch

 Fun Fact

Black grouse use low sounds to call to mates through dense forests. These birds can also hear the low rumble of a faraway thunderstorm.

An owl uses its hearing to find prey in the dark. One ear is set higher on the head than the other. This helps the owl know where a quiet sound, like a mouse rustling in the leaves, is coming from.

Prey animals such as rabbits and deer often have large ears that can move around. Their ears help them hear sounds from every direction.

Listen Up!

Like eyes, the direction an animal's ears face can tell us if that animal is prey or a predator. Predators have forward-facing ears. Prey animals have side-facing ears.

SPECIAL SENSES

Some animals have developed senses that humans don't have.

Sharks, platypuses, and some fish can sense the electric fields of other animals in the water. Some birds can sense Earth's magnetic field. They use it to find their way when migrating.

Most bats, whales, and dolphins use sound to track prey. First, they make a sound. The echo that bounces back gives them information about their surroundings. This is called **echolocation.**

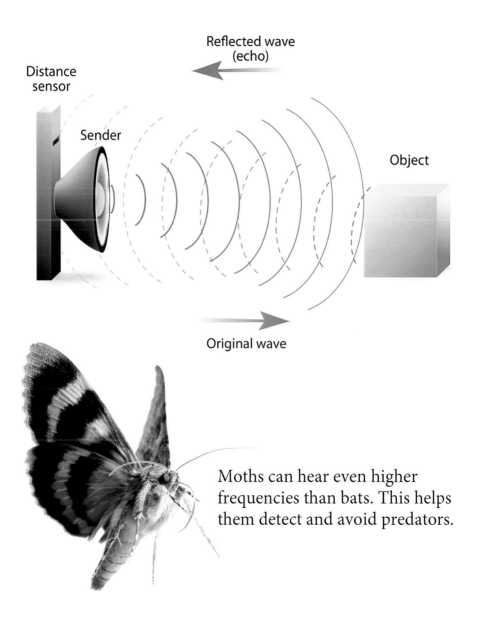

Reflected wave
(echo)

Distance
sensor

Sender

Object

Original wave

Moths can hear even higher frequencies than bats. This helps them detect and avoid predators.

Vampire bats drink the blood of other animals. They find their prey using a patch of skin on their face called a nose leaf. This organ can sense heat from another animal, and even help the bat zero in on a vein.

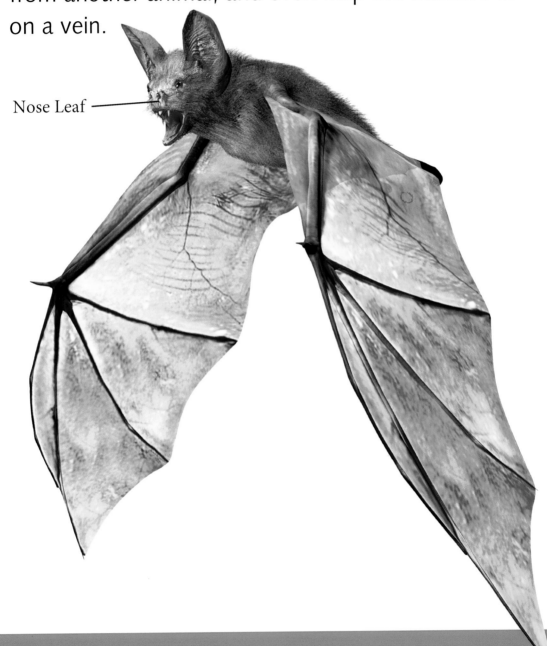

Nose Leaf

A blind cave fish can't see. It finds food using its lateral line organ. Many fish have this type of organ. It detects changes in water pressure. This allows the fish to feel nearby movements in the water.

Superior Senses

Compared to humans, many animals have amazing senses. Technologies such as virtual reality may give us the chance to experience the world through the senses of different animals.

GLOSSARY

cells (selz): the smallest units of an animal or a plant

detect (di-TEKT): to notice or discover something

echolocation (EK-oh-loh-KAY-shuhn): the ability to locate faraway objects by sending sound waves and sensing them as they bounce off the object

environment (en-VYE-ruhn-muhnt): the natural surroundings of living things, such as the air, land, or sea

interprets (in-TUR-prits): figures out what something means

mates (mates): the male or female partners of animals

organs (OR-guhns): parts of the body, such as the heart or the kidneys, that have a certain purpose

prey (pray): an animal that is hunted by another animal for food

receptors (ri-SEP-tors): nerves that detect a particular chemical or force

tentacles (TEN-tuh-kuhls): the long, flexible limbs of some animals such as jellyfish, octopuses, squid and sea anemones

INDEX

brain(s)   5, 13, 14, 17

echolocation   27

electric fields   26

hearing   7, 22, 24

organ(s)   5, 14, 28, 29

predators   25, 27

prey   7, 10, 19, 22, 24, 25, 27, 28

receptors   16, 18

sensors   19

sight   8

smell   4, 12, 13

taste buds   14, 15

touch   4, 18, 21

SHOW WHAT YOU KNOW

1. List some of the ways animals use their senses to survive.

2. Why do animals develop certain types of senses?

3. How do taste buds work?

4. What are some of the ways animals use their sense of touch?

5. Name a sense that some animals have, but people don't.

WEBSITES TO VISIT

www.faculty.washington.edu/chudler/amaze.html

www.kids.nationalgeographic.com/animals

www.sciencenewsforstudents.org/article/sense-danger

ABOUT THE AUTHOR

Jodie Mangor writes magazine articles and books for children. She is also the author of audio tour scripts for high-profile museums and tourist destinations around the world. Many of these tours are for kids. She lives in Ithaca, New York, together with Mishka the dog, Olaf the crested gecko, Pippo the cat, and her family.

Meet The Author!
www.meetREMauthors.com

PHOTO CREDITS: Cover and title page: ©animalnige; table of contents: ©Andrea Izzotti; p.4: ©UrosPoteko; p.5, 10: ©GlobalP; p.6: ©Oktay Ortakcioglu; p.7: ©YasserBadr.Bennthere; p.8: ©Milan Lipowski; p.9: ©Dr Schmitt, Weinheim Germany, ©arlindo71; p.10: ©Steve Mcsweeny; p.11: ©Ekaterina Shvigert; p.12: ©nicholas belton; p.13: ©David Yang, ©MikeSPb; p.14: ©purple_queue, ©KirsanovV; p.15: ©LPETTET; p.16: ©abadonian; p.18: ©Dieter Meyrl; p.19: ©Carlos Alvarez; p.20: ©fmajor, ©shaunl; p.22: ©Johan Swanepoel; p.23: ©MikeLane45; p.24: ©Vasiliki Varvaki; p.25: ©Voren1; p.26: ©RamonCarretero; p.27: ©ttsz, ©Antagain; p.28: ©Geerati; p.29: Public Doman, ©Daniel Chetroni

Edited by: Keli Sipperley
Cover design by: Rhea Magaro-Wallace
Interior design by: Kathy Walsh

Library of Congress PCN Data

Animal Senses / Jodie Mangor
 (Science Alliance)
  ISBN 978-1-68342-350-8 (hard cover)
  ISBN 978-1-68342-446-8 (soft cover)
  ISBN 978-1-68342-516-8 (e-Book)
 Library of Congress Control Number: 2017931194

Rourke Educational Media
Printed in the United States of America,
North Manchester, Indiana

**Power,
Empire
Building, and
Mergers**

Power,
Empire
Building, and
Mergers

Stephen A. Rhoades

LexingtonBooks

D.C. Heath and Company
Lexington, Massachusetts
Toronto

Library of Congress Cataloging in Publication Data
Rhoades, Stephen A.
    Power, empire building, and mergers.

    Includes index.
    1. Consolidation and merger of corporations—United States. 2. Indus-
trial concentration—United States. 3. Power (Social sciences) 4. Industry
and state—United States. I. Title.
HD2746.5.R48 1983   338.8'3'0973   82–49255
ISBN 0–669–06439–4

Published simultaneously in Canada

Printed in the United States of America

International Standard Book Number: 0–669–06439–4

Library of Congress Catalog Card Number: 82–49255

To my wife, Sharon

Contents

	Preface and Acknowledgments	ix
Chapter 1	Introduction	1
Chapter 2	The Problem in Perspective	5
Chapter 3	Competitive Capitalism at Work: A Microeconomic View	11
Chapter 4	Business in Pursuit of Profits: The Good and the Bad	19
Chapter 5	Is the Profit Motive Waning?	29
Chapter 6	The Drive for Power: Some Preliminaries	39
Chapter 7	Power as a Concept in Philosophy	45
Chapter 8	Power as a Concept in Psychology	53
Chapter 9	Mergers for Monopoly Profits	61
Chapter 10	The Antitrust Laws Harness the Drive for Profit	75
Chapter 11	A New Breed of Merger	81
Chapter 12	What Does the New Breed of Merger Accomplish?	89
Chapter 13	The Power Motive Revealed along with Other Costs of Mergers	103
Chapter 14	Let Power Beget Power: A Proposed Blueprint for Monolithic Capitalism	121
Chapter 15	Let Power Beget Power: A Catch	133
Chapter 16	An Alternative Blueprint for U.S. Capitalism	143
Chapter 17	Conclusion	151
	Index	155
	About the Author	159

Preface and Acknowledgments

My research during the past ten to fifteen years has convinced me that the desire for power—to build an empire—is the primary motivator of business executives and that mergers are the primary means of attaining power. The drive for power is largely responsible for the massive merger movement in this country since 1960. It has resulted in the disappearance of thousands of independent businesses in all sectors of the economy. These mergers are reshaping the basic structure of the U.S. economic system. The economy is moving away from *competitive* capitalism to *monolithic* capitalism—a system dominated by relatively few large, diversified companies. The long-run effects of this tendency on the economic and sociopolitical systems will be profound and in my opinion unattractive to most citizens. Some who support the move toward monolithic capitalism claim that it is inevitable, that technological requirements of modern industry dictate large, diversified firms with few competitors. The evidence, however, does not support that view.

The antitrust laws of the United States are intended to inhibit mergers and other business behaviors that are likely to have an adverse effect on the economic system. They are aimed at preventing those mergers that are likely to result in monopoly and the attendant monopoly profits and misallocation of resources. Current antitrust laws are predicated on economists' belief that all mergers are motivated by profits. Consequently, the antitrust laws are impotent as a constraint on mergers that are motivated by the desire for power but are not likely to result in monopoly profits. To the extent that mergers are, as I believe, motivated by the desire for power, merger activity will continue unabated as the evidence clearly shows it is doing. Though monopolies may not result from many of today's mergers, society will pay other important costs over the long run—both economically and sociopolitically. These costs will arise as the economy evolves from competitive capitalism to monolithic capitalism as a result of mergers.

Many noneconomists are unaware of the important issues raised by mergers. The reason is that macroeconomic issues and policies (for example, inflation, unemployment, interest rates, the money supply, and government spending) capture the headlines and provide the basis for short-term financial speculation. In contrast, microeconomic problems caused by mergers evolve very slowly and subtly. I am writing this book because of my concern that changes of a microeconomic nature are taking place that will have dire consequences for our society. The drive for power through mergers is the root of the problem. Until widespread attention is attracted to this problem, it will be impossible to get congressional support for remedial legislation. For that reason, this book is not directed strictly to an academic audience.

This is not another of the recently popular doomsday books. It is my opinion that under competitive capitalism private enterprise in the United States will assure a dynamic and technologically progressive economic system. If, however, we ignore the persistent drift toward monolithic capitalism brought on by mergers, there will certainly be a public outcry for direct control over business in this country. That would be a disaster, but it is not inevitable. New antitrust laws provide an alternative. Even though U.S. businessmen are generally opposed to the antitrust laws, these laws help to keep business private. They establish the rules of the business game in order to assure that the game is played in the best interests of society. These laws are a constraint on business, but within the laws business is free to compete vigorously without direct government controls or intervention. Unfortunately, existing antitrust laws are inadequate to prevent business behavior (mergers in particular) with adverse consequences that will someday lead to direct government intervention in the economic system. It is my view that new antitrust laws designed to constrain the desire for power are needed to assure that capitalism will remain dynamic and progressive and to keep government out of the marketplace.

Numerous people contributed to this book in one way or another. While I was a graduate student and during my early years as an economist, Willard Mueller and Douglas Greer stimulated my interest in the implications of mergers and diversification. Joe Cleaver has for many years provided moral support, encouragement, and antagonistic questions in connection with my research. Helpful comments on the manuscript were provided by Oscar Barnhardt, Douglas Greer, Margaret C. English, Donald Savage, and Alice White. Gerald Hanweck and my father made some very useful suggestions to me. Skillful editing was provided by Margaret Hunanian. My wife, Sharon, contributed with typing, encouragement, and useful suggestions. In addition, a number of bright, young students who have worked for me have helped maintain my enjoyment for research through their open and enthusiastic interest in my various research projects. These students include Grant MacEwan, Loren Weeks, Steve Anderson, Jack Campbell, Joe Dempsey, and Melanie Law, William Conner, and Katharine Lauer, all from Dartmouth College; Wagner Jackson and Michael Greene from Harvard University; Susan Kessler from Smith College; and Susan Altemus from Denison University. Art Buchwald graciously granted me permission to quote one of his newspaper columns. I extend my thanks and appreciation to all of these people.

I must also emphasize that my employer, the Federal Reserve Board, is not responsible for and does not necessarily share the views expressed herein. This book was written on my time without financial support.

Power,
Empire
Building, and
Mergers

1 Introduction

Capitalism in the United States is approaching a turning point. We are drifting relentlessly toward monolithic capitalism—a system ultimately dominated by a few very large, diversified companies. The government will be called upon to control these companies. Already there are calls for requiring the largest U.S. corporations to obtain charters from the federal government. This is the result of subtle but momentous changes taking place in the structure and organization of our economic system, which will cause profound changes in our sociopolitical system in the end. We have the means at our disposal to counteract these tendencies and to preserve competitive capitalism and our pluralistic society. To do so, it is essential to attract attention to the problem so that appropriate public policy will be adopted.

It may seem peculiar that a shift of such magnitude in our system would not be generally apparent. There are, however, three reasons for this. First, the drift toward monolithic capitalism is subtle. It is a change that can be likened to an incoming tide. It progresses rather slowly and it is not very dramatic. Only at the end of the process are we aware of what has occurred and the immensity of the changes that have been wrought.

Second, the problems with which I am concerned are *micro*economic in nature, but *macro*economic issues capture the daily headlines. This is no great surprise. Macroeconomics deals with such visible matters as inflation and unemployment, and macroeconomic policy works through the money supply, interest rates, and government spending. The issues and policies of macroeconomics can change sharply in a matter of weeks or even days—interest rates may leap upward, unemployment may surge, or the Federal Reserve Board may report a precipitous rise or fall in the money supply. The problems in the realm of microeconomics that I am outlining are manifested in the structure and organization of the hundreds and thousands of industries and firms that form the basic fabric of our economic system. On a day-to-day basis, the changes that take place in connection with these firms and industries are not awe inspiring. For example, how many people are aware when, on a given day, Gulf and Western Industries or U.S. Steel Corp. acquires some other company?

The third reason that fundamental changes taking place in our economic system are going unnoticed arises from economists' approach to analyzing microeconomic phenomena. A basic assumption in microeconomic theory is that business people are motivated strictly by profits. Business behaviors such as advertising, pricing, and mergers are all assumed to be in the pursuit of profits.

1

Consequently, if some dimensions of business behavior are not motivated by profits the traditional economic analysis and predicted implications of that behavior may be wrong. The business behavior that is leading us toward monolithic capitalism is not easily explained in terms of the profit motive.

It is my contention that business executives (and government officials) are motivated by the desire for power—power in the sense of control over people and events. The great twentieth-century philosopher Bertrand Russell has observed that "love of power is the chief motive producing the changes which social science has to study,"[1] and that "the fundamental concept in social science is Power, in the same sense in which Energy is the fundamental concept in physics." The failure to recognize this "has caused some of the principal events of recent times to be misunderstood."[2] The assumption that power is an important motivator of business executives provides a basis for explaining the behavior that is leading us toward monolithic capitalism. The desire for power in the economic arena seems likely to be manifested in the achievement of size, a wide range of operations, access to large-scale financing, and dramatic short-run changes in financial reports.

Mergers are made to order for satisfying the desire for power in business and are therefore the prime mover in the trend toward monolithic capitalism. Certain kinds of mergers have been largely preempted by the antitrust laws. These are the so-called horizontal mergers; that is, mergers between competing firms. Profit maximization provides a logical explanation for horizontal mergers. Economists can show that such mergers often create a monopolistic situation that results in higher prices and restricted output for consumers as well as higher profits for business. The antitrust laws were gradually shaped so that while profits remain as a driving force in capitalism, the profit drive is constrained or channeled away from gaining monopoly profits by way of horizontal mergers. Even with this constraint, merger activity in this country continues unabated. It simply takes a different form—that of the so-called conglomerate merger, which involves firms that are not direct competitors. Interestingly, conglomerate mergers are generally not consistent with the assumption of profit maximization in traditional microeconomic theory because they do not generally yield monopoly profits or an increase in efficiency which would also increase profits. Thus, analyses of such mergers, guided by the profit maximization axiom, yield no clear results. However, the conglomerate merger is consistent with the assumption that business executives are motivated by a desire for power. Indeed, the new wave of unfriendly takeovers—that is, the acquisition of companies in which management, and frequently owners, are opposed to the acquisition—provides a striking illustration of the drive for power. The unfriendly takeover is an adversary proceeding. One business executive is a winner and the other is a loser. The results of conglomerate mergers provide no indication that profits are the motive.

Until is is accepted that power, in addition to profit, is a motivator of business behavior, merger activity will lead the march into monolithic capitalism.

Existing antitrust laws, which were originally formulated out of concern about the consolidation of resources as well as the formation of monopolies, remain useful for impeding the drive for monopolies and monopoly profits through merger. Unfortunately, the narrow emphasis on the monopoly-profit effect of mergers renders the laws next to useless in halting mergers that consolidate resources yet have no predictable effect on prices and profits, according to traditional models of microeconomic theory. Conglomerate mergers will continue to take place outside the scope of the antitrust laws and the U.S. economy will gradually be transformed into a system of fewer and larger diversified firms—monolithic capitalism.

There are two ways of dealing with the trend toward monolithic capitalism. One is to follow the prescription of John Kenneth Galbraith. Essentially this involves doing nothing. Galbraith contends that monolithic capitalism is inevitable. He arrives at this conclusion by arguing that "technological imperatives" of modern industrial society require ever larger firms and fewer competitors in order to cope with the risk in investment and research in increasingly sophisticated products. But we are told not to worry. As business power and influence increases, government can offset this power—an application of Galbraith's concept of countervailing power. Unfortunately, the noneconomic (as well as the economic) implications of Galbraith's scenario are highly unattractive. For one thing, it means increased power in government. It means far more direct government intervention in the economic system. Most fundamental of all is that as the economic system changes from competitive capitalism to monolithic capitalism, other major institutions in society must change accordingly. The pluralistic philosophy of society in the United States is thoroughgoing. The emphasis on individualism and the diffusion of power is apparent in the structure and function of the federal government, the economic system, local government, and in our educational system. If we encourage or even allow the development of monolithic capitalism, the nature of the other institutions must, in time, change as well. This would be the first step toward a profound change in the philosophical foundation or our society.

Since all available evidence indicates that the trend toward monolithic capitalism is not a technological imperative, there is another and better way to deal with the problem. That is to adopt an appropriate antitrust policy. The present antitrust policy has been fairly effective in channeling the profit motive so that it remains as a driving force but its adverse consequences aimed at obtaining monopoly profits are impeded. What we must do now is develop an entirely new set of antitrust laws (to complement, not replace, existing laws) that are based on the recognition that business behavior is motivated by a desire for power. Such a policy would not and should not emasculate the power drive; it is, along with profits, a driving force in our free-enterprise system. But the drive must be constrained. Just as the profit drive leads to the attempt to create monopolies, the power drive leads to the grasp for control and power over more economic resources. This policy approach to the control of the power drive will preserve the dynamic elements of capitalism, and will also preserve the kind of institutional arrangements in the economic and sociopolitical systems that are consistent with a pluralistic society.

Business is traditionally opposed to antitrust policy, but if business is to remain reasonably free over the long run we must rely on antitrust policy. This is the only way we can preserve competitive capitalism and avoid direct government involvement in business decisions. Assuredly the growth of monolithic capitalism will elicit a popular demand for government to offset and control business power. I for one would not want to see that. The keys to the preservation of competitive capitalism are the recognition that power, in addition to profits, motivates business behavior, and the development of widespread public awareness of the problem and its implications.

Notes

1. Bertrand Russell, *Power: A New Social Analysis* (New York: Barnes and Noble, 1962), p. 11.

2. Ibid., p. 9.

2 The Problem in Perspective

Popular attention to economics has focused on macroeconomic problems and issues, such an inflation and interest rates, which are associated with the economy in the aggregate. Most people know that a decrease in the discount rate, an increase in the money supply, or an increase in government spending all tend to stimulate economic activity or cause inflation. In contrast, few people are familiar with microeconomic problems (for example, market concentration and aggregate concentration) or with microeconomic policy such as enforcement of antitrust law. Many reasonably well-informed people can tell you that the nation's money supply, a basic tool of macroeconomic policy, is controlled by the Federal Reserve Board. However, it is a safe bet that few could say who administers the antitrust laws, a basic tool of microeconomic policy. (The answer is the Department of Justice and the Federal Trade Commission.) This lack of knowledge is unfortunate because the problems and issues of microeconomics are connected with the basic fabric of an economic system. There are several explanations for the unfamiliarity with microeconomics among educated noneconomists.

I suspect that most people familiar with macroeconomics have taken an introductory course on economics in college. Although these courses cover microeconomics as well as macroeconomics, a student's formal education in the former is not reinforced in newspapers and periodicals. Furthermore, textbooks on money and banking are devoted primarily to the role of money in macroeconomic theory. At best, microeconomics is dealt with by describing the Federal Reserve System, or explaining bank income statements and balance sheets and the simple mechanical shuffling of checks, currency, and coin around the country. Rarely do authors try to develop microeconomic theory, which could be used to analyze the nature of the competitive interrelationships that determine the prices and services provided by banks and other thrift institutions. The result is that there is, from an analytical standpoint, no *banking* in a course on money and banking. It is also interesting that courses on industrial organization, the microeconomic counterpart to money and banking, are not required of undergraduate majors in business administration in many schools. Yet a course in money and banking is widely required.

The failure of undergraduate education to create awareness of microeconomic issues probably indicates that economists themselves have relegated microeconomics to stepchild status. This could be because of the fact that macroeconomics is in some respects an easier subject for study. Certainly the

5

issues that it deals with are topical because measures of macroeconomic phenomena can change rapidly. Its major problems are relatively few and highly visible.
Similarly, the policies traditionally used to combat these problems are highly
visible, few in number, and their implementation is theoretically (although not
necessarily politically) straightforward. Further, these policies are changed frequently and they often alter short-term investment opportunities, which gives
them a lot of appeal in a society that seems preoccupied with short-term financial performance. These policies include fiscal policy, in which the federal
government uses taxation and spending to directly affect aggregate demand
(spending by government, consumers, and businesses), and monetary policy, in
which the Federal Reserve Board uses the money supply to control interest rates
or the amount of money available, thereby affecting aggregate demand. Finally,
money and notoriety comes to those who are willing to make pronouncements
regarding interest rates and GNP over the next few weeks or months.

In contrast, microeconomic problems are neither so highly visible nor so
uniform across the industries and institutions that make up the economic
system. The problems of microeconomics tend to emerge slowly and are manifested only in the long run. The implementation of microeconomic policies is
complex, even theoretically. Nevertheless, it is essential to focus attention on
microeconomic issues to provide the basis for sound long-run economic policy
in this country.

There is another explanation for the neglect of microeconomics. This is a
tribute to the tremendous influence of John Maynard Keynes's book on macroeconomics, *The General Theory of Employment, Interest and Money*, which
appeared during the Great Depression.[1] It attracted little serious professional
interest among economists at first, but the thoughtful interpretations of this
book by Dudley Dillard and Alvin Hansen helped Keynes's ideas take the economics profession by storm after the economic and academic disruptions of
World War II.[2] Keynes's work dominated the profession for the next twenty-five
years, and not surprisingly so. The book was rich with ideas for hypothesis testing, so it generated much research and many published papers. Furthermore, the
theory and policy developed by Keynes appeared to provide the prescription for
some of the most serious economic ills of society. His ideas seemed to offer the
prospect of ending, or at least ameliorating, the business cycle that carries us
into inflation and then into recession or depression.

Keynes's influence did not remain confined to academics. With an emphasis
on active government involvement in the economic system, especially through
government spending and taxation, Keynes's ideas eventually became the re-
spected and trusted credo of liberal policymakers. To be an adherent of Keynesian economics was to be a right-thinking (no pun intended), socially sensitive
individual. Indeed, Keynesian economics became a fashionable topic for discussion among U.S. presidents and congressmen starting with the Kennedy administration. Keynesian-style macroeconomic theory and policy reached their

golden age during the 1960s. Under President Kennedy, government policies of spending and taxation appeared to effectively stimulate growth in the economy, maintain a high level of employment, and avoid inflation all at once. The Keynesian cure gave every indication of being the correct one. The Johnson administration pursued the economic policies of its predecessor.

The cure, however, began producing undesirable side effects in the late sixties and early seventies. Inflation and unemployment increased simultaneously—impossible according to the Keynesian formula. At first, the adherents of Keynesianism attributed these problems to the distortions of the Vietnam War and to misguided policy under President Johnson. It was said that the economic system had simply been pushed beyond the limits of available resources with the "guns and butter" policy of the Johnson administration. By the early seventies, the most severe economic stresses of the Vietnam War had largely disappeared, yet the two supposedly antithetical problems of inflation and high unemployment intensified. In spite of this evidence, many economists maintained their faith in Keynes and devoted their energies to refining and developing the Keynesian macroeconomic model.

The persistence of the problems of inflation and unemployment led to a spreading rebellion within the profession, and an increasing number of economists began to accept, at least tentatively, an alternative to Keynesian policy. This alternative is called *monetarism*. The basic idea of monetarism is that control of the money supply by the Federal Reserve Board, rather than fiscal policy through government spending and taxation, is the appropriate policy for influencing overall economic performance. Monetarism is not new, although it has only recently achieved wide acceptance. Milton Friedman, a recent Nobel prize winner in economics, has advocated it for years.

With the apparent failure of Keynesian policy and the unflagging efforts of Friedman, monetarism is finally receiving attention beyond academic circles. Beginning with Richard Nixon, U.S. presidents have publicly acknowledged the importance of controlling the money supply in order to cure inflation. Perhaps even more important in the implementation of monetarism as a tool of macroeconomic policy, chairmen of the Federal Reserve Board have at least partially supported the monetarist approach. Arthur Burns, who chaired the Board throughout most of the 1970s, increasingly leaned toward the monetarist position, although he remained somewhat skeptical. His skepticism was reflected by the Board's continued focus on achieving interest rates, through open-market operations and discount-rate policy, that would encourage or discourage consumer and business spending.

Monetarists would urge that the money supply, not interest rates, deserved strict attention. The Federal Reserve Board can, at least theoretically, control either interest rates or the money supply, but not both at once. Nevertheless, the seed of monetarism had been planted; the idea began to receive consideration in monetary policy under Burns.

Some believe it was Paul Volcker, appointed as chairman of the Federal Reserve Board by President Carter in 1979, who gave monetarism formal sanction. In October of 1979, the board issued a statement indicating that henceforth it would seek to control the money supply by controlling bank reserves and let interest rates go where they might. Throughout 1980, interest rates fluctuated dramatically. The prime rate reached an all-time peak of 21 percent in April and fell to 11 percent in July. By February of 1981, the prime rate had risen to 21.5 percent.

The basic money supply has fluctuated widely on a weekly basis rather than growing at a slow, steady rate to accommodate growth in the economy, as would be required under monetarism. Thus, adherents of monetarism argue that the monetarist approach has not been given a fair test. Perhaps, however, this experience demonstrates that strict control of growth in the money supply within a specified range is not technically feasible over short periods, although the longer-run average (one or two years) might conform to growth targets. The answer is not clear. What is clear is that macroeconomic policy in the United States, of either the Keynesian or the attempted monetarist variety, continues to be woefully ineffective in influencing overall economic performance. We are well into the decade of the 1980s and we are still facing relatively high inflation and high unemployment.

With continuing apparent macroeconomic problems, and with two relatively tidy theoretical and policy alternatives, professional and popular attention have remained preoccupied with macroeconomics. The neglect of microeconomics is remarkable considering that the problems we are observing and trying to correct with macroeconomic policy may very well have microeconomic origins. For example, the powerful labor unions that monopolize the labor supply for automobile production have been cited as partly responsible for the U.S. automobile industry's lack of cost competitiveness with the Japanese because of the large wage settlements unions have imposed upon the industry. An example at a local, more personal level suggests the pervasiveness of this microeconomic problem. The bargaining power of the union representing the bus drivers and subway personnel in Washington, D.C.'s new Metro system has pushed fares so high (even though the system is subsidized) that it is cheaper for a commuter to carpool and pay high parking fees and transportation costs than to ride the buses and subways. Such wage agreements result in higher prices and the observation of the apparently, macroeconomic problem of inflation. However the basic problem is microeconomic—a problem of labor-market power created by unions. In many instances, an industry creates what is called product-market power—the situation in which there are few firms in an industry, and they decide that it is in their best interest to band together (like a union) and charge consumers a high price rather than compete with one another. This has the same effect on prices as the labor-market power created by unions. Here again, as the result of a microeconomic problem we observe the apparent macroeconomic problem of inflation. If, in fact, the problems on the macroeconomic level are a reflection of problems on the microeconomic level, than macroeconomic policies are doomed to failure until the microeconomic problems are isolated and addressed.

There is an even more important reason for concern over the lack of attention paid microeconomics. The institutional and organizational arrangements of an economic system, which are the subject of microeconomics, largely determine the performance of businesses (in terms of prices, efficiency, productivity, and so forth). More broadly, they determine the sociopolitical makeup of the society. Although the institutional and organizational arrangements of the economic system are based upon the society's philosophical disposition, over the long run they influence both the society's philosophical disposition and the structure of other institutions in the society. The arrangements of the U.S. economic system both reflect and sustain the long-standing philosophy of a pluralistic society, with its emphasis on individual freedoms within the political and social systems. Consistent with this philosophy, economic activity in the United States is organized according to competitive capitalism, in which the means of production and economic power are fairly widely dispersed.

I am concerned that we are drifting away from competitive capitalism toward monolithic capitalism—a system of very large corporations and industries that are dominated by a few large, diversified companies. This may be happening partly because most people are simply unaware of just how important institutional arrangements (one of the subjects of microeconomics) are in the economic system. These arrangements affect not only economic performance but also the entire sociopolitical system. Unfortunately, several eminent economists, most notably John Kenneth Galbraith, have heralded this movement away from competitive capitalism as both desirable and inevitable. With the increased role of government in society, their views are quite fashionable. However, when the institutional arrangement of the economic system is not viewed in isolation; when, instead, its interdependence with the sociopolitical system is considered, the implications of this decline of competitive capitalism (and its underlying philosophy of individualism and pluralism) will be seen. The implications for the sociopolitical system are probably unattractive, or even unacceptable, to most U.S. citizens. Even if the economic system is considered in strict isolation, no available research evidence supports the view that the move toward monolithic capitalism is inevitable or will improve economic performance. It is my contention that the persistent movement away from competitive capitalism toward monolithic capitalism will eventually harm economic performance, if it has not already. Furthermore, it will have serious implications for the sociopolitical system.

Notes

1. John Maynard Keynes, *The General Theory of Employment, Interest and Money* (New York: Harcourt, Brace and Co., 1936).

2. Dudley Dillard, *The Economics of John Maynard Keynes* (New York: Prentice-Hall, Inc., 1948); and Alvin H. Hansen, *A Guide to Keynes* (New York: McGraw–Hill Book Co., Inc., 1953).

3

Competitive Capitalism at Work: A Microeconomic View

Many years ago Thomas Malthus (1766-1834) dubbed economics the "dismal science." I do not think his phrase accurately characterizes economics today. Macroeconomic issues are constantly in the headlines. They consume much of the energy of U.S. presidents. Their importance has become strikingly apparent to the average citizen, with the recent double-digit inflation, 21-percent interest rates, a scarcity of energy resources (for whatever reason), and an unpredictable, perverse stock market. No, economics is not the dismal science any longer. In this book, I am attempting to highlight important microeconomic issues. To place the subject in perspective, I shall present some basic concepts of micro-economic theory. This is preceded by a brief description of economics in general and the differences between the capitalist and socialist economic mechanisms.

Essentially, economics deals with the manner in which a society's scarce resources (land, labor, and capital) are allocated for different uses. Economists attempt to develop a logical analytical framework to explain such things as why and how more small cars and fewer large cars are being produced, why more chickens and fewer beef cattle are being raised, and why more government spending often fuels inflation. There are two fundamentally different institutional frameworks for allocating resources in a society—capitalism and socialism.

Under capitalism, consumers and producers interact directly to determine what and how much business will produce; businesses determine how to produce whatever consumers want them to produce. The way this system of resource allocation works is that the consumers indicate to producers what goods and services they want more than others through their expenditures, or dollar votes, and the producers respond by offering more or less of these various goods and services in order to capture the profits from the consumers' dollar votes. Resources are allocated from the production of one product to the production of another as businesses attempt to supply what consumers demand.

Under socialism, an additional institution is heavily involved in the resource-allocation mechanism—the government. In this considerably less direct approach, the government acts as an intermediary. Government bureaucrats (perhaps highly skilled technicians, but bureaucrats nonetheless) attempt to evaluate consumer demand for various goods and services, and then they assign different production quotas to various industries based on their estimates of the total amount of resources available for allocation. In addition, because a socialist government directly participates in the resource-allocation process, it can divert resources to the production of whatever goods and services its leaders decide are in the best interests of society more easily than a capitalist government can. In short, under capitalism, private institutions are the primary determinants of resource allocation; under socialism, government is the primary controller of resources. Because this book is concerned with evolving problems of capitalism, the discussion of microeconomic concepts will focus on the theory developed to explain the resource-allocation process within the institutional framework of capitalism.

Microeconomic theory is one of two major branches of economics. The other is macroeconomic theory. Whereas macroeconomic theory deals with the function and performance of the economic system as a whole, microeconomic theory deals with the components of the system that ultimately influence its overall performance. Microeconomics deals with how alternative institutional and organizational arrangements affect the allocation of resources. It involves the analysis of the institutions in the economic process—businesses, industries (groups of businesses), workers, and consumers—and the way in which these institutions are organized. A company may be very large or very small; it may be organized as the producer of a single product or service or many different products or services. An industry may be composed of one company (a monopoly) or many competing companies. Workers may be organized in groups such as labor unions, or they may offer their labor services individually. A primary goal of the student of microeconomics is to determine the implications of different institutional and organizational arrangements in the economy for the allocation of the society's scarce resourcess. It is my concern that institutional and organizational relationships in the system are changing in a manner that will undermine the basis of competitive capitalism and a pluralistic society.

The broad outline of modern microeconomic theory can be traced to Adam Smith's superb classic, *The Wealth of Nations,* (1776).[1] Smith outlined a theory designed to explain how a capitalist economic system provides and allocates the goods and services wanted by the inhabitants of a country. The capitalist system is based on private ownership of productive resources—land, capital, and labor. Land and capital are owned by private businesses or individuals and labor services are owned by individuals. The system requires these three basic productive resources in varying quantities and qualities. For example, agriculture uses a lot of land but relatively little labor and capital, whereas steel production requires a lot of capital but relatively little land and labor. The computer industry requires highly trained labor; the trucking industry needs unskilled labor. The basic goal of the economic system is to allocate the great variety of scarce resources in order to supply the goods and services needed and wanted by the society. This is the supply side of the economic system. There is a demand side of the system as well, which is essential to the process of resource allocation.

The demand side of the capitalist economic system also relies on the private sector. Thus, capitalism is based on a concept that economists call *consumer sovereignty.* Individual consumers, via their spending patterns, tell producers what and how much they want produced. The automobile industry provides a recent, vivid example of the effects of consumer sovereignty. Many consumers have stopped buying large automobiles; inventories of these large cars have built up, and Detroit is involved in an unprecedented effort to convert its productive capacity to small, fuel-efficient automobiles. This is very simply the producers' response to consumer demand through a dollar vote. Although the federal government has nudged the automobile industry to produce smaller cars by mandating specific miles-per-gallon requirements, consumer demand for Japanese cars has forcefully shoved the U.S. companies into the production of small automobiles. It is apparent that consumer sovereignty is affecting the use of resources in this industry.

The private ownership of productive resources and the concept of consumer sovereignty are basic elements of a capitalist economic system. One more element must be added—the motivation of businesspeople. The profit motive, or profit maximization, has been a basic assumption in the technical, analytical development of microeconomic theory since Adam Smith developed the broad outlines of that theory. There had to be some reason why people would invest their time and energy and risk their money in building facilities and hiring employees to produce a product. The prospect of financial gain—profits—was seen as the producer's primary motivator. The interrelationship of the three basic elements of a capitalist system—private property, consumer sovereignty, and profit maximization—were succinctly summed up by Smith in his observation that each individual, in pursuing his own self interest, is "led by an invisible hand" to a course of action that promotes the general social welfare.[2]

Smith's insights into the functioning of a capitalist system were remarkable. It is perhaps even more remarkable that Smith recognized, at that very early stage of modern capitalist development, how various organizational arrangements of producers could exist within the basic framework of capitalism. He realized that some organizational arrangements might benefit society less than others. The key difference among the alternative arrangements is very simply the number of producers in an industry. The arrangement that Smith regarded as most beneficial to society is that of pure competition. Under this organizational arrangement, each industry is composed of many different producers, none of which dominates the industry, and labor monopolies (unions) do not exist.

The beneficial effect of the competitive organization of industries in the system is twofold. First, because there are many sources of each product or service, producers are forced to charge a competitive price. This price covers cost of production and provides enough return to keep the capital from being moved into the production of other goods or services. The competitive price is forced upon producers because if any one producer tries to charge a higher price, he will be unable to sell his product. Consumers will simply go to other producers who are charging the competitive price. A further benefit of the competitive system of capitalism is that all producers must strive to keep production costs as low as possible, and this includes resisting the wage demands of labor. If a producer does not minimize costs, he will be unable to charge a price as low as that of his competitors and will be driven out of business. The drive for cost minimization under competitive capitalism encourages producers to constantly seek out methods of reducing production costs through invention and innovation. This leads to technological progress, increased productivity, and ultimately a higher material standard of living in the society.

Smith expressed concern about the implications of the alternative organizational arrangements for the economic system. These other arrangements, monopoly and oligopoly, differ in number of producers. Monopoly, at the opposite extreme from pure competition, is an arrangement in which an industry has only one producer. Smith expressed his concern with monopoly very concisely, observing that, "The price of monopoly is upon every occasion the highest which . . . can be squeezed out of the buyers."[3] The consumer has no alternative place to shop, and thus little constraint is placed on the price charged by the monopolist. In addition, the monopolist has little incentive to minimize costs with existing production facilities and little incentive to innovate and increase productivity. High costs can be passed along to consumers in the form of higher prices.

The potential for monopolistic pricing behavior is not just a theoretical abstraction. It is quite evident upon a casual glance at the world around us today. Take, just for example, the situation of a monopolist car dealer. Imagine what you would pay for a new automobile if there were only one dealer in town. You would, in all likelihood, pay the full list price because there is little if any reason for a dealer with no competitors to charge anything less. Yet, the fact is that the list price on conventional automobiles is typically anywhere from $800 to $2,000 above the dealer's cost. As your own experience has probably shown you, by shopping among several dealers you can easily purchase a car for substantially less than the list price; often for a couple of hundred dollars over dealer cost. So it seems wise to heed Smith's concern with monopoly.

Relatively few instances of pure monopoly exist in U.S. industry today. Of course, utilities and telephone services are generally exceptions, but these are special cases where the government has, for sound economic reasons, awarded a monopoly. In these cases, the government has recognized the pricing power of monopolies and therefore regulates the prices that these monopolists charge.

Although few monopolies exist, many situations in U.S. industry fall between the extremes of monopoly, with only one producer, and pure competition, with many producers. The situation in which an industry has a few producers is called an oligopoly. Smith recognized this possible form of organizational arrangement under capitalism and worried that the outcome would probably be more like that under a monopoly than like that under pure competition. The profit motive provides strong incentive for producers to coordinate or collude in establishing prices—to establish a common front. By agreeing on a price rather than competing for customers with lower prices, the producers in an industry can earn monopoly profits. This type of producer behavior is generally feasible only if an industry has a relatively small number of producers—an oligopoly.

The importance of the number of producers in determining whether firms in an industry charge a monopolistic or competitive price appeals to common sense as illustrated by a simple analogy. Imagine yourself in a room with one or two other people. Then suppose that you are asked to agree on a mutually satisfactory dinner menu or agree on what card game to play. I suspect that most of you would be able to reach agreement fairly quickly. Suppose, however, that you are in the same room but with fifteen or twenty other people rather than just one or two. Again, you are asked to agree on the menu for dinner or a specific card game. Even though you all would have an incentive to reach an agreement—a good meal or some fun—I think it is a safe guess that you would have more trouble getting this many people to agree. Smith recognized the incentive (profits), and thus the potential for collective efforts by producers to reach pricing agreements that would yield monopoly profits for all. He observed that, "People of the same trade seldom meet together, even for merriment or diversion, but the conversation ends in a conspiracy against the public, or in some contrivance to raise prices."[4]

Smith's observation makes businessmen sound rather evil. The inclination to collude is made to seem immoral. But the simple fact is that profits provide a strong incentive for producers to avoid price competition. If they operate in an industry with relatively few producers, such collusion becomes feasible. It is, in other words, rational economic behavior. It is apparent that the profit motive, which gives us new products, new technology, and increased productivity, can have undesirable effects.

A striking example in recent history of the conditions for and practice of successful price collusion is provided by the Organization of Petroleum Exporting Countries (OPEC). This example also illustrates the incentive and benefits to be achieved by participants in a collusive price arrangement. Only a few countries are significant exporters of petroleum—thus one condition necessary for successful collusion is met. These countries also control production of a product that is needed or desired. Of course, if the product were not needed or strongly desired, consumers would resist higher prices by simply not purchasing the product. In 1970, while the petroleum-producing nations were still competing, a barrel of oil sold for about $3.00. After OPEC agreed on a formal cartel in 1974, prices rose dramatically and continued to rise throughout the decade. By 1982, a barrel of oil sold for about $35.00. As part of the cartel agreement, the participants consciously limit output of petroleum so that the artificial monopoly price will hold. The financial gain and thus the incentive for collusion is obvious. Perhaps the biggest surprise about the whole OPEC experience is that it took the participants so long to recognize the potential in their situation and to act upon it.

Collusion among producers in an industry is rational, profit-motivated behavior. Unfortunately, monopolist behavior, whether by a single monopolist or by several producers in collusion, results in pricing and resource allocation that are rarely in the best interest of society at large. Not only do consumers pay higher prices (as OPEC so vividly demonstrates), in addition, inadequate economic resources are devoted to such industries because producers have to restrict output (also demonstrated by OPEC) to keep prices above the competitive level. The development and implementation of inventions and innovations may also suffer.

At this point, you have probably noticed an apparent contradiction. On the one hand, I have extolled the virtues of competitive capitalism and the material benefits to society arising from the drive for profits. On the other hand, I have noted that the prospect of increasing profits provides the incentive for producers to collude and charge a monopoly price; and I noted that in many industries the number of producers is small enough that collusion is feasible. To allay any confusion, a few words on an important form of microeconomic policy—the antitrust laws—are warranted. These laws are intended to preserve the profit motive's beneficial effects (low prices, low costs, and technological progress) in competitive capitalism and to inhibit the undesirable effects such as price collusion. The likelihood of price collusion has not gone unrecognized nor been neglected at policy levels. The antitrust laws of the United States, in particular the Sherman Act (1890), declare price collusion along with certain other anticompetitive behaviors to be illegal. Obviously, laws proscribing certain kinds of behavior do not automatically eliminate such behavior. Although there are laws against robbery, rape, and murder, as well as price collusion, the prisons are overfilled and the Justice Department continues to prosecute and win price-fixing cases against U.S. businesses. Nevertheless, the antitrust laws clearly reduce anticompetitive business behavior. Unfortunately, efforts to enforce antitrust law are weak.

Enforcement of the antitrust laws is hampered by the paltry sums Congress provides to the Antitrust Division of the Department of Justice and the Federal Trade Commission for antitrust enforcement. The 1982 budget for the Antitrust Division was about $50 million and the budget for the Federal Trade Commission, of which only a portion goes to antitrust activity, was about $80 million. This lack of funding for antitrust enforcement reflects, in part, the lack of awareness of microeconomic issues and problems. With no interest from their constituents, many congressmen show little support for antitrust policy. In addition, the business interests that oppose antitrust policy are strong, with a definite incentive to marshal forces against antitrust policy.

The effort to maintain some semblance of competitive capitalism through the antitrust laws clearly faces difficulties both from lack of popular and congressional support, and from strong business opposition. These factors alone could lead to pessimism about the future of competitive capitalism in the United States. But another factor presents far more of a problem for the future. That factor is power—the power of control over people and events. The desire for power may be as important as the profit motive for managers of large corporations in the United States today. Present enforcement of the antitrust laws inhibits anticompetitive business behavior that is aimed at obtaining monopoly profits. This concern of antitrust enforcement with the obviously anticompetitive behavior of business reflects economists' basic assumption, underlying microeconomic theory, that the sole objective of business is maximization of profits. If, however, power is an important objective of the leaders of large corporations, then existing antitrust laws cannot stem the trend away from competitive capitalism to monolithic capitalism. I believe, power, like profits, is a strong motivating force in a modern capitalist society. But, where the drive for profits through collusive pricing and other anticompetitive behavior has been constrained by the antitrust laws, the drive for power is largely unconstrained. The implications for the economic and sociopolitical systems are profound.

Notes

1. Adam Smith, *An Inquiry into the Nature and Causes of the Wealth of Nations,* ed. Edwin Cannan (Chicago: The University of Chicago Press, 1976). Originally published in 1776. Reprinted by permission of The University of Chicago Press.

2. Ibid., p. 477.

3. Ibid., p. 69.

4. Ibid., p. 144.

4

Business in Pursuit of Profits: The Good and the Bad

In the previous chapter, I noted that the profit motive is a crucial element of microeconomic theory. Since a capitalist system is driven by the personal motivation of businessmen, it is useful to bring the profit motive and its benefits to society out of the realm of theory and observe the effects in practice. The drive for profits has clearly been important in the rapid industrial development and continued economic progress of the United States. I shall describe several events from industrial history that suggest the importance of the profit motive. All but one of these events highlight Adam Smith's observation that each individual, in pursuing his or her own self-interest (assumed to be profits in the case of businesspeople), is led as if "by an invisible hand" to a course of action that promotes the general welfare. Thus, the prospect of profits leads businesspeople to allocate resources in response to consumer demand and to seek ways of reducing the cost of production and increasing productivity. Everyone benefits from this impersonal process of the market mechanism. Business response to consumer demand provides the goods and services wanted, and productivity increases provide a higher standard of living.

The last event that I will describe is a major price conspiracy. This event is the most clear-cut illustration of the drive for profits, as opposed to some other possible motive. It also dramatically illustrates that the drive for profits can have adverse side effects. Thus, it demonstrates the necessity of constraining and channeling the profit drive of businessmen if this motive is to yield a course of action that promotes the general welfare. That is the purpose of the antitrust laws.

The developments leading to mass production provide good examples of how business pursuit of profits has benefited society. (Although, as I will show later, the pursuit of profits has imposed costs on society as well.) Typically the movement to mass production involves a change in basic technology, a change in the organization of production, or both. The results of innovations in technology and in the organization of the production process are direct; the contribution to productivity and a higher standard of living is fairly easy to document. The profits that result can often be documented as well. The benefit from increased productivity is that more goods and services are available to all. If, for example, the productivity of every person in a society could be doubled somehow, twice as many goods and services would be available. Since a doubling of productivity implies a doubling of output for the same amount of input, *total* cost of production would remain unchanged but *unit* cost would be cut in half.

So, assuming competitive pricing, prices would decrease by one half. Even if the wages of individuals did not change, each person could purchase twice as many goods and services as he could before the productivity increase. This is the basis for increases in the material standard of living in a society. The benefits to business are lower costs of production and higher profits—at least temporarily, until competitors increase productivity too. By achieving increased profits in this manner, the businessman promotes the general material welfare of society.

The illustration of the profit motive in action can begin with an example provided by Adam Smith. Smith wrote during the early stages of industrial capitalism, when division of labor in manufacturing was becoming prevalent. Division of labor means that each worker performs a very narrow, specific task instead of all of the different tasks required to produce the finished product. Smith believed that the division of labor greatly improved the productivity of labor and the skill and dexterity of individual workers in eighteenth century England. It also saved time otherwise spent as the worker moved from one task in the production process to the next. Presumably, the primary reason that eighteenth-century businesses adopted the division of labor in their operations was to increase their profits by reducing costs. In doing so, they just happened to promote the general welfare as well.

Adam Smith's classic account of the adoption of the division of labor and its benefits focuses on the manufacture of pins.

> To take an example, therefore, from a very trifling manufacture; but one in which the division of labour has been very often taken notice of, the trade of the pin-maker; a workman not educated to this business (which the division of labour has rendered a distinct trade), nor acquainted with the use of the machinery employed in it (to the invention of which the same division of labour has probably given occasion), could scarce, perhaps, with his utmost industry, make one pin in a day, and certainly could not make twenty. But in the way in which this business is now carried on, not only the whole work is a peculiar trade, but it is divided into a number of branches, of which the greater part are likewise peculiar trades. One man draws out the wire, another straightens it, a third cuts it, a fourth points it, a fifth grinds it at the top for receiving the head; to make the head requires two or three distinct operations; to put it on, is a peculiar business; to whiten the pins is another; it is even a trade by itself to put them into the paper; and the important business of making a pin is, in this manner, divided into about eighteen distinct operations, which, in some manufacturies, are all performed by distinct hands, though in others the same man will sometimes perform two or three of them. I have seen a small manufactory of this kind where ten men only were employed and where some of them consequently performed two or three distinct operations. But though they were very poor, and therefore but indifferently accommodated with the necessary machinery, they could, when they exerted themselves, make among them about twelve pounds of pins in a day. There are in a pound upwards of four thousand pins of middling size.

Those ten persons, therefore, could make among them upwards of forty-eight thousand pins in a day. Each person, therefore, making a tenth-part of forty-eight thousand pins, might be considered as making four thousand eight hundred pins in a day. But if they had all wrought separately and independently, and without any of them having been educated to this peculiar business, they certainly could not each of them have made twenty, perhaps not one pin in a day; that is, certainly, not the two hundred and fortieth, perhaps not the four thousand eight hundredth part of what they are at present capable of performing, in consequence of a proper division and combination of their different operations.[1]

Smith's example provides an impressive illustration of an increase in productivity. Though no profit data were provided, the businesses that first adopted this cost-cutting process certainly reaped fine profits. The laggards also had a profit incentive. They could either adopt the more efficient procedure and remain in business, or they could maintain the status quo, suffer losses, and possibly fail.

Early developments in the tobacco industry provide a more recent illustration of the benefits to society arising from the drive for profits. In the early 1880s, four firms dominated cigarette manufacturing. They were Allen and Ginter, William S. Kimball and Co., Kinney Tobacco Co., and Goodwin and Co. The firm W. Duke Sons and Co. was a distant fifth in the industry. Even though the industry consisted of only five firms, they were all relatively small. The product was comparatively new, and skilled workers made cigarettes by hand, which tended to limit the growth of these firms. In the 1880s, however, a major technological advance was introduced when James Bonsack invented and patented a cigarette-rolling machine. The machine pushed tobacco on to a continuous tape of paper, compressed it into a round form, wrapped it, shaped it, pasted the paper, and cut the finished product to the proper length.

The effect of the Bonsack machine on the cost of producing cigarettes was truly amazing. At the time, a skilled worker could produce 3,000 cigarettes per day. A single machine could produce 120,000 cigarettes per day. The machine also eliminated the need for a large number of skilled workers. Labor costs were cut to two cents per thousand cigarettes. Even after the cost of the machine, including royalties and depreciation, was taken into account, the cost of producing cigarettes dropped an astonishing sixfold. As so often seems to be the case in U.S. industrial history, it was not the largest firm that was first to adopt the machine. The smallest of the five U.S. cigarette manufacturers, W. Duke Sons and Co., first used the machine in its factory. The benefits to the Duke Company came rapidly, and within a few years it dominated the industry. Shortly thereafter, the other cigarette manufacturers, unable to catch up with the Duke Company, joined with it to form the American Tobacco Co., which came to be known as the Tobacco Trust.

The early history of the petroleum industry again illustrates the general benefits resulting from business pursuit of profits. In the United States, the petroleum industry began on August 29, 1859 when a former railroad conductor by the name of "Colonel" Edwin L. Drake struck oil at 69 feet in Titusville, Pennsylvania. The industry developed rapidly as rail lines were built into the region and special cars were invented to permit bulk transport of petroleum. At the same time, innovations began improving the refinining process. Refining output was significantly increased by applying more intense heat, so a super-heated steam-distillation process, already in use in sugar refining, was adopted by the petroleum industry. The *cracking* process was also developed. This involved applying higher temperatures to reshape the molecular structure of crude oil, and increased output by 20 percent per still. Changes in the construction and design of the stills increased output still further. In addition, methods were developed to move the crude through a plant continuously from one refining process to the next. Only about ten years after oil was discovered in the ground, the unit cost of refining was cut in half, dropping from six to three cents per barrel. Productivity continued to increase, and additional resources were attracted to the industry. From 1880 to 1899, labor costs declined—as the value of output from U.S. refineries increased almost threefold, from $43.7 million to $123.9 million, the number of workers in the industry increased only about 20 percent, from 8,869 to 12,100. While the new energy source which would soon drive the country was being developed, corporate and family fortunes were being amassed. The names Rockefeller and Standard Oil stand out in the early years of the industry's development.

In the early years of the iron and steel industry, numerous major product and process innovations were introduced as business sought profit opportunities from the growing demand for steel, particularly for the nation's rapidly growing rail system. Between 1850 and 1900, these innovations produced large increases in output with corresponding declines in costs. In the 1860s, iron and still mills were very labor intensive. Then in the 1870s the Bessemer process was introduced, which produced quality steel at a low cost. Along with the advances in product quality, important advances in the production process were made. Steel plants were integrated so that several processes could be undertaken on a continuous basis within a single plant. The engineer Alexander Holley played a major role in designing the new integrated plants precisely and systematically to achieve large-scale output as efficiently as possible. For example, the plants that Holley designed for Andrew Carnegie, which included more powerful blast furnaces, increased production from Carnegie's Lucy furnace from 13,000 tons in 1872 to 100,000 tons by the late 1890s. The technological innovations and improved plant and process design spread through the industry as competitors of Carnegie sought to maintain cost competitiveness. Additional resources were drawn to the steel industry. Between 1869 and 1899, the average yearly output of U.S. blast furnaces increased from 5,000 to 65,000 tons, and the output of steel works and rolling mills from 3,000 to 23,000 tons.

The product and process innovations developed or adopted by Carnegie had two benefits. First, they dramatically increased steel and iron production at ever lower cost. This provided an important foundation for industrial development in the United States. Second, Andrew Carnegie grew extraordinarily wealthy. In 1878, Carnegie's rail mill showed a profit of $401,000. Only two years later profits stood at $2 million. By 1900, profits from all of Carnegie's operations were $40 million—an immense sum for that time.

Henry Ford's innovations in automobile production rapidly turned the automobile from a novelty and luxury enjoyed mostly by the well-to-do into an important means of transportation within the reach of many U.S. citizens. It quickly became a dominant feature of the landscape and has had a pervasive influence on all of our lives. Of course it has influenced where we all work and live, but in addition, about one out of seven workers in this country today depends, for his or her job, directly or indirectly on the automobile industry.

Gasoline-powered vehicles were being produced commercially in Europe by 1885. In the United States, the gasoline vehicle produced by Charles and Frank Duryea in 1893 marked the beginning of commercial production. The automobile was a novelty at first—only 300 were owned in the United States in 1895—but demand grew rapidly between 1900 and 1910. During this period, the number of firms producing automobiles increased from twelve to sixty-nine, and sales increased from 4,000 to 187,000. Nevertheless, the price of the automobile was still beyond the budget of the average consumer.

In 1909, Henry Ford, who had produced cars since 1896, began producing the Model T Ford. His stated intention was to keep exactly the same design and concentrate on cutting production cost. His efforts at cost reduction went right down to the paint of the car. Ford declared that, "Any customer can have a car painted any color that he wants so long as it is black." Ford made all motor and chassis parts so that they would be interchangeable among cars. He used tough new alloys and adopted advanced machinery. But Ford's most important innovation was the assembly line. His assembly line was a moving belt that brought the automobile to workers and machines located in carefully determined sequences along the line. Each worker did a highly specialized job at his position on the assembly line. The results of Henry Ford's innovations were indeed impressive. The labor required to produce a Model T dropped from 12 hours 8 minutes to 1 hour 33 minutes. The precipitous drop in production costs lowered prices and expanded the market enough that the profit margin could be smaller on each unit. The price of the Model T decreased steadily from $950 in 1909 to $290 in 1925. Production of Model T's rose from 10,000 in 1909 to 2 million in 1923. The automobile was no longer a novelty. It had been made affordable to the great masses of consumers. At the same time, Ford Motor Company came to dominate the automobile industry and Henry Ford amassed one of the great personal fortunes in the world.

I could go on with other illustrations. For example, a whole new era in television entertainment is unfolding as major U.S. and foreign firms are responding to the huge profit potential in video disks and cassettes with large investments in research and product development. During the past fifteen years we have witnessed dramatic advances in electronics technology as many firms have invested heavily in research to develop new products for which there is a large demand. One result has been a remarkable increase in the capabilities and convenience of hand and desk calculators. At the same time, prices have plummeted so that now even a small home computer is within the budget of many people.

The drive for profits by business has provided us with new products and increased productivity that has raised the standard of living. These examples have also illustrated the crucial role of profits in allocating productive resources for different uses. For example, the potential profitability of petroleum induced businesses to commit vast resources to the industry so that within a few decades of the initial discovery of oil, petroleum had become a major industry. Similarly, as soon as it became apparent that the automobile could be something other than a novelty, the profit opportunities rapidly attracted huge amounts of capital and other productive resources. This is the essence of the capitalist system at work; the allocation of scarce resources by private firms in response to the exercise of consumer sovereignty. One reward for such effort is profits.

The last historical example of the drive for profits is less laudable. It describes a conspiracy among major electrical-equipment manufacturers to fix prices, rig bids, and share markets—in short, to avoid competition. Top executives of some of the largest corporations in the United States flagrantly violated the antitrust laws in the quest for profits. They were able, over a period of years, to charge prices as much as 50 percent higher than competitive levels on billions of dollars of electrical equipment. The story illustrates three points. First, it shows how important profits are as a motivator of business behavior. Second, it demonstrates that although profit-motivated behavior benefits society, it must be constrained and channeled to avoid its adverse effects on society. Third, it dramatizes how firms in industries with a small number of producers can reach agreements on the prices to charge. Their incentive, of course, is the prospect of higher profits for all in the absence of price competition. The discussion is based on a detailed account by John G. Fuller.[2]

The story begins in Knoxville, Tennessee in May of 1959. Julian Granger, a reporter for the *Knoxville News-Sentinel*, found a release from the Tennessee Valley Authority (TVA) noting that a contract for transformers had been awarded to Westinghouse Electric Corp. by TVA for $96,000. The release went on to say that Allis Chalmers Corp., General Electric Co. and Pennsylvania Transformer had all quoted identical prices of $112,712 on the contract. This seemed strange since, in order to get competitive bids on their contracts, TVA required secret, sealed bids. Reading further, Granger found that two other companies had quoted identical prices of $273,200 on another contract, and seven companies had quoted $198,438.24 on a contract for conductor cable. Granger contacted TVA and learned that the volume of business involved was immense.

The market for turbine generators alone amounted to about $400 million per year. Only a few companies, led by General Electric and Westinghouse, accounted for most of the heavy electrical equipment produced in the United States. A search of TVA records confirmed suspicions about the bidding procedures of the firms. Many more identical bids were discovered. Granger reported his findings in the *Knoxville News-Sentinel* and followed with a more detailed report later in the month.

Granger's articles were brought to the attention of Senator Kefauver, chairman of the U.S. Senate Subcommittee on Antitrust and Monopoly. Sen. Kefauver immediately traveled to Knoxville to obtain more detailed information. After seeing the material firsthand, Senator Kefauver conducted formal hearings to determine whether the identical bids were the result of a conspiracy to fix prices. If so, the matter would be turned over to the antitrust agencies—the Department of Justice and the Federal Trade Commission—for prosecution. The hearings revealed that prices of electrical products such as radios, stoves, and refrigerators (for which there are many competing producers) had remained constant or even declined since 1951, but prices of heavy electrical equipment (for which there are few producers) had actually increased by 50 percent since 1951. Furthermore, list after list of identical bids was produced at the hearing. Another pattern in the bidding also emerged. It was a pattern of rotation of the winning bid among the producers. For instance, one bid for an oil circuit breaker in 1957 looked like this:

General Electric	$7,440 (low)
Westinghouse	7,455 (middle)
Allis Chalmers	7,455 (middle)
Federal Pacific	7,610 (high)

But the next time around the bids might be:

Westinghouse	$6,465 (low)
Allis Chalmers	6,470 (middle)
General Electric	6,470 (middle)
Federal Pacific	6,480 (high)

It certainly looked like the firms involved had devised and agreed upon a mechanism for allocating the business among themselves. The evidence that there was a major price conspiracy in the sale of electrical equipment became compelling. In June 1959, only shortly after Granger's articles appeared and Senator Kefauver had begun hearings, the Antitrust Division of the Department of Justice impaneled a grand jury in Philadelphia to examine pricing in the electrical-equipment industry.

Documents and testimony developed by the grand jury revealed that executives of the companies used code names for themselves and their companies and held clandestine meetings.

The grand jury in Philadelphia handed down twenty indictments against twenty-eight companies and forty-five of their executives. The indictments were officially announced on February 16, 1960 and the first one read in part as follows:

> At these periodic meetings, a scheme or formula for quoting nearly identical [bids] to electric utility companies . . . [was] designated by them as a "phase of the moon" formula. Through cyclic rotating positioning inherent in the formula, one defendant manufacturer would quote the low price, others would quote intermediate prices, and another would quote the high price; these positions would be periodically rotated among the manufacturers. This formula was so calculated that in submitting prices to these customers, the price spread between the defendant manufacturers' quotations would be sufficiently narrow so as to eliminate actual price competition between them, but sufficiently wide so as to give an appearance of competition. This formula permitted each defendant manufacturer to know the exact price it and every other defendant manufacturer would quote on each prospective sale.[3]

It took Judge Ganey, who presided over the investigation, only two days to levy fines and sentences. The most startling factor in the sentences was that seven of the individual defendants were sent to jail in their pin-stripe suits. Even though the jail terms were only thirty days, the sentences sent a shock wave through the business community. It was one of the first times in U.S. history that anyone had been sent to jail for violation of the antitrust laws.

It was obvious that the involved executives knew what they were doing was patently illegal under the antitrust laws. Then why did they do it? The amount of business involved annually was enormous—industrial control equipment, $262 million; turbogenerators, $400 million; voltage-distribution equipment, $200 million; and so forth through a long list of equipment. The profits to be made by colluding to avoid price competition were also enormous. The incentive to collude and fix prices as through this were a monopoly was great.

This type of profit-seeking behavior is strictly illegal under the antitrust laws because it robs the capitalist economic system of one of its greatest virtues —providing consumers with that they want at the lowest possible price. It also stultifies innovation by removing the pressure to beat competitors. From the standpoint of equity, this form of profit-seeking business behavior takes money out of the pockets of the mass of consumers and gives it to businesses and their stockholders. It is important, if capitalism is to remain dynamic and progressive and is to allocate resources efficiently, that managers of U.S. business are strongly motivated. However, it is also clear that some of the behavior this motivation causes must be constrained and channeled.

Notes

1. Adam Smith, *An Inquiry into the Nature and Causes of the Wealth of Nations,* ed. Edwin Cannan (Chicago: University of Chicago Press, 1976), pp. 8 and 9.

2. John G. Fuller, *The Gentlemen Conspirators* (New York: Grove Press, 1962), © 1962, Grove Press, Inc.

3. Ibid., p. 65.

5 Is the Profit Motive Waning?

Even though profits have been a strong motivator of businessmen, there are reasons for suspecting that profits are declining as a motivating force in U.S. capitalism. Three factors could be diminishing the importance of profits for business behavior. These are the increased affluence of society in general, the possibility that the economic system is experiencing a long-term decline in profitable investment opportunities, and the fact that hired managers rather than the actual owners run virtually all of the major corporations in the United States today.

This society has become highly affluent during the twentieth century. Much of this rise in the living standard has occurred in just the past thirty-five years. For example, only about 50 percent of the families in the United States owned automobiles in 1945; now more than 90 percent of the families own automobiles, and the two-car family is common. Around 35 percent of all meals are purchased away from home today as compared to an extremely small percentage in 1945. The civilian per-capita consumption of meat, an expensive but popular source of protein, has increased from 129 pounds per year in 1900 to almost 200 pounds per year today. In 1945, almost no families owned television sets, yet today ninety-seven percent of the families have at least one set, and about 60 percent of these are color sets. Technological advances have made television commercially available, but the television was an additional item for the home in 1945 rather than the replacement item it is today.

The remarkable increase in expenditures on what are to a large extent luxuries reflects an increase in per-capita disposable income in the United States of almost 250 percent (from $1,886 to $4,418) between 1929 and 1978. That is after adjusting for inflation. The distribution of this income among various categories of expenditures provides further testimony of our affluence. According to U.S. Bureau of Census data, in 1909 consumers spent about 19 percent of disposable income on housing as compared to only about 15 percent today; spent 26 percent of income on food as compared to only 19 percent today; and spent 3 percent of 1909 income on recreation as compared to almost 7 percent today. George Katona estimated that by the early 1970s about one-half of all family units had discretionary income (income beyond what is needed for necessities) as compared to only 25 percent of the family units in 1946 and 15 percent of families during the 1930s.[1]

Spending patterns show that U.S. citizens have, in a relatively short time, become more affluent. There are, however potentially more significant signs of our rising affluence. Particularly notable is the increasing willingness to trade work (and presumably more income) for more leisure time. This trade-off is reflected in the decline of the average work week in manufacturing from 59 hours in 1900 to 39.8 hours in 1970. The International Labor Organization in Geneva reported that, in 1980, the United States had the world's shortest work week with an average of 35.6 hours. One of the major demands in union bargaining today is for a reduction in the number of hours or days worked. The demand for a four-day, 35-hour week is common and it is actually showing up at some companies. This apparent willingness to sacrifice additional income for more leisure time even shows up at the executive level. Business periodicals report that more and more executives are declining moves to new locations that would provide higher salaries.

The obvious desire to trade off work and income for increased leisure or a better life reflects a phenomenon that economists call the *diminishing marginal utility* of money. The concept of marginal utility has its origins in the writings of W.S. Jevons, M.E.L. Walras, and C. Menger of the Austrian School of Economics during the 1870s. The basic idea is simply that as a person has a larger amount of money, the utility of an extra (marginal) dollar becomes smaller. For example, the utility of a marginal, or additional, $100 to the person earning $5,000 per year is most likely greater than it is to the person earning $50,000 per year.

Businesspeople, especially those in the large corporations, occupy a unique station in society, but they are not immune to the broad social forces in society, including the affects of affluence. The decline in the marginal utility of money resulting from rising affluence in general might also be reflected in the diminution of the profit motive among businesspeople. It is not uncommon to read about executives of major corporations who have stated publicly that business is interested not only in profits—that business should have a social conscience and accept civic responsibilities. Statements of this kind may be partially self-serving attempts to provide a benevolent corporate image. They may also, however, reflect a diminishing marginal utility of money and profits. The large corporations must earn enough profits to satisfy stockholders and attract new investors, but they could all earn less than maximum possible profits and remain equally profitable and attractive to investors. Consequently, the possibility that affluence has dulled the edge of the profit motive is quite real.

The view that capitalist economic systems will experience a long-term decline in the rate of profit has been espoused by such noted economists as Adam Smith, David Ricardo, Karl Marx, and John Maynard Keynes. Such a decline in the rate of profit has generally been attributed to one of several causes. First, competition among firms with increasing amounts of capital will drive down the returns on capital. Second, as more capital is used in place of labor, which is in the Marxian view the source of profits, profits must decline. Third, as the supply of capital becomes more abundant over time, the returns arising from capital scarcity will decline, and investment opportunities will disappear. Many who have anticipated a long-term decline in profits also conclude that this tendency would not be favorable for a capitalist system. The results they have predicted range from increasingly severe depressions, to a decline in the motivation of business, to the complete demise of the system. My interest in this persistent view arises from the possibility that, if we experience a continued decline in the rate of profit, the role of profits as a motivator of business will likely diminish.

Adam Smith was one of the first economists to argue that the long-run rate of return in a capitalist system will steadily decline. For example, he contended "The increase of stock, which raises wages, tends to lower profits. When the stock of many rich merchants are turned into the same trade, their mutual competition naturally tends to lower its profits."[2] Smith presented some empirical evidence from historical experience. This evidence, he believed, affirmed his view that the long-run rate of profit tends to decline. Based on his argument that interest rates and the return on capital must move up and down together, Smith traced interest-rate movements from the time of Henry VIII on through the reigns of Edward VI, James I, and Queen Anne in England. He also traced these trends in Scotland, France, and Holland, reaching the conclusion that interest rates, and thus profits, had been steadily declining. Smith did not dwell on this issue. He never did carefully tie the rate of profit to interest rates, and he did not speculate on the implications of the tendency for interest rates to fall.

David Ricardo also wrote about a long-run decline in the rate of profit in his book, *Principles of Political Economy and Taxation* (1821). Ricardo's analysis of a long-run decline in the rate of profit had its origins in the work of Thomas Malthus. Malthus contended that population growth would necessitate the increasing use of less fertile land as more land had to be used to provide enough food for a larger population. As a result, Ricardo argues, wages must rise so that the worker would have enough income just to pay for the more expensive food required for survival. The necessity of paying higher wages would, in turn, cut into the profits of business. Since Ricardo stressed that the motivating force of capitalist production is the entrepreneur's expectation of profit, he concluded that progress in capitalism involves a diminution in the motive for capital accumulation. Ricardo's analysis of diminishing profits focused on agriculture and the diminishing return to land. It is a further affirmation of Adam Smith's remarkable insight into the workings of capitalism that, although he wrote forty-five years earlier than Ricardo, his analysis focused on trade and factory production, which became the dominant features of capitalism.

In 1867, Karl Marx published volume I of his penetrating critique of capitalism, *Das Kapital*. Undoubtedly it is Marx's arguments concerning a declining rate of profit, rather than those of his predecessors and followers, that have attracted the attention of economists to this issue. He presented a piercing and critical view of capitalism and predicted a highly pessimistic outcome for capitalism as a result of declining profit rates. Marx argued that as capital accumulates over time, it replaces labor in the production process. (In Marx's terms, the "organic composition of capital" increases as "fixed capital" replaces "variable capital".) Since labor (variable capital) is the basic source of "surplus value" (the value added over and above the value of materials used in production) and thereby profits, the decline in labor input relative to capital input would reduce the rate of profits.

According to Marx, since the rate of profit depends upon the surplus value created by labor, the only way that capitalists would be able to maintain the rate of return as capital increasingly replaced labor would be to continually reduce the wage paid to labor. Marx regarded this as one of the fundamental contradictions of capitalism. The continual expansion or accumulation of capital is essential to capitalism; but this process cannot proceed indefinitely because, as capital replaces labor, wages must be continually reduced in order to maintain the rate of return. In Marx's scenario, the workers ultimately rebel against declining wages. The private property of the capitalists would be expropriated and production would then be established on the basis of common ownership, that is, socialism. Marx did believe, however, that certain forces could postpone the final stages of capitalism—for example, increased exploitation of labor, new colonies or foreign trade to provide cheaper raw materials, and technological advances that result in less expensive capital. Nevertheless, the end result was, in his view, inevitable.

In the twentieth century, the most eminent believer in a long-run decline in profits is John Maynard Keynes. In *The General Theory of Employment, Interest and Money,* he gave particular attention to the problems of unemployment and underutilization of productive capacity, and appropriate monetary and fiscal policies. However, in the latter part of the book, Keynes reflected rather casually on a number of subjects.[3] One of these was the prospect for a long-run decline in the rate of profit in modern industrial countries. He expected this decline because the "marginal efficiency of capital" (Keynes's terminology for the rate of return over cost of capital) would tend to diminish as capital becomes more abundant. When the marginal efficiency of business investment equals the rate of interest (which is the cost of money to business for purchasing capital equipment), there will no longer be an incentive to purchase additional capital equipment. This process would, according to Keynes, be marked by depressions because of insufficient business spending for the investment required to maintain employment and income.

Even though the government might be able to offset this tendency by reducing interest rates to near zero, thereby encouraging investment through reducing the cost of capital, it could not reduce interest rates below zero. Consequently, there must come a point at which capital equipment in itself no longer produces a return—it will have lost its scarcity value. Then there will no longer be an incentive to accumulate capital. As Keynes observed, "There can be no doubt that this criterion will lead to a much lower rate of interest than has ruled hitherto; and, so far as one can guess at the schedules of the marginal efficiency of capital corresponding to increasing amounts of capital, the rate of interest is likely to fall steadily, if it should be practicable to maintain conditions of more or less continuous full employment." He also noted that "it is to our best advantage to reduce the rate of interest to that point relative to the schedule of the marginal efficiency of capital at which there is full employment."[4]

Unlike earlier economists, Keynes looked favorably on the prospect of a decline in the return to capital. He commented that "a properly run community . . . ought to be able to bring down the marginal efficiency of capital in equilibrium approximately to zero in a single generation."[5] He anticipated that ultimately the return to capital would "just cover their labor costs of production *plus* an allowance for risk and the costs of skill and supervision."[6] As a consequence, this "would mean the euthanasia of the rentier."[7] By this, Keynes meant that there would no longer be a return to capital simply because of its scarcity. The purely financial investors (his rentier class or coupon clippers), whom Keynes regarded with a jaundiced eye, would gradually die out. This outcome—the declining rate of return to capital and euthanasia of the rentier—was essentially inevitable in Keynes's analytical framework. Keynes apparently did not expect, or at least did not speculate about the kind of adverse implications for capitalism arising from a declining rate of profits that some of his predecessors anticipated.

The views of the economists discussed thus far do not represent an exhaustive survey of those who have argued that capitalism will experience a long-term decline in the rate of profit. It is a credible view that has been held by numerous outstanding economists over a long period of time. However, historical experience provides no support for the notion. Mark Blaugh reported some relevant evidence developed by a Marxist economist for the years 1849 through 1950. The findings reveal that in U.S. manufacturing the capital-output ratio (and thus, Marx's "organic composition of capital") did not rise between 1849 and 1950.[8] Thus, there had been no overaccumulation of capital, which would lead to falling profits as Marx and others predicted. Furthermore, profit rates in manufacturing from 1919 to 1950 showed no tendency to decline. My own examination of rates of return in U.S. manufacturing revealed no persistent decline between 1950 and 1980. It is apparent that the declining rate of profit is one of several of Marx's dire predictions for capitalism that have generally failed to materialize. (Others include an ever larger reserve army of unemployed labor, increasing misery of the proletariat, polarization of classes, and concentration of capital.)

Even though we can probably agree that the rate of profit has not yet shown a tendency toward long-run decline, it is reasonable to ask about future prospects. Is a decline likely in the near future? In my opinion, the answer is a

resounding no. The expected decline in profits has been predicated on a declining opportunity for investment accompanied by an overabundance of capital.
Significant developments in capitalism have prevented such an outcome. The
extent and magnitude of technological advance in modern industrial society,
which Marx simply could not foresee when he was writing during the early
stages of industrial capitalism, have been the major counteracting forces. Technological advances have opened up entirely new and profitable investment
opportunities as well as opportunities for the labor force. This sort of progress
is almost certain to continue.

For example, the development of the automobile and aviation industries
has provided a remarkably wide range of investment opportunities for large and
small firms during the first three-quarters of the twentieth century. These include steel, rubber, glass, motels, fast-food restaurants, petroleum, and gas
stations. The rapid spread of affluence and technological advances in the United
States just since World War II have opened up innumerable, profitable investment opportunities in televisions and stereos, cameras, fashionable apparel, furniture, food processors, microwave ovens, and citizen's band radios, for both
large and small businesses to cater to the desires of the average consumer.

The future holds more of the same opportunity. Today the computer-
electronics industry appears to be only emerging from its infancy. Individual
homes may be computerized through their telephones and televisions for financial, recreational, and security purposes. The field of genetic engineering is
getting off to a fitful start, raising significant moral questions. If, however, the
stock-market appeal of the many new, small firms in this field is any indication,
it has a tremendous future. Rather ironically, the seemingly devastating actions
of the OPEC cartel have opened up a vast range of profitable investment opportunities—solar energy, nuclear energy, garbage energy, forest management, new
forms of transportation, new types of housing, and myriad methods for con-
serving energy with relatively conventional products. The range of possible
investment opportunities titillates the imagination of any capitalist.

Assuming there is a reasonable public policy that encourages saving and
investment, widespread affluence in our society will assure that capital will be
available at a reasonable cost to finance new investment. Of course, business
investment in research and development and in new plants and equipment is
essential to achieve the increases in productivity that yield a higher standard of
living. The assumption of a reasonable public policy toward saving and investment may seem a bit shaky in light of the experience of the 1960s and 1970s.
Following the Keynesian prescription, government policies leaned heavily
toward encouraging consumption at the expense of saving and investment. The
savings rate in the United States is the lowest of all major industrial countries.
For example, saving as a percent of disposable income in the United States has
been around 6 percent during the past fifteen years (as low as 3.4 percent during
1979 and 1980), while it has been around 20 percent in Japan, 14 percent in
Germany, and at similar high levels in other industrial countries.

Recent laws, however, reflect a change in public policy. For example, the removal of Regulation Q ceilings and other limits on the interest rates that banks and other thrift institutions may pay savers should result in a reasonable return for savers. This should stimulate saving. The elimination or raising of the usury-law ceilings on how much interest borrowers may be charged will require borrowers to pay the market rate for money. When this occurs, spending is likely to be much less attractive in relation to saving than it has been for many years. Such policies to encourage saving should provide the funds required by business for investment. A change in public policy is also reflected in recent legislation reducing the tax burden on business and shortening the depreciation write-off period for new capital equipment. This too should encourage investment.

In summation, historical evidence provides no indication of a long-term decline in profits of U.S. capitalism. The conditions that are required in order for such a decline to occur seem unlikely to materialize for many years. Investment opportunities should be abundant, and public policy is leaning toward encouraging saving and investment.

The last factor I will consider in assessing the possibility that the role of profits as a motivator of business is diminishing concerns the predominant legal form of modern U.S. business—the corporation. Before 1900, the corporate form of business organization was relatively uncommon. Businesses were typically organized as proprietorships or partnerships. The corporate form of organization emerged as a mechanism for reducing the legal liability of owners. It also came about because of the nature of modern business. The development of new and technically sophisticated products and manufacturing methods often required such a large amount of capital that most individuals or small groups of individuals could not come up with the financing. The corporate form of business organization provided a way of enlisting the funds of thousands, even millions, of owners for a business enterprise through stock ownership. Of course, the willingness of many small investors to participate in the ownership of a business was greatly facilitated by the limited liability of the owners, which the corporate form of organization provided.

The evolution of modern manufacturing and the corporate form of business organization created the need for and the means of accumulating large amounts of capital from stockholders. It had other effects as well. In the early stages of capitalism, owners of a business also ran the business, but that is no longer true. Large corporations, which dominate economic activity in the United States, are usually run by hired managers rather than by the owners, who are absentee stockholders. The trend toward the manager-operated rather than owner-operated firm is striking. In their landmark book, Adolph Berle and Gardiner Means reported that as early as 1929, 44 percent of the 200 largest nonfinancial corporations in the United States were controlled and operated by managers rather than the owners.[9] In his update of the Berle and Means study, Robert Larner reported that as of 1963, over 80 percent of the 200 largest nonfinancial businesses in this country were manager controlled.[10]

The marked tendency toward the manager control and operation of business is interesting in itself. However, the implications of this tendency are even more interesting. The manager of a business who also owns the business will have an incentive to maximize profits, since he will be the recipient of whatever profit he can make. The early founders of microeconomic theory, who lived in a world where owners typically ran their businesses, adopted a very reasonable assumption of business behavior in constructing the theory—the assumption of profit maximization. This remains a fundamental assumption of microeconomic theory today.

In today's world where large businesses are usually run by hired managers rather than owners, it is questionable that the drive to maximize profits is as strong as it was in the past. Robert Gordon examined this question and found that in 149 of the 200 largest U.S. nonfinancial corporations in 1935, the leading executives were compensated primarily through salary and bonuses rather than stock ownership.[11] This suggested that the profit motive of businessmen might in fact be diminished. However, evidence indicates that ownership incentives still exist. A more recent study by Wilbur Lewellen found that for top executives of the 50 largest manufacturing firms from 1960 to 1963, stock was a more important source of income than salary and bonus.[12] The fact still remains that the incomes of managers of large U.S. companies do not depend entirely, and may not depend primarily, on profits.

If the compensation of business managers does not depend entirely on profits, does this reduce the drive to maximize profits? A recent study reviewed the evidence and presented a test that is relevant to this hypothesis. The study found, as have some other studies, that owner-controlled firms (which tend to be small) are more profitable than manager-controlled firms.[13] Although the evidence reviewed is mixed, it leads me to the conclusion that the profit motive is probably somewhat diminished in manager-controlled firms. Since the great majority of large U.S. businesses are operated by managers, it seems fair to conclude that the profit motive has diminished for an important and influential segment of business.

In this chapter, I have reviewed some developments and arguments that provide a basis for suspecting a diminution in the role of profits as a motivator of business in modern U.S. capitalism. These are increasing affluence, a secular decline in profits, and a trend toward manager rather than owner control of firms. Overall, what can be concluded?

First, we can dismiss outright the notion that a long-term decline in profits will rob the capitalist system of profits as a motivating force. Evidence from the past 130 years and prospects for the future provide no support for this notion in spite of its long and illustrious heritage. I think, however, that the observed tendencies toward greater affluence and manager rather than owner control of businesses are a different matter. The tendency toward greater affluence is an established fact. Moreover, it appears that as a result of affluence, the marginal utility of money is diminishing in U.S. society at large. What cannot be demonstrated, but is at least a reasonable possibility, is that the affluence and diminishing marginal utility of money may have affected businessmen as well as others and thereby may have reduced the potency of profit as a motivator of business. The trend toward manager instead of owner control of business led to the hypothesis that profits may not be as important to managers as they are to owners. I think the evidence, on balance, suggests that owners are more profit oriented than managers, and the fact is most large businesses in the United States are manager controlled.

Two out of the three developments I have reviewed point to the possibility that profits have weakened as a motivator of business managers. Nevertheless, they are still an important stimulus. For one thing, managers of corporations are ultimately answerable to the stockholders and they must earn enough (although not necessarily maximum) profits to attract new investors and finance further growth. The discussion in the previous chapter suggested that profits have, in the past, been a strong motivator of business behavior. Many studies by economists indicate that businesses will generally earn higher profits whenever the opportunity permits. In particular, studies show that when a business has some degree of monopoly, it will normally take advantage of such a situation and earn higher profits than firms having no monopoly power. Consequently, the inclusion of the profit motive as a basic assumption of microeconomic theory regarding business behavior would seem to remain on fairly solid ground. However, it seems very likely that there are other factors besides profits that motivate businessmen.

If we hope to understand business behavior and thus to develop public policy that maintains competitive capitalism, it is essential to be realistic in the assumptions used in the analysis of business behavior and the public policy adopted in this area. In the next three chapters I propose to show that the drive for power is an important motivator of business behavior.

Notes

1. George Katona, *Psychological Economics* (New York: Elsevier Scientific Publishing Co., 1975).

2. Adam Smith, *An Inquiry into the Nature and Causes of the Wealth of Nations,* ed. Edwin Cannan (Chicago: University of Chicago Press, 1976), p. 98.

3. John Maynard Keynes, *The General Theory of Employment, Interest and Money* (New York: Harcourt, Brace and Co., 1936), especially chapters 16 and 24.

4. Ibid., p. 375.

5. Ibid., p. 220.

6. Ibid., p. 375.

7. Ibid., p. 376.

8. Mark Blaugh, *Economic Theory in Retrospect* (Homewood, Ill.: Richard D. Irwin, 1962), p. 234.

9. Adloph Berle and Gardiner Means, *The Modern Corporation and Private Property* (New York: Macmillan, 1932).

10. Robert Larner, *Management Control and the Large Corporation* (Cambridge, Mass.: Dunellen, 1970).

11. Robert Gordon, "Ownership and Compensation as Incentives to Corporation Executives," *Quarterly Journal of Economics* (May 1940), pp. 455-73.

12. Wilbur Lewellen, "Management and Ownership in the Large Firm," *Journal of Finance* (May 1969), pp. 292-322.

13. Cynthia Glassman and Stephen A. Rhoades, "Owner vs. Manager Control Effects on Bank Performance," *Review of Economics and Statistics* (May 1980), pp. 263-70.

The Drive for Power: Some Preliminaries

Profits remain an important motivator of U.S. businessmen and should not be underestimated. I am proposing, however, that profits may not be as important as they used to be and that *power*—that is, the desire for power and control over resources, people, and events—also motivates business behavior. It is notable that while political scientists have long recognized the role of power in influencing behavior the influence of power on behavior is ignored altogether in economics. Economists pride themselves on being the leaders among the social scientists in adopting, at least to some extent, the rigor and scientific method of the natural sciences. They have developed abstract theoretical models to lay out neatly the theoretical foundations of the discipline, as exemplified by Paul Samuelson's *Foundations of Economic Analysis* (1947), or any issue of the profession's leading journal, *The American Economic Review.* In addition, economists have developed testable hypotheses from these theories and have applied the scientific method in the course of quantifying and statistically testing these hypotheses.

Unfortunately, focusing strictly on mathematically tractable and quantifiable phenomena causes problems. In order for the theoretical models of economists to be manageable, it has been necessary to resort to numerous simplifying assumptions. In a discipline dealing with the functioning of the economic system in which so many diverse influences are at work, the risk of losing touch with reality exists. The result is that the discipline becomes irrelevant. There is a trade-off between attaining mathematical rigor in theories and describing reality. The effort to apply the scientific method for hypothesis testing in economics also has pitfalls. In particular, in order for a hypothesis to be testable, the factors or influences to be taken into account must be quantifiable. Because of the diversity of influences at work in the economic system, including elements of human behavior, the emphasis on the strictly measurable influences in the system may exclude important factors, with a corresponding loss of reality and relevance. In short, if some element of the economic system is not amenable to differential calculus or direct measurement, economists will generally ignore it. Power is such an element. Even Keynes, who was himself a statistician, was concerned with the tendency of economists to eschew realities of the world in favor of mathematical rigor. He observed that, "Too large a proportion of recent 'mathematical' economics are mere concoctions, as imprecise as the initial assumptions they rest on, which allow the author to lose sight of the complexities and interdependencies of the real world in a maze of pretentious and unhelpful symbols."[1]

In the area of microeconomics, you will recall that economists have embraced profit maximization as a fundamental assumption of the theory. Profit maximization is assumed to be the sole objective of business. One reason that economists rely on this assumption (aside from the fact that profits are indeed important to business) is that profits can be neatly manipulated mathematically in theoretical models. Moreover, profits can be quantified for use in hypothesis testing. Data on profits are readily available or can be constructed from information published by the U.S. Bureau of the Census, the Internal Revenue Service, the Federal Trade Commission, *Moody's, Standard and Poor's,* and *Fortune,* among others. Thus, the assumption of profit maximization is not only reasonable, it is also quite convenient. Some economists have recognized, however, that the assumption of profit maximization as the sole objective of business sacrifices realism for the sake of convenience and rigor.

William J. Baumol was one of the first economists to gain widespread acceptance for the idea that profits may have to share their position as the motivator of businessmen with another factor. Baumol argued that businessmen attempt to maximize their sales. He acknowledged that they must also maintain profits at a high enough level (although probably not a profit maximizing level) to attract investors. This has come to be known as the *constrained sales maximization* hypothesis.[2] It could just as well be called the "constrained profit maximization" hypothesis because, while sales growth is an objective, so are profits. In the context of Baumol's model, the drive for profits is constrained by the businessman's objective of increasing sales. The point is that Baumol's hypothesis does admit, and even argues, that profits are not the sole objective of business.

More recently, the economists Harvey Leibenstein and Oliver Williamson, building on the work of Robert Gordon in the 1940s, have developed related hypotheses. Essentially, they posit that since large corporations are run by hired managers rather than owners, expenses of these firms may not be kept to the minimum possible level. Since the income of the hired manager does not depend strictly on profits, the drive to maximize profits by way of minimizing expenses is weakened. Indeed, Williamson argues that managers actually have an incentive to increase expenditures that will provide them with certain executive perquisites (for example, a company plane, a plush office, and so forth). Nevertheless, like Baumol, Leibenstein and Williamson recognize that profits also remain an objective of business managers.

The recent works aimed at extending traditional microeconomic theory to incorporate business objectives other than profit maximization have four points in common. First, they attempt to inject more realism into theoretical models. Second, although alternative objectives are proposed, the profit motive is not discarded. Third, and particularly interesting I think, each hypothesis has introduced objectives—such as sales maximization and expense preferences—that are amenable to mathematical manipulation. Fourth, these objectives are quantifiable, which makes them amenable to statistical hypothesis testing. As a result, these recent developments in microeconomic theory meet what seem to be the necessary conditions for serious consideration by economists.

A few economists have explicitly recognized and acknowledged the potential significance of unquantifiable psychological factors, such as power, for business behavior. For example, Wesley C. Mitchell sought to establish the importance of the study of human nature for the discipline of economics. In 1914, Mitchell perceived the tendency among economists to eschew the immeasurable.

> A slight but significant change seems to be taking place in the attitude of economic theorists toward psychology. Most of the older writers made no overt reference to psychology, but tacitly imputed to the men whose behavior they were analyzing certain traits consistent with common sense and convenient as a basis for theorizing. By recent writers, on the contrary, non-intercourse with psychology, long practiced in silence, is explicitly proclaimed to be the proper policy.[3]

Mitchell was clearly disturbed by the tendency he observed. He went on to say, "For when economic theory has been purified so far that human nature has no place in it, economists become interested perforce in much that lies outside their theoretical field."[4] Nevertheless, Mitchell's review of the application of human behavior in the development of economics and the advances being made at that time in the fields of psychology, sociology, physiology, neurology, and political science led him to conclude on an optimistic note:

> Happily, the preceding reviews justify the belief that the situation is changing for the better. For Parmelee and Thorndike, Wallas, Veblin, and Lippmann, even in a measure Sombart and Walling, are endeavoring to explain how men act. . . . It is because they are developing a sounder type of functional psychology that we may hope both to profit by and to share in the work of contemporary psychologists.[5]

Even Joseph Schumpeter, an economist widely noted for his contributions toward making economics a more rigorous discipline, recognized the significance of the psychological element in business behavior. He remarked that businessmen are not motivated solely by profit but also by the "desire to found a private dynasty, the will to conquer in a competitive battle, and the joy of creating."[6]

Among recent economists, George Katona stands out for his attempts to analyze the psychological dimensions of economic behavior. He wrote two major books on this subject, *Psychological Analysis of Economic Behavior* (1951) and *Psychological Economics* (1975). In his first book, Katona recognized that a primary reason economists have ignored the psychological foundations of economic behavior is the lack of solid empirical evidence on the subject. In response to this problem, Katona spent many years at the University of Michigan researching consumer behavior. Unfortunately, in spite of Katona's recent work and Mitchell's optimistic outlook in 1914, on the prospect for focusing on human behavior in economic analysis, there has been little movement in that direction.

I am proposing a step in that direction and will discuss power as a basic motivator of humans. The drive for individual power is a historical fact. It is neither new nor confined to a particular culture or time, though some cultures, and even religions, may have tended to stimulate the drive for power.[7] One cannot reflect on the actions of such historical figures as Alexander the Great, Julius Ceasar, Napoleon Bonaparte, and Adolph Hitler without recognizing a remarkable drive for power.

Most civilized societies today frown upon the kind of blatant drive for power exhibited by these historical figures. Consequently, the drive for power is likely to be found in subtler forms that are socially more acceptable. This by no means implies that the desire for power is weak. One obvious and easily documented indication of an apparent drive for power in the United States today is provided by business executives who move into government service. A recent case is that of G. William Miller who was reportedly making around $700,000 a year as president of Textron, Inc., when he accepted an appointment from President Carter to be chairman of the Federal Reserve Board. The salary of the chairman at that time was about $60,000 per year. William McNamara left a highly lucrative position as a vice-president of Ford Motor Company to become Secretary of Defense in the Kennedy administration. W. Michael Blumenthal gave up the presidency of the Bendix Corporation to become Secretary of the Treasury during the administration of Jimmy Carter. What could motivate these people, or the many other high-salaried business executives who accept such appointments, to take such a tremendous pay cut? There may be some element of a diminishing marginal utility of money, but the typical trade-off of work (and money) for more leisure is certainly irrelevant here. Although the prospect of an even larger salary upon returning to private life is one possibility, prestige must also be considered a motive. In the United States, an achievement-oriented society, the prestige of a position is usually directly related to the amount of power the position bestows upon the holder. Public-opinion polls of recent years found that the chairman of the Federal Reserve Board is regarded as one of the most powerful people in the country behind the president of the United States. Though the pay is low, the job has something to offer—power.

Notes

1. John Maynard Keynes, *The General Theory of Employment Interest and Money* (New York: Harcourt, Brace and Co., 1936), p. 298.

2. William J. Baumol, *Business Behavior, Value and Growth* (New York: Macmillan, 1959).

3. Wesley C. Mitchell, "Human Behavior in Economics: A Survey of Recent Literature," *Quarterly Journal of Economics* (November 1914), p. 1.

4. Ibid., p. 2.

5. Ibid., p. 47.

6. Joseph Schumpeter, *The Theory of Economic Development,* trans. Redvers Opie (Cambridge, Mass.: Harvard University Press, 1934), p. 93.

7. See, for example, R.H. Tawney, *Religion and the Rise of Capitalism: A Historical Study* (New York: New American Library, 1937).

7 Power as a Concept in Philosophy

The obvious and blatant drive for power exhibited by some individuals might result from a flaw in their character or mentality; it might be a product of paranoia, inferiority, or delusions of grandeur. Indeed, psychologists often cite the careers of Napoleon and Hitler, both of whom were short in stature, and Franklin D. Roosevelt, who suffered a physical handicap, as examples of extraordinary efforts to compensate for perceived shortcomings and inferiority. Considering the apparent excesses in the drive for power by some historical figures, the argument that the power drive is unique to individual people would seem to have some merit. To propose convincingly that power motivates businessmen, the drive for power must be established as a general, if not universal, element of human nature. It must be determined, therefore, whether the power drive can be regarded as a common trait in people—a common denominator. A logical place to search for the role of power, if any, in human behavior is in the work of the students of human nature and behavior—the philosophers and psychologists.

The search begins among the philosophers. Although I consulted a variety of sources, including original works, in investigating the thinking of various philosophers, I have relied heavily on Will Durant's *The Story of Philosophy* (1926) as both a guide and a source.[1] This search reveals that the notion of power as a motivator of humans has occupied the thoughts of philosophers for over two thousand years.

The view that power motivates human behavior can be found as far back as the ancient Greek philosophers. We usually associate Greek philosophy with Socrates, Plato, and Aristotle. However, the foundations of Greek philosophy were laid by the Sophists, who were traveling thinkers and teachers before and during the life of Plato (427–347 B.C.). The Sophists observed a drive for power by individuals, and some actually regarded it as desirable. In addition, one of the two major lines of thought among the Sophists, exemplified by the teaching of Protagoras, emphasized the relativity of things. This provided the basis for their view on power. Nothing in their view, including nature, is intrinsically good or bad, true or false; it depends on how we think about it. The Sophists argued that all men are by nature unequal. Accordingly, morality restricts human freedom; it is simply an invention of the weak to inhibit the strong. These Sophists contended that the strong should not be bound by such conventions and that they should strive to achieve their preferences. Power, therefore, was regarded as a virtue and a primary desire of man. These views sound very much like those of

Nietzsche, the nineteenth-century philosopher and poet whose philosophy is commonly regarded as synonymous with power.

Plato disagreed with the Sophists. He emphasized the value of the individual. He felt that the inherent good and intrinsic value of individuals should lead to a utopian society with no private property. Nevertheless, he recognized that his notions were futile, human nature being what it is. In *The Republic,* Plato observed that the attributes of human nature included acquisitiveness, ambition, competitiveness, and jealousy. This observation stemmed from Plato's argument that human behavior arises from three sources—desire, emotion, and knowledge. He contended that these characteristics are in all men to varying degrees. Desire leads some to be restless and acquisitive. Emotion begets ambition along with spirit and courage. There is a dichotomy in the philosophy of Plato—what he thinks human nature should or could be on the one hand and what he observes human nature to be, in fact, on the other hand. Plato's observations on human nature do not specifically refer to power. Power can, however, easily be read into the characteristics of human nature outlined by Plato.

The Prince, although written about five hundred years ago, is studied today by statesmen, political scientists, and others interested in the use of power. Its author was an Italian diplomat, Niccolo Machiavelli (1469-1527). Machiavelli was primarily a man of political affairs. He was not a philosopher in the same sense as the others whose work is being examined here. However, the concepts of statesmanship and politics developed in *The Prince* reflect a clear understanding of politics, history, and ethics. Because Machiavelli's study has been of such enduring interest and general applicability, it must be regarded as a classic in the area of political philosophy.

Machiavelli believed that politics is independent of morality. From this position, he developed generalizations regarding political behavior. These generalizations were based on how people in fact behave rather than on how they should behave. Instead of analyzing human nature, Machiavelli presented a detailed account of how to gain political power and to maintain it against those who would take it. Power was the key in his analysis—power is desired and should be used. Indeed, the entire thrust of *The Prince* is based on the assumption that the desire for power is a fundamental part of the human condition. Machiavelli's own observations convey a cold and calculating view of the use of power. In connection with taking power, Machiavelli observed:

> Whence it is to be noted, that in taking a state the conqueror must arrange to commit all cruelties at once, so as not to have to recur to them every day, and so as to be able, by not making fresh changes, to reassure people and win them over by benefiting them. . . . For injuries should be done all together, so that being less tasted, they will give less offense. Benefits should be granted little by little, so that they may be enjoyed.[2]

On maintaining power, Machiavelli warns that one must be alert to the desire for power by political subordinates and notes,

> ... when they are not bound to you of set purpose and for ambitious ends, it is a sign that they think more of themselves than of you; and from such men the prince must guard himself and look upon them as secret enemies, who will help to ruin him when in adversity.[3]

He offers his ultimate rule on attaining and maintaining political power:

> A prince should therefore have no other aim or thought, not take up any other thing for his study, but war and its organization and discipline, for that is the only art that is necessary to one who commands, and it is of such virtue that it not only maintains those who are born princes, but often enables men of private fortune to attain that rank.[4]

There is certainly nothing subtle in Machiavelli's philosophy on the use of power for political ends. He also assumes that those who have achieved either political or financial position in society will seek to maintain or increase their power.

Francis Bacon (1561-1626) had a varied and successful career as both a philosopher and a politician in England. In 1583, he was elected to Parliament and in 1618 assumed the legal post of Lord Chancellor. Though Bacon expressed concern about his two-tiered career, it is likely that his experience in the world of political affairs helped develop his keen insights on human nature. Probably this experience also inspired his admiration of Machiavelli and other similar writers. Unlike Plato, such writers analyze what men *do*. Thus, in his essay, "Advancement of Learning", Bacon observed, "We are beholden to Machiavelli, and writers of that kind, who openly and unmasked declare what men do in fact, and not what they ought to do."[5] In Bacon's philosophy, the drive for power is less a central theme than an implicit assumption. His view is evident in his assumption that people strive for and compete for power. He expresses a rather heartless view of human nature that is reminiscent of Machiavelli. For example, in his essay "Of Dissimulation," Bacon even treats friends primarily as a means to obtain power. His prescription for dealing with friends is: "Love your friend as if he were to become your enemy, and your enemy as if he were to become your friend."[6]

Baruch Spinoza (1632-1677) was born in Amsterdam and was primarily a philosopher throughout his life. Unlike Bacon, but like Machiavelli and later Nietzsche, Spinoza used individual power as a central theme. *Ethics,* his major work, reflected his primary interest in studying man in relation to society and the universe. He sought to develop a psychology of the emotions as forces in man. For Spinoza, who saw virtue in terms of the power of the individual, power became a primary factor in man's relation to society: "By virtue and power I mean the same thing. . . . the more a man can preserve his being and seek what is useful to him, the greater is his virtue."[7] Because of his emphasis on the virtue of power, Spinoza had little use for humility, noting that "he who repents is twice unhappy and doubly weak."[8] Thus he contends that, "The foundation of virtue is no other than the effort to maintain one's being; and a man's happiness consists in the power of so doing."[9] Some of the similarities to Nietzsche are indeed striking. The power of a man is a virtue; thus power is something to strive for and to wield.

Throughout his life, Immanuel Kant (1724-1804) was a scholar writing prolifically in natural science as well as philosophy. His major works in philosophy were *Critique of Pure Reason* (1781) and *Critique of Practical Reason* (1788). His philosophy in connection with power, however, appears most distinctly in a shorter work on political theory.[10] In this work, Kant recognized the existence of strife among individuals. He argued that this is a desirable trait in man. It is the means of developing the capacities of life and is essential for progress. If men were strictly social, he proposed, they would stagnate without individualism and competition. He describes the benefits and source of such strife as essentially deriving from a power drive. "Without those qualities of an unsocial kind . . . men might have led an Arcadian shepherd life in complete harmony, contentment and mutual love; but in that case all their talents would have forever remained hidden in their germ." Fortunately, in Kant's judgment, this is not the way of human nature. "Thanks be then to nature for this unsociableness, for this envious jealousy and vanity, for this insatiable desire of possession or even of power!"[11] Drawing the distinction between what is and what ought to be, Kant, in preferring what *is,* differs sharply from Plato. He notes that, "Man wishes concord; but nature knows better what is good for his species, and she will have discord."[12] And further, "The natural impulses that urge man in this direction impel him to exertion of his powers, and consequently to further development of his natural capacities."[13] Kant sees power as a motivator in man and, unlike the utopian philosophers, he regards power, along with envy and jealousy, as desirable traits. Although these traits may have unpleasant side effects, Kant sees them as crucial in the advancement of man. Today we can see similarities in the role of profits as a motivator of business behavior in a capitalist economy—advancing our material progress but sometimes despoiling the environment and causing some of the socially less desirable actions of men.

Like Kant, Arthur Schopenhauer (1788-1860) was a German, but he wrote almost entirely in the field of philosophy. In his major philosophical work, *The World as Will and Idea* (1819), Schopenhauer viewed everything as subjectively determined—the world is man's idea. Basically, Schopenhauer regarded man's will or desire as the essence of man, though he thought it to be fundamentally evil. Thus, rather than simply accepting will as fact or providing a utopian alternative as to what ought to be, Schopenhauer sought to explain why this was so. He concluded that man's desires are infinite and therefore can never be satisfied. When one desire is satisfied, others arise to take its place. This notion of Schopenhauer anticipates the concept of a hierarchical theory of motivation in modern psychology most often associated with the works of A.H. Maslow (discussed in the next chapter). Schopenhauer sees the desire for power as basic in all of nature.[14] Schopenhauer did not care for what is, and was pessimistic about human nature. Yet, by focusing on what is in human nature, Schopenhauer nevertheless reached the same general conclusion that Kant reached—that the desire for power is inherent in human nature.

In the writing of another German philosopher, Friedrich Nietzsche (1844–1900), we find the work most widely associated with the importance of power in human behavior, except perhaps for Machiavelli's *The Prince*. Power plays a central role in many of Nietzsche's philosophical works. The power theme is apparent in his central concepts of superman, the will to power, sublimation, master morality, and slave morality. Nietzsche even proposed that the will to power is expressed in all human activity—that it may even be the basic energy of the entire cosmos. Nietzsche started from the idea that if life is a struggle in which the fittest survive, then strength must be the ultimate virtue. Nietzsche's harsh views on power and its use by man were tempered somewhat as he suggested that man seek, the "superhuman" power of such men as Goethe and Leonardo da Vinci rather than the "all-too-human" power of military despots. However, his belief in strength as the ultimate virtue led Nietzsche most often to favor the use of force. Nietzsche's admiration for power and strength is captured in his reactions to the cavalry on display in Frankfurt. "I felt for the first time that the strongest and highest Will to Life does not find expression in a miserable struggle for existence, but in a Will to War, a Will to Power, a Will to Overpower!"[15]

In developing his notion of the superman, Nietzsche focused on the relation of the individual to society. He noted that the role of society is the enhancement of the power of the individual. In drawing together the major conclusions of his works in *Thus Spake Zarasthustra* (1890) Nietzsche observed, "What is good? All that increases the feeling of power, the will to power, power itself, in man." According to Nietzsche, power itself and the achievement of power are the essence of life.

Bertrand Russell (1872-1970) was a mathematician as well as a philosopher, and he wrote extensively in both fields. Russell attached a great deal of importance to the role of power in human behavior and devoted an entire book to the subject. Underlying Russell's extensive treatment of the concept of power was his view that power is one of the primary desires and motivators of man. The relevance of his view to the U.S. sociopolitical and economic systems is direct.

Of the infinite desires of man, the chief are the desires for power and glory. These are not identical, though closely allied: The Prime Minister has more power than glory, the King has more glory than power. As a rule, however, the easiest way to obtain glory is to obtain power; this is especially the case as regards the men who are active in relation to public events.[16] (p. 8)

Where no social institution, such as aristocracy or hereditary monarchy, exists to limit the number of men to whom power is possible, those who most desire power are, broadly speaking, those most likely to acquire it. It follows that, in a social system in which power is open to all, the posts which confer power will, as a rule, be occupied by men who differ from the average in being especially power-loving. Love of power, though one of the strongest of human motives, is very unevenly distributed, and is limited by various other motives, such as love of ease, love of pleasure, and sometimes love of approval. (p. 10)

We should, of course be mistaken if we regarded it as the sole human motive, but this mistake would not lead us so much astray as might be expected in the search for causal laws in social science, since love of power is the chief motive producing the changes which social science has to study. . . . I shall be concerned to prove that the fundamental concept in social science is Power, in the same sense in which Energy is the fundamental concept in physics. (pp. 9 and 11)

Russell also regards the study of power as essential in economics and he becomes quite explicit on this point.

The orthodox economists, as well as Marx, who in this respect agreed with them, were mistaken in supposing that economic self-interest could be taken as the fundamental motive in the social sciences. The desire for commodities, when separated from power and glory, is finite, and can be fully satisfied by a moderate competence.

When a moderate degree of comfort is assured, both individuals and communities will pursue power rather than wealth; they may seek wealth as a means to power, or they may forgo an increase of wealth in order to secure an increase of power, but in the former case as in the latter their fundamental motive is not economic. This error in orthodox and Marxist economics is not merely theoretical, but is of the greatest practical importance, and has caused some of the principal events of recent times to be misunderstood. It is only by realizing that love of power is the cause of the activities that are important in social affairs that history, whether ancient or modern, can be rightly interpreted. (p. 9)

Russell's argument here would certainly explain why high-salaried business executives accept relatively low-paying government positions. These people have certainly assured themselves of a "moderate degree of comfort." Furthermore, it seems clear that their "fundamental motive is not economic."

Russell cites the work of Berle and Means, which I discussed earlier in connection with the prospect of a long-run decline of profits in capitalism, to support his contention that power is essential in understanding the behavior of businessmen.

They (Berle and Means) contend that, although ownership is centrifugal, economic power is centripetal; by a very careful and exhaustive investigation they arrive at the conclusion that two thousand individuals control half of the industry of the United States. They regard the modern executive as analogous to the kings and Popes of former times; in their opinion, more is to be learnt as to his motives by studying such men as Alexander the Great than by considering him as the successor of the tradesmen who appear in the pages of Adam Smith. The concentration of power in these vast organizations is analogous—so they argue—to that in the mediaeval Church or in the National State, and is such as to enable corporations to compete with the State on equal terms. (p. 87)

Russell's philosophy on power in general and in relation to economics in particular is clear. After a lengthy discussion of the evils of power, Russell attempts to deal with power as a fact of life and discusses the ethics of power. He adopts the pragmatic position that power is a primary desire of man. The evils of power, therefore, are best dealt with by harnessing or channeling the power drive toward socially desirable ends rather than by trying to eliminate it. Russell proposed that, "It is not enough that there should be a purpose other than power; it is necessary that this purpose should be one which, if achieved, will help to satisfy the desires of others." (p. 179) Further, he believed that:

The forms that a man's love of power will take depend upon his temperament, his opportunities, and his skill; his temperament, moreover, is largely moulded by his circumstances. To turn an individual's love of power into specified channels is therefore, a matter of providing him with the right circumstances, the right opportunities, and the appropriate type of skill. (p. 181)

I agree with this line of thinking in Russell; it is precisely what I propose later in this book. I think that harnessing or channeling the power drive is the only means of maintaining the dynamic features of competitive capitalism in the United States while preventing this power drive from destroying the economic system and the sociopolitical system as well.

In conclusion, it is evident that the role of power has been an important idea in the work of some philosophers and a central idea in the work of others—most notably Machiavelli, Spinoza, Nietzsche, and Russell. Philosophers have been concerned with the role of power in human behavior for many years. The power motive is *not* just an idle or isolated thought.

Notes

1. Will Durant, *The Story of Philosophy* (New York: Pocket Books, 1953). Originally published in 1926.

2. Niccolo Machiavelli, *The Prince* (New York: New American Library, 1952), p. 62.

3. Ibid., p. 64.

4. Ibid., p. 81.

5. xii, 2.

6. viii, 2.

7. IV, 20.

8. IV, 54.

9. IV, 18 note.

10. Immanuel Kant, "The Natural Principle of the Political Order," *Kant's Principles of Politics,* ed. and trans. by W. Hastie (Edinburgh: T. and T. Clark, 1891).

11. Ibid., p. 11.

12. Ibid., p. 11.

13. Ibid., p. 12.

14. I, 191.

15. Forster-Nietzsche, *The Young Nietzsche* (London: 1912), p. 106.

16. All quotes and passages of Bertrand Russell in this chapter come from *Power: A New Social Analysis* (New York: Barnes and Noble, 1962). Reprinted with permission.

8 Power as a Concept in Psychology

While philosophers study the nature of things in general, the field of psychology has a far more narrow focus that is directly relevant to our interest—the study of human (and animal) behavior. This search reveals that one of the major systems of psychology today is founded on the proposition that the desire for power is the primary motivator of human behavior.

Psychology as an independent field of study is quite new. The person generally regarded as the founder of modern psychology is the German Wilhelm Wundt (1832-1920). He did his major work in the latter part of the nineteenth century while Francis Galton (1822-1911) was developing similar methods of psychology in England. The approach to psychology developed by Wundt and Galton sought to apply the scientific method in investigating cause-effect relationships in human behavior, often in laboratory settings. This approach laid the foundation for what has become one of the two major schools or systems of psychology today. It may be called the experimental-positivistic-behavioristic school, which relies on careful, systematic observation and experimentation.

The other major school of modern psychology today is psychoanalysis, which was founded by Sigmund Freud (1856-1934). In its early stages, the Freudian school gave impetus to the development of another school of psychology—individual psychology. Individual psychology regards the desire for power as the primary motivator of human behavior. This latter school is of particular interest here. Since it grew from Freud's system with which many people are familiar, I will start with Freud in tracing its history.

Sigmund Freud was a Viennese physician whose approach to understanding human behavior did not rely on laboratory experimentation, as did the earlier work of Wundt and Galton. Instead, Freud developed theories of human motivation based on careful observation of individual cases. These case studies were used by Freud to provide a systematic method of analysis and treatment of mental illness. The crucial elements in Freud's psychoanalysis are the *id,* the unconscious, and sexual motivation. It was Freud's theory that human behavior is directed by the id dimension of personality organization. This is the dimension of the personality reflecting the biological and instinctual parts of the psyche and is governed by pleasure seeking. In addition, the unconscious, or that which is driven out of awareness, has an important influence on human behavior. In Freud's theory, the *ego* (the conscious, organizing part of the psyche) and the *superego* (the conscience that inhibits instinctual behavior) play relatively unimportant roles in determining human behavior.

According to Freud, unconscious motives are very strong and are primarily sexual in nature. Freud's views attracted considerable attention among professional psychologists and physicians. Beginning in the 1890s, Freud invited a group of Viennese colleagues to his home on a weekly basis to discuss the theories of human behavior he was developing. As a result of these meetings and lectures to professional audiences, interest in psychoanalysis spread. The circle of adherents to Freud's theories grew as it became evident that Freud's system of analysis provided a potentially fruitful method for analyzing and treating mental illness. In 1899, Alfred Adler, a nerve specialist, attended one of Freud's lectures. He came away convinced that Freud was developing an exciting new approach to psychology. Adler was invited to join Freud's circle in 1902.

During the next several years, Alfred Adler was stimulated by the theories of human behavior developed by Freud. However, Adler developed an analysis of human motivation that contrasted sharply with Freud's. In 1907, Adler published his *Study of Organ Inferiority,* which contained the foundations of his line of thinking in psychology. In that book, Adler developed the principle of *overcompensation.* The basic idea was that people with physical problems strive to compensate for their problems and, in doing so, they sometimes overcompensate. Although Adler's principle of overcompensation was discussed in connection with physiological functions, it had important psychological implications. This was the origin of the now well-known *inferiority complex.* A subsequent paper by Adler, "The Aggression Drive in Life and Neurosis" (1908), further established his idea that the desire for power, driven by feelings of inferiority, is the basic motivator of human behavior.

By this time, Adler's differences with Freud's system of analysis had sharpened enough to become apparent to many observers. Although Adler accepted Freud's basic contentions that human behavior results from specific motivations and drives, he could not accept the argument that sex was the primary motivator. Nor was Adler able to accept Freud's view that the id and subconscious were the basic sources of human behavior. Instead, Adler contended that the primary motivator of human behavior was the drive for power and superiority over people and things in order to compensate for real and perceived weaknesses. Further, he believed that it was not the id but the ego dimension of the personality—the conscious, organizing part of the psyche—that dominates human behavior. Adler continued to develop his line of thinking and, along with C.G. Jung, to take issue with Freud's theory. The friction between Freud and Adler grew until in 1911 they formally broke off their association. A number of Adler's adherents left Freud's circle at the same time. This began the systematic development and spread of a new school of thought in psychology. In 1913, it was named *individual psychology* by Adler and his adherents to distinguish it from Freud's psychoanalysis.

The relevance of Adler's work to my study is clear in the following quotation, which sums up the essence of Adler's system of psychology: "the goal of superiority, of power, of the conquest of others, is the goal which directs the activity of most human beings." (p. 161)[1] This goal is a basic motivator in every human being—it arises out of the feeling of weakness and inferiority that begins in infancy.

> Every child, dependent as he is on the help of the community, finds himself face to face with a world that gives and takes, that expects adaptation and satisfies life. His instincts are baffled in their fulfillment by obstacles whose conquest gives him pain. . . . He realizes at an early age that there are human beings who are able to satisfy their urges more completely and are better prepared to live. . . . He learns to over-value the size and stature which enable one to open a door, or the ability to move heavy objects, or the right of others to give commands and claim obedience to them. . . . A desire to grow, to become as strong or stronger than all others, arises in his soul. To dominate those who are gathered about him becomes his chief purpose in life. (pp. 33 and 34)

According to Adler, the infant's desire to grow stronger and dominate others continues to develop throughout childhood. The striving for power by the child is, in Adler's view, reflected even in the child's play.

> The goal of superiority, another factor obvious in play betrays itself in the child's tendency to be the commander and the ruler. We can discover this tendency by watching how the child pushes himself forward and to what degree he prefers those games which give him an opportunity to satisfy his desire to play the leading role. (p. 92)

Adler noted that the widely observed adverse effects of power have resulted in attempts to socialize children, in the sense of making them sensitive toward others, and to control their power drive. Like the philosopher Bertrand Russell, Adler regarded the drive for power as a fundamental element of human nature. He felt that rather than fruitlessly trying to eliminate this drive, we should attempt to control and channel it. Adler viewed the role of the mother as instrumental in developing the social feeling that will modify the striving for power in children. The results of this influence may actually make the job more difficult because children quickly learn that the unabashed drive for power is not socially acceptable. He noted that "children do not express their striving for power openly, but hide it under the guise of charity and tenderness, and carry out their work behind a veil. Modestly, they expect to escape disclosure in this way." (p. 74) We can see the same effects of socialization in adults, among whom, "The goal of superiority is a secret goal. The existence of a social feeling prevents its frank development. It must grow in secret and hide itself behind a friendly mask!" (p. 165)

Just as the id, the unconscious, and the sex drive are fundamental to the psychoanalysis of Freud, the *ego* and the *power drive* are the crucial determinants of human behavior in Adler's individual psychology. In that system, the drive for power is pervasive in the lives of individuals. The conscious drive for power is a basic element of human nature. It arises in infancy and is apparent throughout childhood and adulthood. It cannot be escaped, only channeled and socialized. The power drive not only resides within the individual but pervades family relationships. It is the basic determinant of all human behavior.

Adler's system of psychology was not widely accepted in its early years because of Adler's acknowledged leanings toward socialism. More recently, however, Adler's system of psychology has become widely influential among psychologists, psychiatrists, and even anthropologists, throughout the world.

The work of Freud and Adler placed great emphasis on motivation as the basis for human behavior. Numerous psychologists and others have studied human motivation, including William I. Thomas, Henry A. Murray, L.F. Shaffer, and E.J. Shoben, Jr. Most students of human motivation have constructed lists of the various motives that are believed to underlie human behavior. There has been one basic difference among the students of motivation. Some argue, like Adler, that various motives are a fundamental element of human nature. Others contend that many if not all motives are socially learned. Which group is correct is not clear. What is clear, however, is that every list of motives contains one or more terms that imply the power motive—for example, *dominance, mastery, achievement,* and *recognition.*

Perhaps the leading student of motivation was the psychologist Abraham Maslow. He is noted for formulating a *hierarchical* theory of motivation. Maslow argued that a list of human needs and motives could be as long as one wished to make it, but such a list would not be terribly helpful. Consequently, Maslow proposed a few basic levels of needs—a hierarchy of needs which are, from lowest to highest level, physiological needs, safety, love, esteem, and self-actualization.[2]

Once a lower-level need or motive is satisfied, an individual's behavior is dominated by the next higher level. When the physiological needs, such as food and water, are basically satisfied the next higher level—safety—dominates behavior. After the safety need (freedom from aggressive and harmful acts) is satisfied, the need for love, that is the need for belonging and affection, arises as the motivator of behavior. Maslow concluded that in our society, the physiological and safety needs of most individuals are satisfied, as is the need for love in most well-adjusted people. As a consequence, the needs or motives that dominate human behavior in our society are esteem and self-actualization. The need for esteem includes the desire for self-esteem as well as the esteem of others. Maslow cites the work of Adler in noting that these needs are reflected in the desire for strength, achievement, recognition, and importance. What we have been calling the power drive is clearly embodied in the need for esteem in Maslow's hierarchy. The hierarchy of needs proposed by Maslow has strong similarities to the argument of Bertrand Russell presented in the previous chapter. If you recall, Russell contended that, "When a moderate degree of comfort is assured, both individuals and communities will pursue power rather than wealth."

Since Adler's system of psychology was based on the notion that people strive for power and control over others from infancy, Maslow's reference to Adler's work is significant. In reaching his conclusion that the esteem and self-actualization needs are the primary motives in our society, Maslow observed that, "These needs have been relatively stressed by Alfred Adler and his followers, and have been relatively neglected by Freud and the psychoanalysts. More and more today, however, there is appearing widespread appreciation of their central importance."[3]

So far, our investigation of the power phenomenon in psychology has focused on what are essentially theoretical developments. Direct, scientific testing of the power drive is very difficult, if not impossible. There has been, however, some relevant indirect investigation, especially that of David C. McClelland. McClelland has conducted both cross-cultural and individual studies of motivation. In a major study, McClelland proposed that, although the extent of economic development of a country traditionally has been attributed to geography and climate, psychological factors are also important. In that study, he attempted to isolate psychological factors by rigorous quantitative methods. Relying on the insights about human motivation provided by the work of such pioneers as Freud and Adler, McClelland developed a method of measuring differences in human motivation. His analysis covered two highly developed countries, Germany and Japan, and two less-developed countries, Brazil and India. The results of the analysis led McClelland to conclude:

> The profit motive, so long a basic analytic element among Marxist and western economists alike, turns out on closer examination to be the achievement motive, at least in the sense in which most men have used the term to explain the energetic activities of the bourgeoise. . . . The basic desire for gain, in and of itself, has done little to produce economic development. But the desire for achievement has done a great deal, and ironically it was probably this same desire that activated the lower middle-class leaders of the Russian Communist Party as well as the bourgeoise they criticized so intensely.[4]

In McClelland's view, the achievement motive is stimulated by the desire for power, social approval, or knowledge. His study indicates that the desire for power, among other factors, more than pecuniary gain was responsible for economic development.

Another empirical study by McClelland focused on the motivation of individual U.S. business managers in large corporations. The findings revealed that most managers (over 70 percent) were higher in power motivation compared with people in general. In this particular study, power was defined as the need or desire to control and influence others. This need was greater in managers than their interest in being liked. The best managers were found to be those whose need for power was directed toward the goals of the institution rather than for personal aggrandizement and empire building.[5] This shares Bertrand Russell's and Alfred Adler's emphasis on the need for controlling and channeling the power drive toward societal interests.

Before ending this discussion of the drive for power in the literature of psychology, it is important to examine the view of an economist who has studied human behavior in economic affairs. Though George Katona's work focused primarily upon consumer psychology and behavior, he has given some attention to business motivation. Katona wrote that "there can be no doubt that in present day American business thinking the function and role of profits are substantial."[6] However, explicitly noting the work of the psychologist. A.H. Maslow, Katona observed that:

> Nonpecuniary motives may loom large in the case of well-established businesses operating under prosperous conditions. Improving the living standards of the firm's employees or even of the town in which the business is located may be viewed as being in the interest of the firm itself. . . . Desire for prestige will be interwoven with more specific business motives.[7]

Along with the desire for prestige, we find once again the emphasis on power as a motivator. In this case, specifically with respect to business executives, Katona observed:

> The urge for prestige may develop into a desire to influence other members of our groups, to control or dominate them—in short, into a striving for power. . . . With respect to striving for power, the ego-centered motivations of business executives often coincide with their business or group motivations. The president of a weak firm may be a dictator in his own office but must assume a subordinate role in negotiating with suppliers and customers. The head or executive of a powerful firm may, however, exercise power all around and thus satisfy personal as well as business drives.[8]

At this point, it is clear that the power motive occupies a significant place in the field of psychology—in fact, its significance is growing. Nevertheless, it must be acknowledged that the psychological literature on the power motive remains largely in the realm of theory. The theory is based on systematic observation of human behavior in the real world, but hard evidence is scanty and tentative. Indeed, how should one go about conducting a rigorous, scientific test of the hypothesis that the behavior of an infant, or an adult for that matter, is motivated by a drive for power. Then too, how does one conduct a rigorous, scientific test of the hypothesis that businesspeople are motivated by profit maximization. Although economists make this assumption regarding business behavior, there is no absolute proof of the hypothesis. The assumption is based on systematic observation of business behavior and there is some empirical evidence that is consistent with the hypothesis.

Why then have economists generally accepted the profit motive as a determinant of business behavior? Probably because it conforms with observed business behavior and it appeals to reason. Furthermore, the assumption of profit maximization is operationally convenient—profits are mathematically tractable and quantifiable. Power is not.

Economics and psychology, along with other social sciences, face similar problems. Given the nature of the subject matter, we do not have the luxury of the natural sciences, where hypotheses can be subjected to carefully controlled laboratory tests or tests based on observation of phenomena subject to fixed laws of nature. This explains why, in the social sciencies, no single test or observation is accepted as definitive proof or disproof of a hypothesis. However, from careful and systematic observation by many scholars over time, generalizations often can be made that tend to hold up against the events of the real world. In light of the observations by philosophers and psychologists, it is reasonable to conclude that the desire for power is an important motivator of human behavior.

The next several chapters focus on the need for constraining and channeling corporate merger activity. It will be seen that certain kinds of mergers are constrained by the antitrust laws because they tend to cause higher prices and profits by restricting competition. That is, they lead to monopolistic prices. It is apparent that such mergers are motivated by the desire for profits. The profit motive is explicitly accounted for in economic models. Thus, the rationale for constraining such mergers is demonstrable within traditional economic models. However a whole new genre of mergers—the conglomerate merger—has become prevalent during the past two decades. There is no evidence that this type of merger is motivated by profits. Because conglomerate mergers show no monopoly-profit effects within the framework of traditional economic theory, conglomerate mergers are not constrained so there are thousands of them each year. The desire for power provides a more plausible motive for such mergers, and the consequences provide a justification for constraining them.

Notes

1. All passages and quotes of Alfred Adler in this chapter come from *Understanding Human Nature,* trans. Walter Wolfe (London: George Allen and Unwin, 1928). Reprinted with permission.

2. A.H. Maslow, "A Theory of Human Motivation," *Psychological Review,* Vol. 50 (1943), pp. 370-96.

3. Ibid., p. 382.

4. David C. McClelland, *The Achieving Society* (Princeton: D. Van Nostrand Co., 1961), p. 391.

5. David C. McClelland, "Power is the Great Motivator," *Harvard Business Review* (March/April 1976), pp. 100-110.

6. George Katona, *Psychological Economics* (New York: Elsevier Scientific Publishing Co., 1975), p. 289.

7. Ibid., p. 303.

8. Ibid., p. 300.

Mergers for Monopoly Profits

Mergers have the potential to erode the foundations of our economic and socio-political systems. This may seem an exaggeration; mergers are but one of many forms of business behavior. Other forms of business behavior encompass advertising, research and development, pricing, marketing, and so forth. However, mergers are unique, because they immediately affect an acquired firm. The effect is final—the demise of that firm. The one inevitable result from the disappearance of a firm through merger is that resources are consolidated and an independent decision-making unit is gone from the system. A second possible outcome is that an industry becomes more like a monopoly, which occurs when the acquiring and acquired firms are in the same industry and are direct competitors.

The influence of mergers on the system is insidious. No single merger has a noteworthy impact on the consolidation of resources in an economy that is so large (about $3 trillion in manufacturing, mining, and banking assets in 1980). Even the 1981 merger of Conoco ($10 billion in assets) and DuPont ($9.5 billion in assets), which was the largest merger in U.S. history, caused no significant increase in the consolidation of resources in the United States. Consequently, it is no surprise that such microeconomic phenomena go unnoticed and that it is difficult to draw attention to the corrosive influence of mergers. Over the long run, mergers that individually seem inconsequential have resulted in an immense consolidation of economic resources. I estimate that in 1981 40 percent of the assets held by the twenty largest industrial firms, and 70 percent of the assets held by the twenty largest banking organizations in the United States, are the result of acquisitions these firms have made. This reflects a huge consolidation of resources (aside from any monopoly effects). Each of these groups of firms controls around a half-trillion dollars in assets. During the merger process, at least 1,200 companies disappeared (into 40 companies).

Just since 1960, over 4,000 banks, having over $100 billion in assets, have been acquired. During this same period, well over 2,000 large manufacturing and mining firms were acquired. These acquired firms held well over $100 billion in assets. Acquisitions of large and small firms in manufacturing, wholesale and retail trade, and services numbered over 40,000. Though most of these were small firms (each with less than $10 million in assets), and some were affiliates of larger companies, these acquisitions represent a remarkable consolidation of economic resources and independent decision makers in only two decades.

Without question, merger activity in the United States has proceeded at a mind-boggling rate. Measures traditionally employed to describe the consolidation of resources usually indicate the proportion of assets controlled by the 100 largest companies in major sectors of the economy. (This is called *aggregate concentration*.) For the manufacturing sector, Federal Trade Commission data indicate that between 1950 and 1980, the top 100 manufacturers increased their share of manufacturing assets from about 40 to 50 percent. My estimates for banking indicate that the 100 largest banking organizations in this country increased their control over banking deposits from about 46 to 55 percent (1958-78). These figures include the substantial growth of foreign assets owned by the big U.S. banks and industrial firms; but of course these assets, be they foreign or domestic, give them economic and political clout in this country or abroad.

The data just presented on recent merger activity are an overview. The dimensions and significance of merger activity can be best appreciated if we look at some of the major consolidations that have taken place in U.S. business. I will begin with an examination of horizontal mergers because until about 1960 mergers were predominantly of the horizontal type.

The phrase *horizontal merger* refers to mergers of firms in the same industry or market, that is, mergers of competitors. Hypothetical examples of horizontal mergers might include General Motors and Ford Motor, or two of your local grocery stores. Such mergers are the most likely to be a manifestation of the profit motive at work. Even if horizontal mergers do not create an absolute monopoly, they do reduce the number of competitors. As I described in chapter 3, if there are few competitors it is possible to reach agreements rather than compete on the prices to charge customers. This was illustrated earlier with the electrical-equipment conspiracy and the OPEC cartel. In short, monopoly-level prices and profits may be achieved even without a true monopoly. That firms in industries with few firms do in fact generally earn relatively high profit or charge prices above a competitive level has been shown in many statistical studies by economists over the past twenty years. Findings of such studies covering the manufacturing sector have been summarized in an article by Leonard Weiss of the University of Wisconsin, and I have summarized those studies in articles dealing with commercial banking.[1]

Although there have been three merger waves in the United States, the one at the turn of the century which I will relate was the most intensive. It involved firms and industries that will be familiar to most readers, and affected a large part of the industrial sector of our economic system. It also involved firms and industries I discussed in chapter 4—U.S. Steel, Standard Oil, American Tobacco, and the automobile industry. There, I used them to illustrate the benefits to society of businesses' drive to maximize profits. Here, they will show that the drive for profits also adversely affects society. Since gaining a monopoly increases profits, business has an incentive to obtain a monopoly by merger.

Unfortunately, this results in monopoly prices to consumers and an increased concentration of economic resources. The consolidation of firms around 1900 left an indelible imprint on the structure of many of our basic industries, leaving them more monopolistic than competitive. Many remain that way to this day. For the details of the events that I discuss, I have relied on several sources.[2]

The United States Steel Corporation emerged in 1901 as a result of the most massive consolidation of firms in a single industry that had ever taken place. This involved some of the legendary figures in U.S. business history. As late as 1890, the steel industry had a fairly competitive structure. Numerous firms were involved in each stage of production. For example, many firms produced crude and unfinished steel, even though three firms were preeminent—Federal Steel, Carnegie Steel, and National Steel. In the production of finished-steel products, there were also numerous producers, though five companies accounted for a large part—American Steel and Wire, American Tin Plate, American Steel and Hoop, National Tube, and American Bridge. Naturally, the finished-steel producers purchased their input from the makers of crude and unfinished steel.

Two factors brought about the end of a steel industry composed of many producers. First and foremost was a strong distaste for vigorous price competition. The other factor was the personalities of two titans of U.S. industry— Andrew Carnegie and J.P. Morgan. At the time, Carnegie's company (Carnegie Steel) was one of the few integrated steel companies in the country. It produced crude as well as semifinished steel. Moreover, Carnegie held iron ore and coal deposits through the Frick Coke Co. and the Oliver Iron Mine Co. He did not make finished steel and thus had to sell crude and semifinished steel to finished-steel producers. Some of the finished-steel producers were also owned by powerful business interests. J.P. Morgan controlled National Tube, and John W. "Betcha-million" Gates controlled American Steel and Wire Co. Under these circumstances, Carnegie feared that he could be financially embarrassed and subjected to a certain amount of control in connection with the pricing and output of his steel. If major customers like Morgan and Gates decided to integrate backward and produce their own crude and semifinished steel, they would be able to force a competitive price on Carnegie or produce enough of their own crude and semifinished steel to satisfy all of their requirements. By the same token, producers like Morgan and Gates recognized that they too could be subjected to some control and pricing discipline if Carnegie integrated forward into their business of producing finished-steel products. They would then face a formidable competitor in finished steel who could, at the same time, control the price of their input.

This episode involved individuals with immense financial resources. John Gates, whose American Steel and Wire Co. bought its semifinished input from Carnegie Steel and Federal Steel (a Morgan interest), started plans to build his own primary steel plant. At about the same time, National Tube (another Morgan interest) and other companies began similar plans. Then Andrew Carnegie announced plans to build a huge tube works in Conneaut, Ohio, incorporating the very latest in technology and production methods. Carnegie also announced plans to build a railroad from Pittsburgh to the Atlantic coast. Carnegie, who was already a supplier to Morgan, would become a major competitor in one segment of the steel industry. In addition, Morgan's Pennsylvania Railroad, which hauled a lot of Carnegie's products, would face direct competition.

J.P. Morgan used his emissary, Charles Schwab, to convince Carnegie of the benefits of cooperation and consolidation rather than unfettered competition. Morgan was prepared to offer Carnegie a handsome price for his company. Details of the plan proposed were subsequently worked out by a shrewd corporation lawyer, James B. Dill. Dill was perceptive enough to recognize that direct negotiations between the two men would be useless. He concocted an approach that he subsequently related to Lincoln Steffens, who wrote of the incident in his autobiography. According to Steffens, Dill said,

> I put Morgan in one room, Carnegie in another, while I took the third room between them with my clerks and stenographers. I knew if they met they would blow up, so I played the part of buffer and negotiator. They could express their opinions of each other to me. I could agree with both of them, sympathize with the generosity and bigness of each one, and share his contempt for the narrow meanness of the other. I was sincere, uninsultable, and true to their agreeable purposes, the one to buy the other to sell.[3]

The price for Carnegie's steel operations, including the Frick Coke Co., was $420 million—a fantastic sum.

Elbert Gary, the president of Federal Steel (a Morgan company) was satisfied with the arrangement worked out by Dill. Nevertheless, in February 1901, Gary also saw the possibility of a huge, self-contained steel company. In a public announcement he declared that "it is probable there will be such ownership of control as to secure perfect and permanent harmony in the larger lines of industry."[4] This plan resulted, in April 1901, in the formation of the United States Steel Corporation.

U.S. Steel was formed by a massive consolidation of firms in the industry that has been called the "combination of combinations." U.S. Steel, a holding company, owned most of the large steel companies in this country in all phases of production. Its holdings ranged from iron ore and coal mines, to railroads and steamships, to water-supply plants and finished-steel products. The original combination in 1901 consolidated about 60 percent of iron and steel production into one firm. The list of companies combined into U.S. Steel in 1901 and the next few years requires four full pages in Moody's *The Truth about the Trusts*.

The consolidation of the steel industry accomplished its ultimate goal. As proponents of the consolidation said, "order" was returned to the industry. This was one way of saying that cooperation was in and price competition was out.

The spirit of cooperation that prevailed is illustrated by the dinner gatherings, "Gary dinners," that subsequently evolved. Elbert Gary, then chairman of U.S. Steel, presided over these gatherings. The purpose of these dinners was expressed in hearings before a congressional committee investigating U.S. Steel in 1911 and 1912. Mr. Gary stated that:

> The question was how to get between the two extremes of securing a monopoly by driving out competition, however good-naturedly, in a bitter, destructive competition or to maintain prices without making any agreement, express or implied, tacit or otherwise. And so, gentlemen, I invited a large percentage of the steel interests of the country to meet me at dinner. Then I said it seemed to me the only way we could prevent demoralization . . . was for the steel people to come together occasionally and to tell one to the other exactly what his business was. . . . Prices were not attempted to be fixed . . . but we have, by the friendly intercourse, prevented . . . sudden, wild extreme fluctuation. . . . We have come together . . . so that competition should be honorable, decent, and reasonable, as opposed to bitter, hostile, destructive competition as used to exist.[5]

The benefit to U.S. Steel along with the smaller firms in the industry from this monopolistic structure was increased profit through cooperation and agreement on prices. The formation of U.S. Steel coincided with a 50 percent jump in pig-iron prices. From 1901 to 1908, U.S. Steel earned from 12 to 14 percent on its investment. Though this was a good rate of return, it is deceptive. Had it not been for the financial strategies surrounding the formation of U.S. Steel that doubled the value of the companies involved from $700 million to $1.4 billion, the rate of return would have been twice as high.[6] U.S. Steel and some of its friends in the industry apparently passed up some of the profit they might have made in order to stabilize prices. One way of doing this is to avoid adjusting prices up and down in response to supply and demand conditions. Not only does this simplify operations, but it helps to avoid price competition that is likely to emerge in an environment of fluctuating prices. The result of this strategy was remarkable price stability. The price for steel rails, for example, remained at $28 per ton from 1901 to 1916.

Without question, the horizontal (and vertical) combination in the steel industry in 1901 and shortly thereafter created monopoly conditions. The participants were able to reap the benefits—high profits and price stability. Adversely, the consumer reaped higher prices, restricted output, and an industry that was not subject to competitive pressure to innovate and develop new production methods. The legacy remains with us today. It is a highly concentrated industry in which competition in pricing and innovation are weak. The Japanese steel industry is taking advantage of that situation now.

The wholesale consolidation of the petroleum industry provides an interesting contrast to the steel industry—not in the end result, but in the means used to accomplish the same end. The dominant firms in the steel industry relied on a policy of cooperation and friendly persuasion along with acquisitions to eliminate competition. The dominant firms in petroleum used a double-barreled policy. They too made acquisitions to eliminate competitors, but they used muscle as well by obtaining discriminatory prices from shippers of petroleum (illegal under today's antitrust laws). The resulting lower costs permitted them to drive competitors out of business—or at least into bankruptcy at which point merger became attractive.

The consolidation of the U.S. petroleum industry began soon after the discovery of petroleum in 1859 in Titusville, Pennsylvania. Small wells and refineries popped up around the region. Three years later, an investor who would irrevocably shape the industry's future entered the picture. In 1862, John D. Rockefeller and his partner in a Cleveland produce business, M.B. Clark, were induced to put $4,000 into an oil refinery. In 1865, Rockefeller became a partner in the business. Two years later, the partnership was enlarged to bring five refineries under common control. The consolidation of the infant petroleum industry was already underway. This was only the first step of a tremendous consolidation movement that would take place in petroleum during the next twenty to thirty years.

Rockefeller's partnership expanded rapidly. The firm incorporated in 1870 under the name of Standard Oil Co. of Ohio to facilitate further expansion. Standard Oil, at that time, controlled only 4 percent of the refining capacity in the country. By 1874, over 50 percent of the refining industry was in the Standard Oil Co. alliance, and by 1879 Rockefeller controlled almost 95 percent of the refining capacity in the United States. This massive consolidation was accomplished, to an important extent, by driving other refiners out of business. The key to this strategy was embodied in the formation of the South Improvement Co. in 1871. The role of this company was to secure preferential rail rates from the railroad companies that transported the refined product. Contracts were completed with the Pennsylvania, New York Central, and Erie Railroads in January 1877. These contracts bore an extraordinary feature. They stated agreement to provide rebates to South Improvement Co. on all petroleum carried by their line and to charge all other parties full rates. The contracts also stated that the railroad companies would furnish Rockefeller's South Improvement Co. the way bills of all petroleum transported over their lines by any party, and would cooperate to prevent loss or injury by competition.

The benefits from such contracts were striking. At one point, the going rate per barrel from Pennsylvania to the coast was $1.44, but for Standard Oil the rate was 80 cents. In order to combat this situation, a group of independent refiners organized the Tidewater Pipeline Co. in 1879. Tidewater built a trunk line from the Pennsylvania fields to a point near New York City to avoid discriminatory rail rates. Standard Oil's arrangements with the railroads destroyed this new competition. The rate for Standard Oil on a 390-pound barrel moving 400 miles by rail was dropped from $1.15 to 10 cents. In addition Standard Oil bought up the refineries served by Tidewater. In 1883, Tidewater was beaten into submission and came under the control of Standard Oil. In the meantime, Standard Oil had acquired twenty-six other pipeline companies that offered competition.

During this period of monopolization, many independent refiners were driven out of business or into the Standard Oil alliance. The monopoly in transportation provided the tool to monopolize refining. Because of Standard Oil's discriminatory rebates for rail transportation and a virtual monopoly over pipeline transportation, independent firms simply could not compete. Upon learning about the emergence of competition through reports from the railroads, Standard Oil would cut prices below costs until any persistent competitor went bankrupt or agreed to merge. Of course, it could support this strategy with monopoly profits earned in other markets. Thus by 1880, the monopolization of the petroleum industry was all but complete. Thereafter, changes that took place were, by and large, legal machinations. The group of twenty companies operating under the umbrella of the Standard Oil alliance were brought into a formal trust arrangement in 1882. Finally, as a result of pressures arising from passage of the Sherman Antitrust Act (1890), the trusteeship was dissolved and emerged as a corporation in 1899. The Standard Oil Co. of New Jersey was born. Even upon its formation it acquired additional petroleum-related companies. The policy of merger was continued aggressively after 1899. Companies that emerged with the huge oil discoveries in Texas and California around 1900 were rapidly acquired. In short order Standard Oil gained control of all of the important wells in these large new oil fields.

The benefits from Standard Oil's monopolization strategy were handsome indeed. From 1897 to 1906, profits ranged between $790 and $850 million for this company which originally invested about $70 million. Average profits on capital stock and trust certificates were 19 percent between 1882 and 1896. From 1896 to 1911, dividends on common stock of Standard Oil ranged from 30 to 40 percent per year.

The virtual monopolization of the petroleum industry was not the result of superiority in economic efficiency. It was the result of a company using its purchasing power to drive competitors out of business to obtain a monopoly. The strategy was a success. The petroleum industry is one of the rare cases in which the monopolistic structure achieved by mergers was reversed. In 1911, the Supreme Court required the breakup of Standard Oil into several companies. Thus, today's industry is not as monopolistically structured as it would otherwise be.

The automobile industry is another of the many industries that experienced a concerted effort toward consolidation by mergers. The only thing that prevented all but total monopolization in the early years of the industry was a cash shortage at General Motors Corp. and the fierce independence and stubbornness of Henry Ford. Even so, the formation and early growth of General Motors left us with an industry that has very few domestic competitors.

The first attempt to establish a monopoly occurred in 1903 with the organization of the Association of Licensed Automobile Manufacturers (ALAM). It included thirty members. The purpose of this association was to monopolize the Seldon motor-vehicle patent. Nonmembers were not allowed to use the patent. Because of the importance of the patent, Henry Ford sought membership in the ALAM but was refused as he was judged to be a fly-by-night operator. Ford was subsequently charged with patent infringement by the ALAM and taken to court. He lost his case in a lower court but the decision was overturned by a circuit court. With that overturn, the basis for the monopoly which the ALAM had been established to achieve was gone, and the ALAM was soon dissolved.

The first attempt to monopolize car production had failed, but there was soon another attempt by William C. Durant. First, Durant successfully reorganized and revitalized the Buick Motor Co. Then, he set out to control the entire automobile industry. He formed General Motors Corp. for that purpose. General Motors was formed as a holding company in 1908 by the purchase of five automobile companies; Buick Motor was the nucleus. By the end of 1909, General Motors had acquired or gained control over more than twenty automobile and accessory companies. These included Cadillac, Oldsmobile, and Oakland. Durant then tried to acquire Ford Motor Co. by the exchange of General Motors for Ford Motor stock. Henry Ford was unwilling to accept an exchange of stock. He wanted $8 million in cash, which General Motors did not have at the time.

The shortage of cash that prevented the purchase of Ford Motor pushed General Motors to take a $12 million bank loan. As a condition of the loan, the bankers took control of the company and Durant was eased out. When Durant left General Motors, he joined Louis Chevrolet in forming the Chevrolet Motor Co. in 1911. This new company produced two highly successful cars—the Chevrolet and the Little. Subsequently, Durant placed the Chevrolet Motor properties in a holding company and proceeded again with his exchange-of-stock strategy. He offered five shares of Chevrolet Motor stock for one share of General Motors stock. By 1919, Durant had acquired the majority of voting shares. Not only had he returned himself to control over General Motors, but he brought with him a successful, independent automobile company (Chevrolet Motor Co.). Five years later, Durant was permanently ousted from General Motors. Nevertheless, he had gone a long way toward accomplishing what he had set out to do—monopolize the automobile industry.

The automobile industry has had a monopolistic structure ever since Durant's time. The performance results of this kind of industry structure are predictable. With few competitors there has been little effective price competition. Furthermore, now that other countries have automobile manufacturers that cater to more affluent consumers (including U.S. consumers), additional problems arising from the lack of competition in the U.S. automobile industry are apparent. The industry has not been particularly aggressive in reducing production costs, introducing new technology, or responding to consumer demand.

For years, the industry yielded to the wage demands of a labor monopoly called the United Auto Workers. As a result, today the labor cost per car is $900 higher in the United States than in Japan. It was easy to give in to the unions when costs could be passed along to the consumer because there was no effective competition. In addition, there was little incentive to be on the leading edge of technology that would outmode existing plant and equipment. Finally, because the biggest profits were made on big cars, the U.S. companies simply chose to ignore the obvious growing interest in small cars. The success of American Motors with its little Nash Rambler in the late 1950s, and the growing sales of the Volkswagen Beetle in the 1960s provided ample evidence that there was a market for small cars. The evidence was ignored.

Things are changing. The emergence of the Japanese automobile industry as an exporter in the late 1960s and the OPEC cartel in the early 1970s have driven home the various consequences of monopolization. The cost of production is high, production techniques and technology lag, and the industry has few of the small cars that consumers want. With the incursion of Japanese automobiles, we also have serious unemployment in the industry and an unfavorable balance of payments. The U.S. automobile industry may come back someday and produce the best cars in the world, but it is the competition from Japan and Europe that will provide the incentive. That is what is so magnificent about a free-market, competitive economic system. If it has plenty of competitors, it will provide the best products at the lowest possible cost.

The means by which the tobacco industry was monopolized are similar to those used in the petroleum industry. As in petroleum, monopoly achieved in one segment of the industry was used to gain monopoly in other segments. Further, as in petroleum, steel, and automobiles, the consolidation of the industry was largely the result of one man's ambition. The tobacco industry began to develop fairly rapidly around 1840. Nevertheless, by the late 1870s the industry was still characterized by simple hand-tool methods employing skilled craftsmen. Tobacco products were manufactured in many small factories; 40 percent of production was in Virginia. The drive to monopolize the industry began in the smallest segment of the industry—cigarettes. The impetus for the consolidation of the industry can be traced to two sources. One was the invention of the highly efficient Bonsack cigarette-rolling machine mentioned in chapter 4. The other was James B. Duke with W.B. Duke and Sons Co., the smallest of the major cigarette manufacturers.

The introduction of the Bonsack machine in the early 1880s meant that production would thereafter be on a larger scale. The disappearance from the industry of some firms was inevitable. This provided no reason, however, to expect the almost complete consolidation of the industry that took place during the next fifteen years. The W.B. Duke Co. began using the Bonsack machine in 1884. At that time, James Duke went to New York in an attempt to make his way into the gentlemanly inner circle of the four companies that dominated the industry. This inner circle maintained a friendly cooperation that assured no serious price competition. Duke's overtures to the group were rebuffed.

Offended, Duke resorted to other means of becoming a recognized force in the industry. He used his cash reserves and his superior machinery as the basis for conducting a major advertising and sales campaign. He also embarked on an aggressive price-cutting campaign. He spent up to $800,000 per year to solidify his position in the industry, forcing others to join him or face bankruptcy. Duke's tactics were successful. In 1890, the American Tobacco Co. was formed. It was a consolidation of all major cigarette manufacturers in the country, accounting for 90 percent of industry production. James B. Duke was president.

The American Tobacco combine went aggressively after the rest of the industry. By this time, however, even smaller independents had adopted the highly efficient Bonsack machine through leases with the Bonsack Machine Co. This enabled them to produce as efficiently as American Tobacco. To eliminate this barrier and complete the monopolization of the cigarette industry, American Tobacco obtained exclusive rights to the use of these machines between 1891 and 1895. Further, the independents lost the use of other machines as American Tobacco acquired the producers of these machines. The monopolization drive proceeded simultaneously on another front. American Tobacco reduced prices to ruinous levels in markets where competition from the independents began to emerge. For example, on one occasion, American Tobacco sold cigarettes at $1.47 per thousand in North Carolina and Virginia after paying a tax of $1.50 per thousand. Of course, losses could be borne by American Tobacco in one market with the monopoly profits it made in other markets where it did not face any competition. In 1891, just one year after its formation, American Tobacco spent $1 million in cash and $5 million in stock to eliminate competitors. These policies were pursued throughout the decade and were effective. Some independents were driven to failure while others were receptive to merger after being financially weakened.

The final blow came in 1899 with the acquisition of the Union Tobacco Co. Union Tobacco had been organized by a syndicate to fight American Tobacco or sell out at a high price. It got the high price. Monopoly was so attractive that American Tobacco paid $12.5 million for the $6 million in assets owned by Union. American Tobacco did not even keep any of the cigarette brands developed by Union. The extra $6.5 million was an indication of the value of monopoly to American Tobacco. Thus, the cigarette industry changed from a competitively structured industry with many producers to a virtual monopoly in just fifteen years.

Just as Duke used his monopoly over cigarette-rolling machinery to fashion a monopoly in cigarette production, he used his monopoly in cigarettes to monopolize other segments of the tobacco industry. Aggressive campaigns of predatory pricing supported by profits from monopoly operations were combined with intensive and costly sales campaigns. The same strategy was used in every phase of the tobacco business and was successful in all but cigars. By 1910, one company (American Tobacco) controlled 86 percent of cigarettes,

97 percent of snuff, 80 percent of fine-cut tobacco, 76 percent of smoking tobacco, 85 percent of plug tobacco, 91 percent of little cigars, and even 14 percent of large cigars. James B. Duke's campaigns of monopolization were most successful.

The fruits of success in the attainment of monopoly were, of course, reflected in high profits. For example, profits from plug tobacco increased right along with the degree of control over the industry. With less than 25 percent of the market, during the campaign to gain control of the plug industry, American Tobacco lost three cents on each pound of plug. By 1900, when it controlled 60 percent of the plug industry, American Tobacco earned nearly four cents per pound, and with 80 percent of the market by 1905, the company made almost eight cents profit per pound of plug tobacco. Earnings patterns were similar in cigarettes and other tobacco products.

The monopoly profits achieved by the consolidation of the tobacco industry provide an obvious explanation for this consolidation—the profit motive. This explanation is consistent with economic theory as well. Under the surface there seems to be another motive. James B. Duke was snubbed, and that set him off on his course of consolidating the industry under his own control. Not only did Duke achieve monopoly, he also obtained power.

The industries discussed in this chapter are not isolated cases. Around 1900, the drive to monopolize through mergers (ignoring technical distinctions between the devices used—for example, trusts or holding companies) took place throughout the economy. Moody reported that shortly after the turn of the century the capitalization of "318 important and active Industrial Trusts in this country is at the present time no less than $7.2 billion, representing a consolidation of 5300 distinct plants and covering practically every line of productive industry in the United States."[7] The industries consolidated through mergers and trust arrangements ranged from locomotives to chewing gum. Hardly a product was untouched by the turn-of-the-century merger movement.

Many of the merger drives in individual industries did not succeed in gaining control over an industry. However, a great many did. For example, of the 92 trusts that John Moody called the "important" trusts, "78 control 50 percent or more of their products and 57 control 60 percent or more. Twenty-six control 80 percent or over."[8] Without question, the breadth and effect of these horizontal mergers on U.S. industrial structure left an indelible imprint on our economic structure. Many of the industries today bear the basic structure that was established at the turn of the century. They are much closer to monopoly than is required for the firms to achieve operating efficiency.

In a detailed analysis of U.S. merger movements, Ralph Nelson concluded that the evidence points toward the desire for monopoly rather than operating efficiency as the primary rationale for the merger movement at the turn of the century.[9] Nevertheless, proponents of merger activity, from 1900 to the present, have relied on the argument that mergers are good for the United States because they increase operating efficiency. For example, recently the *Wall Street Journal* noted that "big mergers don't bother William Baxter" (the Attorney General for Antitrust in the Reagan administration). "He believes big businesses are very valuable things because they tend to be the most efficient."[10] The evidence from numerous systematic analyses such as Nelson's does not support the argument. Under the circumstances, it is remarkable that this old argument is still widely accepted. Unfortunately, it has become the conventional wisdom in spite of the facts.

Profits are one important motivator of business behavior. Consequently, horizontal mergers in general and the sweeping horizontal combinations around 1900 to achieve monopoly constitute rational business behavior. Unfortunately, this particular avenue of the drive for profits imposes major costs on the economic system—high prices and restricted output for the consumer, less efficient allocation of the nation's economic resources, and lagging efficiency and technology. Competitive capitalism depends on strong motivations (whether profit or power) of individuals to have a dynamic, technologically progressive and efficient economic system. However, it was decided as a matter of public policy that in the long-run interests of society the profit drive would have to be harnessed. The objective was not to destroy a driving force in U.S. capitalism but rather to channel it and give it direction. That is a primary purpose of our antitrust laws, the subject of the next chapter.

Notes

1. Leonard Weiss, "The Concentration-Profits Relationship and Antitrust," *Industrial Concentration: The New Learning,* eds. H.J. Goldschmid, H.M. Mann, and J.F. Weston (Boston: Little, Brown, 1974), pp. 183–233; Stephen A. Rhoades, "Structure-Performance Studies in Banking: A Summary and Evaluation," *Staff Economic Studies* No. 92 (Federal Reserve Board, 1977); and Stephen A. Rhoades, "Structure-Performance Studies in Banking: An Updated Summary and Evaluation," *Staff Studies* No. 119 (Federal Reserve Board, 1982).

2. John Moody, *The Truth about the Trusts* (New York: Moody, 1904); Harry W. Laidler, *Concentration of Control in American Industry* (New York: Thomas Y. Crowell, 1931); and Martin L. Lindahl and William A. Carter, *Corporate Concentration and Public Policy,* 3rd ed. (Englewood Cliffs, N.J.: Prentice-Hall, 1959).

3. Lincoln Steffens, *Autobiography* (New York: Harcourt, Brace and Co., 1931), p. 192.

4. Laidler, *Concentration of Control in American Industry,* p. 39.

5. Ibid., pp. 47 and 48.

6. Douglas F. Greer, *Industrial Organization and Public Policy* (New York: Macmillan, 1980), p. 152.

7. Moody, *The Truth about the Trusts,* p. 486.

8. Ibid., p. 487.

9. Ralph Nelson, *Merger Movements in American Industry, 1895-1956,* National Bureau of Economic Research (Princeton: Princeton University Press, 1959), p. 103.

10. *Wall Street Journal* (July 8, 1981).

10 The Antitrust Laws Harness the Drive for Profit

The antitrust laws in the United States sprang from the tremendous horizontal-merger movement that began in the 1870s and showed such a costly side of the drive for profits (monopoly). After seventy years of development, these laws—the Sherman Act, Clayton Act, and Federal Trade Commission Act—have finally become an effective impediment to horizontal mergers. The first of these laws was the Sherman Antitrust Act of 1890. It was passed in response to widespread public fear and concern over the huge horizontal combinations of the two preceding decades. During the presidential campaign of 1888, both the Democratic and Republican parties promised antitrust legislation in their platforms. Agrarian interests were most vocal in calling for some form of government control over the trusts. Farmers saw they were receiving low, sometimes declining prices for their produce while they paid high, stable prices to various trusts for farm equipment and other manufactured products. The high cost of rail transportation for farm products was also identified with the trusts.

The farmers, along with many others, were concerned about the increasing concentration of economic resources, aside from any concern about monopoly. This is not surprising in a country that, from its origins, has consciously sought to prevent the concentration of power of any kind. Thus, the individual states did not and will not surrender all of their powers to the federal government, and the federal government itself is set up in three branches with a system of checks and balances among them. The public outcry against the trusts was a logical outcome of the deeply imbedded philosophy of the people. This philosophy is an important underlying principle of U.S. antitrust laws.

Making good on his campaign promise, President Harrison sent the Sherman Antitrust Act to Congress and it was passed in 1890. Nevertheless, the Sherman Act was little more than a gesture by Congress to placate public concern. No major hearings were held and only a brief debate took place before passage of the act. Little attention and less money were devoted to administering our nation's first antitrust law. Neither the Cleveland (Democratic) administration nor the McKinley (Republican) administration made any real effort to enforce the law. There was not enough congressional support and little commitment at the agency level. There should have been little confusion over the basic objective of the Sherman Act. The essential provisions of the Sherman Act were contained in the first two sections as follows:

Section 1. Every contract, combination in the form of trust or otherwise, or conspiracy, in restraint of trade or commerce among the several States or with foreign nations, is hereby declared to be illegal.

Section 2. Every person who shall monopolize, or attempt to monopolize, or combine or conspire with any other person or persons to monopolize any part of the trade or commerce among the several States, or with foreign nations, shall be deemed guilty of a misdemeanor.

Perhaps as a result of the consolidation movement around 1900, in 1904 the administrations of Roosevelt and later Taft (both Republicans) began to enforce the Sherman Act more vigorously. Two landmark decisions in favor of the Justice Department were handed down by the Supreme Court—the American Tobacco and Standard Oil of New Jersey decisions of 1911. Both cases were tried under the Sherman Act on charges of blatant efforts to achieve monopoly. Found guilty, both defendants were required to divest themselves of major components of their businesses. By this time, however, pressure had built up for additional antitrust laws to supplement the broad but vague prohibitions of the Sherman Act. There was some concern that the Sherman Act was only effective after monopoly was actually achieved.

Two new antitrust laws were passed in 1914—the Clayton Act and the Federal Trade Commission Act. In contrast to events leading to passage of the Sherman Act, these new antitrust laws received extensive debate and discussion before their passage. The Clayton Act introduced more precision in describing illegal business activity than the Sherman Act. For example, section 2 of the Clayton Act forbade price discrimination—the practice of charging one customer more than others for the same product or service. Section 3 of the act prohibited tying arrangements, whereby the seller will sell one of its products only if another of its products is also purchased. Section 3 also prohibited exclusive dealing arrangements, in which a seller will provide a customer with its product only if the customer agrees not to buy competing products from the seller's rivals. Section 8 of the Clayton Act prohibited interlocking directorates between corporations if such a relationship might reduce competition. It was section 7 of the act that was aimed at mergers. It was intended to stop mergers that would reduce competition even though the merger might not lead to monopoly. Thus, unlike the Sherman Act, section 7 was preventive; it was intended to halt monopoly in its incipiency. Its goal was to maintain a competitive market system rather than to allow merger activity to proceed until an industry was effectively monopolized. Unfortunately, section 7 prohibited only the acquisition of the stock of a company but not the assets. This asset loophole was quickly exploited by business. It was not until the Celler-Kefauver amendment to the Clayton Act in 1950 closed this loophole that the Clayton Act became a useful impediment to horizontal mergers.

The Federal Trade Commission Act (1914) established the Federal Trade Commission. The basic antitrust provision in the Federal Trade Commission Act, as amended in 1938, is embodied in section 5. That section declares that unfair or deceptive acts or practices in commerce are unlawful. This is a sweeping prohibition that arguably covers any violation covered under sections 1 and 2 of the Sherman Act. In fact, the commission has used section 5 primarily as a tool to stop false and misleading advertising, which can have anticompetitive effects and also gives consumers bad information.

In addition to having its own antitrust power, the commission was established as an administrative agency to complement the Justice Department in the area of antitrust enforcement. The Federal Trade Commission was granted broad administrative powers to gather data for investigations of U.S. businesses. Unlike the Justice Department, the Federal Trade Commission has no power to prosecute criminal violations of the Sherman Act. Such cases are tried in the court system by the Justice Department. The commission can, however, bring civil cases under section 7 of the Clayton Act or section 5 of the Federal Trade Commission Act. When it does, the case is heard before one of the commission's own administrative law judges, whose decision is forwarded to the full five-member commission for review. The commission's findings of fact are final and binding on the appeal courts in the event that the commission's decision is disputed by a defendant and taken to court.

The Justice Department can undertake either criminal or civil proceedings under the Sherman Act and civil proceedings under the Clayton Act. Under criminal proceedings, the Justice Department can seek punishment of the offenders in the form of fines (of up to $1 million for corporations and $100,000 for individuals) and imprisonment (up to three years). However, if the activity being challenged has achieved a monopoly already, the punishment will not change that situation. In such cases, the department may choose to bring a civil suit, because the remedies allowed in civil suits enable the department to restore a more competitive situation in an industry. For example, it can order divestiture to break up an illegally obtained monopoly. Criminal and civil charges are sometimes brought concurrently if blatant violation of the Sherman Act appears to warrant punishment by fines or imprisonment and if the result of the behavior has led to monopoly that should be broken up to restore competition.

These three antitrust laws are the heart of our national microeconomic policy. Their purpose is to maintain a reasonably competitive marketplace and to prevent a high degree of concentration of economic resources. These laws were initially passed to control the trusts. The alternative means of control would have been direct government regulation, but such an approach was eschewed. The chosen approach was intended to permit society to benefit from the increased efficiency and technological advance that arise from the pursuit of profits. But it was also intended to control the antisocial effects of monopoly and resource concentration.

The antitrust laws are designed to accomplish social control over business by prohibiting mergers and certain business practices, such as predatory pricing, that may lead to monopoly. This is a highly unusual and unobtrusive form of regulation. Essentially, these laws lay down the rules of the business game. The regulator, like a referee, remains out of the game unless the rules are broken. Within these rules, the participants may operate freely. These laws differ widely from many other forms of government regulation, in which the prices charged, profits earned, or services offered are regulated. Not only are the antitrust laws a unique form of regulation, they are unique to the United States, although in recent years other countries have adopted some type of antitrust law.

The antitrust laws, without question, are a success. Though it took some time for the Sherman Act to become institutionalized after its passage in 1890, it has inhibited mergers and business practices that result in monopoly. Because of the Sherman Act, the U.S. economy could probably never again be subject to a massive horizontal-merger movement such as that which occurred around 1900. The Clayton Act (1914), at least after amendment in 1950, has demonstrably played a significant role in preventing horizontal mergers that reduce the number of competitors. Several major court decisions under the amended Clayton Act established this act as an effective tool in maintaining a competitive market system. In the industrial sector two decisions stand out: a lower court decision in the *Bethlehem Steel–Youngstown Sheet and Tube* case (1958), and the Supreme Court decision in the *Brown Shoe–Kinney Shoe* case (1963). These decisions indicated clearly that significant horizontal mergers would have little chance of passing under the Clayton Act. This position was forcefully reiterated in banking. The Supreme Court decision in the *Philadelphia National Bank–Girard Trust* merger case (1963) indicated that section 7 is applicable to banking and that in banking, as in the industrial sector, significant horizontal mergers are unacceptable.

These early decisions under the amended Clayton Act had a marked effect on horizontal-merger activity. Horizontal mergers were a major form of business combination throughout most of U.S. industrial history. However, data on mergers since World War II indicate that the Clayton Act and subsequent judicial interpretations greatly diminished horizontal-merger activity. For example, horizontal mergers in the industrial sector accounted for almost 40 percent of all mergers from 1948 to 1951, but from 1960 to 1963 they accounted for about 13 percent, and by 1968 only 4 percent.[1] An equally marked reduction took place in banking as well.

In spite of the effectiveness of the Clayton Act in preventing the most common type of merger, overall merger activity has not diminished in the slightest. Business simply turned to mergers not involving direct competitors— the so-called *conglomerate* merger. Conglomerate mergers are mergers of firms that are neither competitors, buyers, nor customers of one another. Existing antitrust laws are largely ineffective in preventing conglomerate mergers. These mergers generally provide no economic benefits to society, but they may reduce competition, and they do increase concentration of economic resources.

A high level of conglomerate-merger activity has persisted since about 1960, because no effective antitrust law deals with such mergers. The following chapter will describe the nature, effects, and motivation of conglomerate mergers. There the underlying drive for power will start to become apparent.

Notes

1. Federal Trade Commission, *Economic Report on Corporate Mergers* (Washington, D.C.: Government Printing Office, 1969), p. 61.

11 A New Breed of Merger

Horizontal mergers were the dominant form of business consolidation throughout most of our nation's industrial history. It is remarkable that after the Clayton Act and judicial decisions all but slammed the door on horizontal mergers in about 1960, merger activity did not decline. For example, in mining and manufacturing from 1960 to 1969, when the policy against horizontal mergers became firmly established, the number of large mergers reported by the Federal Trade Commission rose from 64 to 175. In banking, where horizontal mergers were largely preempted at about the same time as those in the industrial sector, merger activity also continued unabated. From 1960 to 1969, I found that the number of bank mergers rose from 89 to 245. Conglomerate mergers immediately filled the gap left by horizontal mergers. They now dominate merger activity in the United States. Conglomerate mergers accounted for 34 percent of all mergers between 1951 and 1955, and 83 percent of all mergers between 1966 and 1970.

Conglomerate mergers, like horizontal mergers, consolidate economic resources. Since conglomerate mergers do not involve competing firms, however, they do not reduce the number of competitors. Thus, the opportunity to achieve monopoly profits is not apparent. Recent experience provides little if any indication that efficiency gains (and thus higher profits) can be expected from conglomerate mergers. In spite of all of the praises about the *synergistic* (a buzzword for the efficiencies that are supposed to result from the superior managerial talent of large conglomerates) effects from acquisitions by large conglomerates, no statistical studies have confirmed such results. This evidently was not confirmed by investors either. In the late 1960s, the stock market mercilessly pummeled the stocks of the glamour conglomerates (for example, Litton Industries, LTV, and Teledyne).

If no apparent profit is to be gained from monopoly or efficiency, then why the shift in the business community from horizontal to conglomerate mergers? After pondering conglomerate mergers and thinking back on some of the personalities and tactics connected with horizontal mergers, I have concluded that the desire for power has been an important motivator of mergers in the United States. The possibility that power is an important motivator of business behavior, especially of mergers, was not readily apparent when horizontal mergers were the order of the day. Profits resulting from the achievement of monopoly, and in some cases from increased efficiency, explained horizontal-merger activity quite plausibly. Economists could be comfortable with this explanation because it was consistent with a fundamental assumption of micro-economic theory—profit maximization. However, with the immediate shift to conglomerate mergers when horizontal mergers were stymied by federal legislation and with the acceleration of often very costly, unfriendly takeovers in recent years, it is difficult to continue believing that profit maximization is the sole or even the primary motive for mergers. The drive for power cannot be ignored. The very nature of conglomerate mergers raises skepticism about the profit motivation and supposed benefits of conglomerate mergers.

My examination of conglomerate mergers focuses on the 1960s. By that time, conglomerate mergers had become the predominant form of business consolidation in this country. In addition, the extent of conglomerate mergers during the 1960s and the meteoric growth of some companies through acquisition make this a particularly interesting period for looking at the nature of conglomerate mergers. The companies whose acquisition activity I will relate here are probably familiar to many readers.

The descriptions of the conglomerate firms in the following pages are based on information from *Moody's Industrial Manual, Standard and Poor's,* and various business periodicals. The examples highlight the internal incongruity of firms that has been a result of conglomerate mergers and illustrate the erosion of rational distinctions between industries. The reason for emphasizing these results of conglomerate mergers is that they suggest something about the motivation for mergers and their implications for the structure of the U.S. economic system. The motivation for conglomerate mergers and their effect on our economic system will indicate whether public policy is required to control them, and if so, what sort of policy is needed.

First, some terminology needs to be cleared up. Thus far, I have used the word *conglomerate* to refer to those companies that went on an acquisition binge during the 1960s. I did this because the term is familiar and generally associated with the phenomenon I am discussing here. But it is inaccurate. According to *Webster's New Collegiate Dictionary* (1965 ed.), the word *conglomerate,* when used as an adjective, means "made up of parts from various sources or of various kinds." As a noun, however, the word *conglomerate* means a "a mixed coherent mass." Here is the problem. If coherence is an essential ingredient of conglomeration, this is not an appropriate term to describe the many business conglomerates that have been tacked together in recent years. The word *agglomerate* would be more to the point. *Webster's* defines the noun *agglomerate* as "a jumbled mass or collection" and the adjective *agglomerate* as "clustered or growing together but not coherent." Although agglomerate is my choice of terminology, because of popular usage of conglomerate I will use the terms interchangeably.

Before 1965, Gulf and Western Corporation did not rank in the *Fortune* list of the 500 largest industrials. By 1969, Gulf and Western occupied sixty-ninth place on the *Fortune* list. Like most of the agglomerates that were so prominent during the 1960s, Gulf and Western experienced a truly stunning growth rate. This did not result from development of important new products or technologies; there was a much easier and faster way to become big. The company's growth was the result of a dizzying acquisition binge. There were large mergers and small mergers including related businesses and unrelated businesses. Gulf and Western alone made roughly 160 acquisitions between 1960 and 1969, ranging from publishing firms to cigar makers. A review of a few of these acquisitions illustrates the grab-bag approach that often characterizes agglomerate acquisitions.

Gulf and Western, like many of the conglomerates, was run by an aggressive leader, Charles Bludhorn, who engineered the acquisition campaign. He provided the stimulus for the company's merger growth from sales of $6 million in 1957 to $1.3 billion in 1968. The company had started out in 1934 as the Michigan Bumper Co. and remained a small auto-parts producer until Bludhorn took over the company in 1957. From that time onward, Gulf and Western seemed to have one major objective—to grow as fast as possible by acquisition. The acquisitions that took place immediately following Bludhorn's move to Gulf and Western appear logical enough. Dozens of small, independent auto-parts distributors and warehouses were acquired. These seemed to mesh neatly with Gulf and Western's basic business. Then the company branched into manufacturing with the acquisition of companies that made automotive ignitions, diecasting, metal stampings, and so forth. Still, the acquired companies seemed to fit logically into Gulf and Western's framework of operation. This logical pattern of acquisition soon came to a halt.

In 1966, the symptoms of conglomeration became apparent with the acquisition of New Jersey Zinc, one of the largest and oldest producers of zinc. Paramount Pictures and Desilu Productions were acquired soon thereafter. Further acquisitions put Gulf and Western into sugar (South Puerto Rico Sugar Co., 1967), cable TV (Halifax Cable TV, 1967 and North Brevard Cable TV, 1968), mining (Herman Mines, Ltd., 1967), cigars (Consolidated Cigar, 1968), publications (Resource Publications, 1968 and East Publishing Co., 1968), paper manufacturing (Brown Co., 1968), music (Parabut Music Corp., 1970 and Infinite Music Corp., 1970), and cosmetics (Polly Bergen Co., 1971).

Many of the acquisitions by Gulf and Western were small; particularly those in the auto-parts distribution and warehousing business. An extreme example is the acquisition in 1963 of Marathon Auto Parts (assets of $5,539). But many of the acquired companies were large. Examples include Universal American (1968), E.W. Bliss (1968), and Consolidated Cigar (1968), which respectively ranked 361, 427, and 492 on *Fortune's* 1968 list. The acquisition campaign of Gulf and Western certainly did not create a monopoly. It did, however, in a very short period of time, result in the consolidation of a large amount of productive economic resources and the disappearance of many independent decision makers. The implications of such an agglomerate structure for independent decision making are suggested in a statement by Bludhorn. He observed, "We're like an investment company, except that they just sit upstairs and watch the horses run. We get down and manage the horses."[1] That may indeed be what Gulf and Western and other agglomerates do, but one can only wonder how, when top management is heavily occupied by planning the financing and consummation of acquisitions, they can manage effectively. Even if top management devoted its entire energy to running such a far-flung agglomeration of subsidiaries, one would still wonder if there were sufficient expertise to do the job effectively. One skeptic was a leading U.S. businessman—Lammont duPont Copeland, a former president of DuPont. He was quoted as saying, "Running a conglomerate is a job for management geniuses, not for ordinary mortals like us at DuPont."[2]

The guiding forces in Litton Industries' rise to conglomeration were Charles B. (Tex) Thornton, its chairman, and Roy Ash, its president. Thornton came to Litton Industries in 1953 after serving as vice-president of Hughes Aircraft. Roy Ash had been the top statistician at Bank of America before moving to Hughes Aircraft where he met Thornton. In 1953, Thornton bought Litton Industries from its founder, Charles Litton. Ash joined Thornton at Litton Industries, and their intent was to build a major electronics firm that would be on the leading edge of technology in this developing field.

Litton Industries made about seventeen acquisitions during the 1950s. These mostly seemed to interface neatly with the company's basic business as well as with the original objectives of its new mentors. Litton acquired such companies as West Coast Electronics (1953), Automatic Seriograph Co. (1955), Triad Transformer Co. (1956), and Digital Control Systems, Inc. (1957). In 1958, however, the direction of Litton's acquisition activity began to show signs of change. By the end of the 1960s, Litton Industries was into products ranging from shipbuilding to paper and trading stamps. It had also branched into services ranging from store design, to general economic studies, to designing education curricula. Sales volume increased at a phenomenal rate, skyrocketing to $1.6 billion in 1966 from $3 million in 1954. In 1960, at the beginning of the glory decade for conglomerates, Litton Industries' assets of $119 million placed it 275th on the *Fortune* 500 list. By 1969, with assets of $1.6 billion, Litton Industries was ranked 55 on the *Fortune* list.

As was the case with Gulf and Western, the ascendancy of Litton Industries was not primarily the result of great successes in product or technological development. It was instead the result of an acquisition spree that swallowed up over one hundred companies. These acquisitions carried Litton into many unrelated activities: printing (Eureka Specialty Printing Co., 1961), shipbuilding (Ingall's Shipbuilding Corp., 1961), paper (Fitchburg Paper Co., 1964), X-ray equipment (Profexray, Keleket X-Ray, Hammer X-Ray, 1964, and Magnuson X-Ray and Wittenberg X-Ray, 1965), stationery (Atlas Stationers, 1964), furniture (Lehigh Furniture, 1965 and Standard Desk, 1968), refrigeration (Mc-Grary Refrigerator, 1966), typewriters (Imperial Typewriter, 1966), business forms (Sturgis Newport Business Forms, 1966), publishing (American Book Co., 1967, Van Nostrand, 1968, and Delmar Publishers, 1969), consulting (Marine Consultants, 1967), food manufacturing (Stouffer Foods Corp., 1967), dental supplies (Fl. Dental Supply, 1968), and a variety of service companies.

What had started as an integrated, logically structured business in the 1950s bore no resemblance to the Litton Industries at the end of the 1960s. The urge to merge had obliterated the firm's identity. It was simply a very big company that controlled many businesses. A lot of economic resources had been con- solidated into one firm along with the loss of independent decision makers. For the economic system, there were no apparent gains.

Why is the federal government widely derided for being cumbersome and inefficient, but such comments are rarely heard in connection with huge private bureaucracies? Presumably the criticism of government arises because of its hugeness, its highly diverse activity, and its freedom from having to turn a profit. If sheer size and diversity of operation are part of the explanation for saying government is inefficient (about which I proffer no judgment), how do huge, highly diverse companies escape the charge? Perhaps the marketing (including lobbying) skills of big business are potent enough to divert concern about the problems of big business while at the same time convince people of the serious- ness of parallel problems of government.

The creativeness behind the agglomeration of LTV Corp. was provided by James J. Ling. At one time during the 1960s, Jimmy Ling was regarded as the merger king of U.S. industry. His company was referred to in the title of a *Fortune* article as "Jimmy Ling's wonderful growth machine." Like Litton Industries, LTV started out in the early 1950s as a small electronics company. What began in California as L.M. Electronics in 1953, became Ling Electronics in 1958, Ling Altec Electronics in 1959, Ling Temco Electronics in 1960, Ling Temco Vought in 1961, and LTV Corp. in 1972. The frequent name changes reflect the company's merger activity.

LTV's growth through merger is as spectacular as any, although it took a somewhat different form. The most notable difference is that LTV (under what- ever name) did not make the large number of acquisitions that many of the other conglomerates had made. It made roughly thirteen acquisitions during the 1960s. This figure is somewhat deceptive because in the case of LTV subsidiaries were encouraged by Ling to make their own acquisitions. The purpose according to Jimmy Ling was that, "Each of the underlying companies will be a conglo- merate in itself."[3] LTV devoted its financial resources and managerial talent to making very large acquisitions, frequently of companies that were already widely diversified. The results of this strategy were just as impressive as those achieved by Gulf and Western, and Litton Industries.

LTV's sales mushroomed from $4 million in 1957 to $148 million in 1960. By 1968, LTV had sales of $1.8 billion, placing it in thirty-eighth place on *Fortune*'s 500 list. LTV's phenomenal overall growth was matched by the expansion in the menu of products it offered. The menu, which had included only electronics equipment in the late 1950s, ranged by the end of the 1960s from airplanes and steel to meat and insurance. LTV's earliest acquisitions involved firms that appeared to logically complement the company's basic business of electronics—Calidyne Co. in 1958, and Altec Co., University Loudspeakers, and Continental Electronics Manufacturing in 1959. From then on, no evidence can be found that the acquisitions were building a coherent, integrated firm.

In 1960, LTV acquired Temco Aircraft Corp. which put it in aircraft manufacturing on a modest scale. Then in 1961, LTV merged with Chance-Vought and overnight became a significant manufacturer of airplanes and missiles with large defense contracts. Over the next several years, LTV made only a few small acquisitions as it attempted to digest Chance-Vought. Then, in 1965, LTV spent over $30 million in cash to acquire Okonite, a leading producer of utility-electrical cable. It followed this with its 1967 acquisition of Wilson and Co. for around $165 million. LTV was instantly propelled into a significant position in meat and food processing, sporting equipment, pharmaceuticals and chemicals. LTV's next major acquisition, though not its largest, provided its widest range of diversification in one shot. The Greatamerica Corp. was acquired in 1968. This put LTV into the airline business (Braniff Airways), banking (First Western Bank and Trust Co.) and insurance (American-Amicable Life and Stonewall Insurance). Apparently LTV was after a really big acquisition because it attempted to acquire Allis Chalmers, the big producer of earth-moving and farm equipment along with various electrical and industrial goods. The acquisition attempt was successfully resisted by Allis Chalmers. Undaunted, and obviously intent on making a big acquisition of a company producing something or other, LTV acquired Jones and Laughlin Steel Corp. which at the time (1968) had almost $3/4 billion in assets.

The ambition, energy, and financial wizardry required to post such an acquisition record as LTV's in so short a time are impressive. However, the objective is not clear, and the company's long-run performance has been rather ordinary. One can only wonder what LTV might have accomplished if its managers had devoted their energy to research and development and the operational side of their business instead of the sophisticated financial strategy required for their acquisition campaign.

Teledyne is the one company discussed in this chapter for which the term conglomerate may actually be more appropriate than agglomerate, although its later acquisitions began to stretch the meaning a bit. Even though Teledyne's growth did not carry it as far afield as the acquisitions of Gulf and Western, LTV, Litton Industries, and others, it was no less caught up in the merger mania of the sixties. In 1968 alone, the company made around twenty-five acquisitions.

Like many other new companies at the time, Teledyne was in the electronics field. In 1961, its first full year of operation, Teledyne sold $4.5 million of electronics components and systems. By 1965, sales had risen to $40 million, and by 1968 they had grown to around $500 million. Such growth was largely a function of the purchase of other companies. The early acquisitions (for example, Sprague Engineering Corp. in 1963, and Microwave Electronics along with Micronetics in 1965) were fairly well confined to the company's basic business. However, while Teledyne continued to focus on areas of high technology, its acquisition pace increased and carried it farther afield.

In 1966, Teledyne bought more than twenty companies. Most of these were related to the basic electronics business but one of the purchases involved a metal company–Vasco Metal Corp. In 1967, another twenty to thirty acquisitions were consummated. These included the purchase of Wah Chang, which like Vasco was in rare metals. Teledyne also picked up AR, Inc., a manufacturer of stereo equipment, and the United Insurance Co. of America. The year 1968 witnessed another twenty to thirty acquisitions; these included Metal Finishers, Rodney Metals, Columbia Steel and Shafting, Irby Steel Co., Ohio Steel Foundry, Oslo Steel Co., Industrial Diecasting, and Mount Vernon Diecasting. With these acquisitions, Teledyne moved firmly into metals. Finally, in 1969, Teledyne moved into dental equipment with the acquisition of Opton Dental Manufacturing and more heavily into insurance with the acquisition of Argonaut Insurance Co., Trinity Universal Insurance, and Guaranty Reinsurance Co.

While Teledyne's acquisitions were perhaps not so diverse as those of some other conglomerates, the number of acquisitions was large. The company began the 1960s as a brand new firm and emerged as a large industrial firm by the end of the decade. This dramatic growth resulted largely from an acquisition program that obtained close to one hundred companies.

There are many other far-flung acquisition campaigns that I will not discuss in detail. For example, Tenneco was basically a gas pipeline company in 1958 with $380 million in sales. By 1968, Tenneco had almost $1 billion in sales from acquisitions that put the company into chemicals, paperboard and cartons, farm machinery, automotive parts, ranching, farming, and shipbuilding. Similarly, International Telephone and Telegraph (ITT) grew from a producer of telecommunications equipment with $740 million in sales in 1959 to a sprawling conglomerate with close to $4 billion in sales by 1968. In those years, Harold Geneen guided ITT on an acquisition campaign that led the company into life insurance, automatic fire-protection systems, manufacturing and operating vending machines, bread baking, frozen foods, hotels and motels, home building, car rentals, chemicals, silica, consumer finance, computer data services, and secretarial schools. Textron rose from obscurity in the textile business with a program that began in the 1950s when over forty acquisitions were made. The pace of acquisitions accelerated in the sixties, increasing Textron's sales from around $300 million in 1959 to well over $1 billion by the end of the decade. These acquisitions carried Textron into chain saws, eyeglasses, iron foundries, bathroom accessories, helicopters, watch bands, cookware, pens, paint, roller bearings, machine tools, men's toiletries, poultry feed, chemicals, and linseed oil.

Some of the companies put together through conglomerate acquisitions remind one of a Rube Goldberg contraption. Rube Goldberg (1883–1963) was famous for his cartoon drawing of highly complicated, illogical, inefficient machines in spoof of our machine age. Some of the true agglomerates might, like Rube Goldberg contraptions, even be laughable but for the fact that the building of these business contraptions resulted in the disappearance of many independent businesses. These independents might have provided significant innovations and ideas; ideas that can get lost or buried in the politics of a large, bureaucratic conglomerate. Large bureaucracies, public or private, tend to encourage the ordinary. Who know what is lost as these companies engage in financial wizardry but ordinary business operation? What Rube Goldberg did on paper, the conglomerateurs did using debt instruments, people, machines, and companies. What has been the result, and what motivated such behavior? I will look at these questions in the next two chapters.

Notes

1. *Fortune,* William S. Rukeyser (March 1968), p. 123, © 1968, Time, Inc. All rights reserved.
2. *Fortune,* Gilbert Burck (February 1967), p. 131, © 1967, Time Inc. All rights reserved.
3. *Forbes* (November 1, 1967), p. 47.

12 What Does the New Breed of Merger Accomplish?

Today the U.S. economy is experiencing a significant merger movement propelled by conglomerate mergers. By way of example, I have illustrated the nature of these conglomerate acquisitions; but an understanding of the effects and motivations of such mergers is also important. Just as surely as the merger movement at the turn of the century reshaped the industrial structure, conglomerate and agglomerate mergers are reshaping that structure again today. However, there are differences. Unlike horizontal mergers, conglomerate mergers have no observable effect on the structure of individual industries because, by definition, the firms involved in an conglomerate merger are in different industries or markets. Further, such mergers have no clearly predictable effects on the basis of economic theory—models of multi market firms are not an integral part of basic economic theory. Theory simply does not cover this facet of economic reality.

The one effect that proponents of conglomerate mergers have told us to expect is synergy. It is said to arise because of the supposedly superior managerial talent of large conglomerates. The end result according to the synergy argument of putting two companies together is not the sum of the parts. There is a two-plus-two-equals-five effect. Even though, as we will see, the merger activity of the 1960s yielded no synergy, the idea of synergy is back in the business lexicon of the 1980s. An article reporting Sears Roebuck and Co.'s acquisition offers in a single week, for Coldwell Banker (the nation's largest independent real-estate broker) and Dean Witter Reynolds Organization Inc. (the fifth largest stockbroker) noted the revival of the synergy argument.

> Sears hopes to capitalize on one of the basic buzzwords of the '60s—synergy: the ability of two or more organizations working together to produce results exceeding anything they would do separately.
>
> Synergistic promises fell from favor when many conglomerates found they could not manage unrelated businesses very well, but are back in the patter of executives talking about mergers in the financial services industry.
>
> But talking about synergy and achieving it are two different things. A top executive at a major brokerage firm admitted that while the concept looks great on paper, individuals do not shop for financial services the way they shop for foodstuffs.[1]

Since economic theory provides no clear indication of the effects of conglomerate mergers, a review of the evidence on the effects of these mergers is in order.

Some of the very short-run effects of the conglomerate mergers during the 1960s partially explain the amazing degree of investor attraction to conglomerate stocks. The companies leading the merger activity of the 1960s seemed to experience unrivaled growth and remarkable earnings performance. In retrospect, however, this remarkable performance rings hollow. The tremendous growth was, in general, attributable to intensive acquisition activity rather than to major breakthroughs in product development and technology. The reason for such impressive earnings performance is more subtle and complicated. Much of it came about from financial maneuvering such as heavy reliance on debt rather than stock to satisfy the need for capital. This way, since there was no increase in the stock issued, as the company grew its earnings per share of stock showed impressive gains from one year to the next. Convertible debentures were one attractive form of debt employed. In the short run, they made earnings per share of stock look great, but at some point in the future the debenture converted to stock. At that point, earnings per share of stock were likely to become much less attractive.

Another example of this financial manipulation was the use of mergers themselves to influence financial data of the conglomerate. Because of their attractiveness to investors who anticipated further remarkable earnings performance, their stock prices were bid upward so that many conglomerates had a high ratio of stock price to earnings (the P/E ratio). If a conglomerate acquired a firm with a low P/E ratio through an exchange of stock, investors in the stock market tended to assume the earnings of the acquired firm would also become impressive. Thus they converted the expected earnings of the new combined firm into a price per share based on the high P/E ratio of the conglomerate. The result was that the stock of the combined firm immediately went up in price. No new productive capacity was built. Nothing new had been invented. The magnificent performance of the stock resulted simply from the purchase of another firm. Like the use of convertible debentures, acquisitions themselves could be used to chalk up impressive financial performance. However as they grew larger, the conglomerates needed ever larger acquisitions to significantly influence their stock price. This could not go on forever. When it came to an end, the luster rubbed off the financial performance.

In view of the speculative fever surrounding the mergers of the 1960s, there may be another explanation for the stock-market success of these companies. Perhaps stock prices reflected awe and admiration for the ambition, energy, and imagination of businesspeople undertaking such immense projects. Whether the projects would really work became a secondary question. However, even in the midst of the dazzling financial maneuvers and the trumpeting of synergy, a strong wind of skepticism began to blow over the conglomerate in the late

1960s. Synergy was beginning to sound more like a sales catchword than a description of the real world. For example in 1969, the dollar value of many conglomerate stocks fell sharply—LTV fell from 97 to 26, Gulf and Western from 50 to 18, Avco from 49 to 23, and Textron from 45 to 23.

The declining stock prices of many conglomerates probably mirrored their deteriorating earnings performance. For example, earnings at Litton Industries fell 17 percent in 1968. LTV's earnings were down by 7 percent during a nine-month period in 1968, while Ogden's earnings fell by 31 percent. Textron, one of the model agglomerates, increased earnings by only 1.4 percent—a miniscule gain for that company. A more general picture of the performance of the conglomerates showed a comparison of growth in earnings per share (1956–1966) between conglomerates and other companies on the *Fortune* 500 list. There was no significant difference.[2]

Business periodicals began raising questions about the entire concept of the conglomerate. For example, an article in *Forbes* stated, "Conservative observers had long questioned whether over the long term it was possible for a single company to cope with the complex problems of operating a half dozen or more different businesses." In connection with those companies that had diversified rapidly by merger, the article went on to note "they too often oversell what they are doing. Many conglomerators glory in the role of big thinkers and long-range planners. Yet in an uncomfortably large number of acquisitions opportunism has clearly played a larger role than planning."[3] Skepticism about management's ability to effectively manage far-flung businesses also appeared in *Fortune*:

> But the headquarters managements of such companies also have one immense problem in common; theirs is a vastly harder and more complex job than managing a homogeneous or single-market company. Top multi-market management is responsible for the whole firm; it justifies its existence only if the divisions perform better or more efficiently as divisions than they could as independent companies. But a multi-market company is also by definition a multi-adversity company. As the trials and tribulations of corporate history testify abundantly, a single-market company, even in good times, runs into troubles that can strain if not floor the most gifted managers. Because a corporation composed of a lot of different divisions can encounter more adversities than the more homogeneous company, it may need more top-level management talent to deal with them.[4]

More concise but equally pessimistic was the view expressed in the subtitle of another article. It read, "Litton's fall from favor has sparked new doubts about the long range future of conglomerates."[5] Some economists expressed similar reservations. For example, Joel Dean argued that:

> The diversity of the conglomerate's operation causes heterogeneity of top management problems. The inevitable lack of specialized industry experience makes the High Command unable to master the intricacies

and ramifications of the highly diverse competitive situations and technologies, of its diverse industries. The conglomerate's chief executive
lacks the industry experience to make good intuitive judgements on the
crucial imponderables.[6]

In connection with the whole idea of synergy and efficiency from conglomerate
mergers John Blair contended that "of all types of merger activity conglomerate
acquisitions have the least claim to promoting efficiency in the economic sense."[7]

It may just be that the logic of conglomerate mergers has been captured best
by Art Buchwald:

> Every five or 10 years the country goes merger crazy. The Conoco-
> DuPont deal is just the tip of the new iceberg. When Wall Street starts
> looking for companies to gobble up they are worse than gypsy moths.
>
> The other day I called Gnu Computers to speak to a pal.
>
> The operator who answered the phone said, "Good Morning, Hy-
> brid Sun International."
>
> "I'm sorry," I said, "I must have the wrong number. I wanted to
> speak to someone at Gnu Computers."
>
> "Hybrid just took over Gnu Computers an hour ago," she replied.
> "I can put you through to your party."
>
> "I want to speak to Walter Lyons."
>
> "Walter Lyons speaking."
>
> "Are you all right, Walter? I hear you were taken over an hour ago
> by Hybrid Sun International."
>
> "That was an hour ago. A half-hour ago, Stellar Joints merged with
> Hybrid, and we're now part of Stellar, Hybrid Inc."
>
> "Is that good or bad?"
>
> "It depends. Miller High Life is now talking to Stellar's lawyers and
> we'll know in an hour whether we're working for High Life or SoBol
> Oil, which is offering our stockholders $85 a share."
>
> "That's a pretty good price," I said.
>
> "It's just the basement. Wango Pinball Machines is making a bid of
> $10 more than SoBol."
>
> "Who are you betting on?"
>
> "Guilford Tennis Shoes."
>
> "How can a tennis-shoe company afford to buy a billion-dollar
> conglomerate?"
>
> "They don't make tennis shoes anymore. They're in high-tech
> micro-relay stations and communications satellites."
>
> "What happened to their tennis-shoe business?" I asked.
>
> "It was spun off and sold to Commonwealth Water Softeners. But
> Guilford never got around to changing its name."
>
> "So right now you're not sure who you work for?"
>
> "Wait a minute, my secretary just put a note on my desk. Our con-
> glomerate has been taken over by Piccolo Instruments out of Baton
> Rouge, La."

"They used to be," I told him. "But Piccolo was bought by a Canadian investment firm in Toronto last month."

"Then," said Lyons, "that means I'm working for Canadians."

"It seems to me The Wall Street Journal said the majority of stockholders in the Canadian firm were Dutch and West Germans," I told him.

"Look, I better call you back, I've got Hong Kong on the other line."

He got back to me in an hour.

"Who was that in Hong Kong?" I asked.

"That was a Mr. Wu. He just bought out the Canadian Syndicate."

"You're now working for someone in Hong Kong?"

"I guess I am, unless Disneyland makes us a better offer."[8]

Clearly the rationale for conglomerate mergers has been called into question. While the financial performance of the conglomerates of the 1960s would seem to have earned such skepticism about their desirability, maybe this was only the temporary result of their financial maneuvering catching up with them. What about agglomerate (and conglomerate) mergers more generally? What does the evidence show about their effects on the firms they acquire? Is there any sign of synergy or increased operating efficiency as a result of their acquisitions? If there is, both the private owners and the public would benefit from a more efficient utilization of the economy's scarce resources. There has been some research that is pertinent to these questions. It should be noted that research into the effects of conglomerate (and agglomerate) acquisitions has faced two difficult problems. One is that traditional microeconomic models provide very little guidance to the researcher. The other is that little good data are available for hypothesis testing.

A study by the Federal Trade Commission is probably the most detailed analysis of the merger-active conglomerates of the 1960s. That analysis focused on nine firms that acquired a total of 348 companies with combined assets of about $10 billion. The study examined the performance of the firms and the companies they acquired. Of the nine conglomerates, over half (five) had a decline in their profit rate between 1960 and 1969—hardly an affirmation of the existence of synergy or gains in technical efficiency. Of eighty-five large companies that were acquired by the conglomerates, all but five were profitable in the year before acquisition; however, their profits were less than the average for companies in their industries. Thus the conglomerates' choices of acquisition candidates suggests that they were not particularly selective or insightful. Overall, the earnings experience of acquired firms before acquisition and that of the entire conglomerate at the beginning and end of the 1960s acquisition spree did not provide any hint of synergy or unique insight.[9]

Some evidence in the Federal Trade Commission study relates to changes in the way acquired units were operated after acquisition. Such changes might provide clues as to how the conglomerates expected to bring about synergy or some other type of efficiency. Since replacement of previous top management of the acquired unit would seem to be one avenue of improving efficiency, let us look at the record. In about 10 percent of the cases, top management left immediately after acquisition; 39 percent left within three years; and 51 percent stayed for at least three years. Clearly, no consistent approach to the management of acquired units was employed by conglomerates to attain synergy (managerial efficiency).

Because conglomerates tend to be large, one might expect that it would be possible to achieve efficiency of administrative functions. Of eleven administrative functions (including accounting, auditing, legal, advertising, and promotion), the conglomerates changed functions in their acquired units in 329 instances, left them unchanged in 498, and partially changed them in 231. Here again, no apparent pattern in the acquired units suggested a strategy for achieving efficiency.

The Federal Trade Commission study explored other areas where a large conglomerate might squeeze synergy or other efficiency out of acquired units. One of these areas was advertising. Twenty-four acquired companies showed increases in advertising relative to their sales after acquisition, and twenty showed decreases. Another area was new investment. Fifteen acquired companies showed an increase in new investment relative to their assets after acquisition while twenty-two showed a decrease. On average, expenditures for new plants and equipment were substantially lower one and two years after acquisition than in the one and two years before. This indicates no consistent approach was employed by the conglomerates to achieve efficiency in acquired units through advertising and investment expenditures.

The conglomerates apparently adopted a variety of strategies in operating the companies they acquired. According to the evidence, the effect on the profitability of the acquired firms was not any more consistent. There was a tendency for the profits of the acquired firms to decline, although the findings were mixed. In view of the mixed results and the acknowledged shortcomings of the study, it is fair to conclude that the merger-active conglomerates of the 1960s made no consistent changes in the operations of acquired companies and had no systematic influence on profits of acquired firms. In short, there is no evidence that synergy or any other form of efficiency can generally be expected from agglomerate-merger activity.

Numerous other studies on this subject have been conducted by economists. Two scholarly works have summarized and evaluated these studies. Peter O. Steiner evaluated much of this work and reached essentially the same conclusion as the Federal Trade Commission study. Steiner concluded that: (1) the firms acquired were pretty much average in their industries in terms of size and profitability (profits were a little low); (2) the acquiring firms displayed no systematic characteristics; and (3) there was no systematic evidence to support any

of the following possible motivations for the acquisitions—real efficiency, monopoly gains, growth, or speculation.[10]

The other major review of the research into the effects of conglomerate
mergers was conducted by Dennis C. Mueller. In concluding his review of the evidence Mueller observed:

> True, the a priori theories of mergers' causes and effects are still in
> conflict, and will probably always remain so. But the empirical litera-
> ture, upon which this survey focusses, draws a surprisingly consistent
> picture. Whatever the stated or unstated goals of managers are, the
> mergers they have consummated have on average not generated extra
> profits for the acquiring firms, [and] have not resulted in increased
> economic efficiency.[11]

Such conclusions are not confined to the effects of merger activity in the
United States. Mueller reached a similar conclusion in a study of merger activity
in seven countries.[12] A major study of merger activity (not just conglomerate)
in the United Kingdom covering most of the post World War II period was
recently completed by G. Meeks. He concluded:

> Firstly, there appear to be financial (and other) incentives to managers
> who have little or no ownership interest in the company to pursue
> growth even at the expense of profitability. Second, the efficiency
> gains, which in public policy statements have been assumed to be the
> saving grace of growth by takeover, cannot in the event be relied upon:
> strong evidence was reported that the efficiency of the typical amal-
> gamation did not improve after merger—it actually appears to have
> declined.[13]

Research on conglomerate mergers in the industrial sector is remarkably
accordant. This is impressive if for no other reason than there are not very many
areas in economics where the evidence is so consistent. What is most surprising
is that the casual, unsupported arguments that mergers are good for the economy continue to have credibility in the popular press and among policymakers.
There is no indication that mergers yield synergy or any other form of efficiency. Academic researchers and practical analysts of the current merger activity seem to reach the same conclusion.

In late 1980, an article appeared in *Business Week* questioning the current
merger movement in general and even proposing the breaking up of firms in
monopolistic industries. The author of the article, Arthur Burck, owns a consulting firm that specializes in advising and negotiating on corporate mergers.
Mr. Burck observed:

> Takeovers of huge companies have become a way of life in industrial
> America. Aren't these huge amalgamations planting the seeds for

further erosion of the nation's industrial position? It should not be for-
gotten that the concentration of the auto industry resulted from the
merger wave that inundated that industry in the '20s, just as the giants
in steel emerged from the nation's first merger binge late in the last
century.[14]

A more recent article bore the euphemistic title "Asset Redeployment."
The opening sentences in the article read,

> A massive redeployment of corporate assets is vigorously reshaping
> American industry. In corporate boardrooms across the country, almost
> everything is for sale, at the right price. Companies are selling dozens
> of their operating units to each other, to private investor groups, or to
> their own units' officers.[15]

According to this article, "Many buyers firmly believe that they can improve
returns simply by managing the acquired operation better by reducing overhead
and inefficiencies, and by installing sharper managers."[16] While the article suggests some short-term problems (inflation and high interest rates) as inducing the
current merger spree, the benefits of such myopic strategies are highly questionable. Particularly notable is the article's observation that, "One motivation
for selling is to undo the mistakes of many companies' diversification binge of
the 1960's. . . . What is more, a lot of the action is in selling part of businesses
acquired during the big merger wave of just the past two years."[17]

The pessimistic evidence from the industrial sector is supported by a growing body of evidence from banking. The first significant study of performance
effects of merger activity in banking was made by Thomas Piper. He examined
the acquisition results of thirty-one bank-holding companies between 1946 and
1967. His analysis revealed that acquisitions did not, on average, improve the
profitability of the holding company and that the acquired banks were not, on
average, unusually profitable or unprofitable.[18]

Since the mid 1960s, acquisitions by bank-holding companies have been
mostly of the conglomerate type. A comprehensive review of the research evidence in connection with such acquisitions was prepared at the Federal Reserve
Board.[19] In one paper Timothy Curry concluded from all available evidence that
the banks acquired by bank-holding companies do not experience an increase in
profitability after acquisition. Another paper in this review focused on studies
concerned with the cost efficiency of banks acquired by bank-holding companies. In that paper, James Burke reported that available research evidence
provides no general indication that banks acquired by bank-holding companies
become more cost efficient. The results of my studies dealing with bank-holding
companies' participation in the mortgage-banking, consumer-finance, and leasing
industries reveal that, if anything, after companies are acquired they are less
efficient than independent firms in these industries. In spite of this apparent

tendency to reduce the efficiency of the firms they acquire, large bank-holding companies have been acquiring a number of the major firms in these industries. For example BankAmerica, the largest banking organization in the United States, acquired GAC Finance (1973). Manufacturers Hanover Corp., the fourth largest, acquired Citizens Mortgage Corp. (1973) and Ritter Financial Corp. (1975).

I think the evidence on the results of conglomerate acquisitions by bank-holding companies in banking as well as the consumer-finance, mortgage-banking, and leasing industries is particularly revealing. The acquiring bank-holding companies are frequently among the largest banking organizations in the United States, whereas the companies they acquire are small by comparison. Further, by law, bank-holding companies may acquire only those companies that are in businesses closely related to banks. Under the circumstances, if there is any reason to expect conglomerate mergers to yield public benefits in the form of increased efficiency (synergistic or otherwise) it should be apparent here—very large firms (the ones that supposedly have the superior management) acquiring smaller firms in businesses where they have related experience and expertise.

If conglomerate mergers such as these do not yield increased efficiency, it is hard to imagine that very many other conglomerate or agglomerate mergers would. Increases in efficiency would instead seem especially unlikely in connection with agglomerate mergers like those described in the last chapter, where the acquired firms are in businesses largely alien to managers of the agglomerates. It is time that the synergy and related arguments be put to rest. For far too long they have provided an unfounded justification for the acquisition of thousands of viable, independent companies in the U.S. economy. There have been no apparent benefits to the system. Unfortunately, it appears that conglomerate mergers have imposed significant costs on the system.

The losses imposed by conglomerate mergers include: (1) a loss of the profit information needed for investors to allocate resources rationally, (2) an increased opportunity for anticompetitive behavior aimed at smaller competitors, and (3) an increasing concentration of economic resources into fewer hands along with an increased bureaucratization of the system.

A loss of profit information in the economic system would weaken one of the extraordinary features of competitive capitalism—the system's ability to allocate resources from one productive activity to another in a timely and efficient manner. Investors allocate capital and individuals allocate energy and talent in response to consumer demand. Profits are a key element in this process. They provide the signal to investors and entrepreneurs as to where the greatest consumer demand is and thus reveal where profit opportunities exist in the system. This contrasts sharply with the resource-allocation process in a socialist system, where government bureaucrats allocate productive resources. A continued high level of conglomerate-merger activity will erode this essential resource-allocation feature of the U.S. economic system by obliterating the profit signals. As more and more companies disappear into large conglomerates, investors will be deprived of profit information on the individual activities in which the firms had been previously engaged.

The Federal Trade Commission's study justifiably expressed concern with the information loss resulting from acquisitions by conglomerates. The nature of the problem was illustrated for each of the conglomerates under study by a breakdown of the sales and profit data shown in the firms' annual reports. Most of the companies reported sales and profit data for broad divisions of the company. For example, in 1971, Textron reported data for its consumer, aerospace, industrial, and metal products divisions; FMC reported data on its machinery, chemical, fiber and film, and ordnance divisions; Norton Simon reported data on its food and service, soft drinks and distilled spirits, packaging, and communications and graphics systems divisions; and White Consolidated provided no divisional breakdown of data.[20] Such a wide range of products and industries are included in these broadly defined divisions that the financial information, including profits, is next to useless for purposes of guiding investment capital. Unfortunately, this sort of consolidated reporting is the norm rather than the exception. Because each conglomerate owns many companies, this information loss seriously hampers the system's ability to allocate resources.

The signals provided by profits are at the very heart of a capitalist system. The consolidated reporting of conglomerates results in a significant loss of information to investors, but that is only part of the information-loss problem. Large diversified firms have trouble determining the actual profits of their various activities because of the problem they have allocating their overhead costs. Where among the various activities do the costs of management, capital, promotion, research and development, and so forth, belong? This is a difficult problem theoretically as outlined by J.M. Clark.[21] It is also a very difficult problem in practice and is discussed in practically any intermediate textbook in business and finance. If a business manager cannot accurately allocate costs of operation among different lines of business, then how can he accurately determine the profitability of the various activities?

The allocation process within the large conglomerate resembles the bureaucratic process of the socialist system, since there are no good, market-determined profit signals. Private sector bureaucrats rather than government bureaucrats are making allocation decisions. Line-of-business reporting to the Federal Trade Commission does not fully overcome the loss of information to the economic system resulting from widespread diversification and the disappearance of independent businesses. While line-of-business reporting is better than highly consolidated financial reporting, it still has serious shortcomings because of the problem of accurately determining where profits are being made within the diversified firm.

A second cost from a high degree of diversification by U.S. business is the possibility that it increases anticompetitive behavior. Extensions of theory suggest only possibilities in this area, and the evidence is scanty. Nevertheless, it should not be ignored. The most notable manifestations of anticompetitive behavior were proposed by Corwin Edwards in his *conglomerate power* hypothesis in 1955.[22] Edwards contended that diversification of large firms afforded them the opportunity to engage in predatory pricing. The large diversified firm could undertake a severe price-cutting program in one line of business in order to drive its single-line competitors out of business. Such a pricing strategy could be financed with profits made in the conglomerate's other lines of business. The temporary use of such a strategy or simply the threat of its use could induce other firms to follow meekly the prices established by the conglomerate. The result of either driving competitors out of business or coercing them into following the conglomerate's prices would permit monopoly prices rather than competitive prices to be set. There are laws which prohibit predatory pricing. However, it is difficult to prove that prices are in fact predatory. For example, one indicator of predatory pricing is pricing below cost. But as I have just noted, it is a difficult matter to establish the actual cost of a particular line of activity in a conglomerate. Furthermore, laws may proscribe certain forms of behavior, but they do not prevent such behavior. The Justice Department continues to win cases against companies that have engaged in illegal anticompetitive behavior.

The conglomerate-power hypothesis of Corwin Edwards provided a rationale for expecting predatory pricing to take place. To show that it is a possibility I will discuss briefly a couple of documented cases of predatory pricing, although it is not known if these are isolated occurrences or if predatory pricing (or the threat its use) is prevalent among agglomerates and conglomerates.

According to a Federal Trade Commission (FTC) study, Anheuser-Busch, one of the nation's largest brewers, engaged in predatory pricing in the St. Louis market during 1954 and 1955.[23] The policy was initiated in October 1953, when Anheuser-Busch and the other national brewers that operated in many markets adopted a general increase in prices in response to a new wage contract. Although local and regional brewers in many parts of the country followed the increase, three brewers in the St. Louis area did not. In response, Anheuser-Busch chose not to institute a fifteen-cent price increase per case in St. Louis. Then, in the face of higher costs and increased prices elsewhere in the country, Anheuser-Busch cut prices in St. Louis by twenty-five cents a case in January 1954, and by an additional thirty-three cents in June. The FTC study noted that the president of Anheuser-Busch indicated he "imagined Anheuser-Busch wouldn't have 'done anything' in St. Louis if the regional St. Louis brewers had raised their prices in response to the increase by the larger brewers outside St. Louis." The FTC hearing examiner found that Anheuser-Busch's president had made these price cuts for two reasons: "to get business away from its competitors, and to punish them for refusing to increase prices when Anheuser-Busch did so in the fall of 1953."[24] These objectives were met, Anheuser-Busch's market share in the St. Louis area increased from 12.5 percent in December

1953 to 39.3 percent in March 1955, while the market shares of the local firms showed a corresponding decline. This punishment apparently taught the local firms a lesson. When, in February 1955, Anheuser-Busch increased prices in St. Louis, the three local brewers followed suit. Anheuser-Busch had effectively used its profits in other markets to support predatory pricing in St. Louis. This pricing strategy repressed competition and allowed Anheuser-Busch to set beer prices in St. Louis.

Another example of a large, diversified firm using its multimarket presence to apply extreme price pressure to local competitors in a specific market is provided by the Kraft Foods Division of National Dairy, the twentieth largest industrial firm in the country in 1961. According to the FTC study, Kraft entered the market areas of Baltimore, Maryland, Washington, D.C., Richmond, Virginia, and Norfolk, Virginia in 1956 with a line of jams and jellies. By 1960, Kraft had become a major factor in Baltimore but was dissatisfied with its market share in neighboring Washington, D.C. So during a twenty-six-day period from January 16 through February 10, 1961, Kraft offered wholesalers and retailers one free case of jams and jellies for every case purchased. Further, there were no quantity limits, which was highly unusual in such promotions. Kraft also assured buyers that it would conduct a major promotional campaign to help move the stock. The impact on sales was remarkable. In all of 1960, National Dairy had sold 169,977 cases of jams and jellies. During the twenty-six-day promotion it sold 400,803 cases. It actually delivered only 153,909 cases and paid cash of $829,005 in place of other deliveries. This promotion, which cost National Dairy $1.3 million, was in essence a price cut. Data in the FTC's study indicate that the ultimate price for the jams and jellies sold was below even out-of-pocket expenses.

The impact on Kraft's regional competitors in the area (Old Virginia, Theresa Friedman, and Polaner) was immediate. During the first month of the promotion, sales by the local companies fell by 27 percent, 33 percent, and 27 percent respectively. There was no way to compete with below-cost prices. National Dairy could take substantial temporary losses in one market because of profits in other markets and products. The local producers simply could not do this. The conclusion of the commission that the cost of the promotion must have been subsidized by other operations was upheld in 1969 by the Seventh Circuit Court of Appeals. The majority opinion of the court held that, "The cost was of necessity subsidized from income and profits earned by petitioner (National Dairy) in its operations elsewhere."[25] Further, testimony from officials of the local companies indicated that it was not possible to match Kraft's prices and remain in business.

This is definitely not the sort of price competition that economists regard as a desirable trait of a competitive market. Such pricing cannot be sustained over the long run. In addition, it can result in a monopoly if independents are run out of business. Even if a monopoly is not gained, the independents may be sufficiently intimidated that they simply follow the prices of the large diversified firm, and meaningful price competition disappears. The inevitable result is monopoly pricing. The situation where companies are driven out of business (or intimidated) by predatory pricing should be clearly distinguished from that in which a firm, by dint of superior efficiency, is able to charge lower prices than its competitors while earning a normal profit. Indeed, this latter situation is the way the system should work. The market rewards the efficient firm and punishes the inefficient. This forces companies to strive to increase their efficiency and leads to greater productivity.

A third major cost to society from unimpeded conglomerate mergers is an increase in the concentration of the nation's economic resources. If economic concentration is permitted to proceed far enough, it will profoundly affect the sociopolitical system. Because of the pervasive impact of increasing economic concentration on society, I have devoted a separate chapter to this problem.

In spite of the growing evidence and experience questioning the benefits of conglomerate mergers, mergers continue at a rapid pace. Though the evidence provides no indication that profits motivate such mergers, the desire for power provides a plausible motive. This explanation for mergers receives strong support from the recent surge of unfriendly takeovers, the subject of the next chapter.

Notes

1. *Washington Post* (October 11, 1981).

2. *Fortune,* Thomas O. Hanlon (June 1967).

3. *Forbes* (January 1, 1969), pp. 77 and 80. Reprinted with permission.

4. *Fortune,* Gilbert Burck (February 1967), p. 131, © 1967, Time Inc. All rights reserved. Reprinted with permission.

5. *Financial World* (February 14, 1968), p. 12.

6. Joel Dean, "Causes and Consequences of Growth by Conglomerate Merger: An Introduction," *Conglomerate Mergers and Acquisitions: Opinion and Analysis,* ed. Lawrence M. Kaye, et al., *St. John's Law Review* (Spring 1970), p. 29.

7. John Blair, "The Conglomerate Merger in Economics and Law," *Georgetown Law Journal* (Summer 1958), p. 679.

8. Art Buchwald, *Washington Post* (August 30, 1981). Reprinted with permission of the author, Los Angeles Times Syndicate.

9. Stanley E. Boyle and Philip W. Jaynes, *Economic Report on Conglomerate Merger Performance* (Washington, D.C.: Federal Trade Commission, 1972).

10. Peter O. Steiner, *Mergers: Motives, Effects, Policies* (Ann Arbor: University of Michigan Press, 1975).

11. Dennis C. Mueller, "The Effects of Conglomerate Mergers: A Survey of the Empirical Evidence," *Journal of Banking and Finance* (December 1977), p. 344.

12. That study analyzed merger activity in the U.S., U.K. and five European countries. See *The Determinants and Effects of Mergers: An International Comparison,* ed. Dennis C. Mueller (Cambridge, Mass.: Oelgeschlager, Gunn and Hain, 1980).

13. G. Meeks, *Disappointing Marriage: A Study of the Gains from Merger* (Cambridge, England: Cambridge University Press, 1977), p. 66.

14. *Business Week* (November 17, 1980), pp. 18 and 23. Reprinted with permission.

15. *Business Week* (August 24, 1981), p. 67. Reprinted with permission.

16. Ibid.

17. Ibid., pp. 69 and 70.

18. Thomas Piper, *The Economics of Bank Acquisitions by Registered Bank Holding Companies,* Research Report no. 48 (Federal Reserve Bank of Boston, March 1971).

19. Federal Reserve Board, *The Bank Holding Company Movement to 1978: A Compendium* (Washington, D.C.: Federal Reserve Board, 1978).

20. Boyle and Jaynes, *Economic Report on Conglomerate Merger Performance.*

21. J. Maurice Clark, *Studies in The Economics of Overhead Costs* (Chicago: University of Chicago Press, 1923).

22. Corwin D. Edwards, "Conglomerate Bigness as a Source of Power," in *Business Concentration and Price Policy* (Princeton: Princeton University Press, 1955), pp. 331-59.

23. Federal Trade Commission, *Economic Report on Corporate Mergers* (Washington, D.C.: Government Printing Office 1969).

24. Ibid., pp. 425 and 422.

25. Ibid., pp. 442 and 440.

13 The Power Motive Revealed along with Other Costs of Mergers

Though the speculative fever underlying the conglomerate-merger activity of the 1960s wore off, agglomerate and conglomerate mergers are reaching record levels in the early 1980s. The mergers and acquisitions recorded in 1981 greatly surpassed, in numbers and dollar volume, the peak year of the conglomerate wave of the 1960s. The acquisition activity of 1981 featured many large companies with household names.[1] Although today's mergers are still conglomerates, there is a new twist in form providing unique insight into the motivation underlying merger activity. Unfriendly takeovers have increased significantly in recent years. In unfriendly takeovers, the management or owners (or both) of the firm to be acquired (the target firm) oppose the acquisition.

Often the target firm openly resists the takeover by legal devices or other strategies. As a result, the personalities involved and the thinking and action behind the takeovers have come to light in the press. The importance of the desire for power as a motivator of business is revealed in the detailed accounts of these takeovers. They illustrate the role of power in direct connection with merger activity. In the first part of this chapter, I will present a collage of quotations from various periodicals and newspapers to emphasize the human element underlying the merger decisions of business executives. Second, I will propose that the recent decline in U.S. business's competitiveness with foreign business has exposed numerous costs associated with merger activity that I did not discuss in the last chapter. These costs include: 1) a preoccupation with short-term financial objectives in business and business schools, 2) the waste of top talent on guiding merger campaigns rather than business operations, 3) large expenditures on Wall Street financiers and on law firms required to consummate an acquisition, 4) the waste of talent and money to defend against the possibility of a takeover, 5) mergers and other business decisions being made to prevent a company from being acquired, 6) a high rate of unsuccessful mergers resulting in the sale of acquired companies, and 7) the bureaucratization of U.S. business.

Before proceeding with this chapter, I will present an overview provided by an article published in 1978 on the nature of much recent acquisition activity. According to the article,

> Not very many years ago, no self-respecting chief executive would make a hostile tender offer for the control of another company. The hostile tender was the weapon of the 'raiders' and raiders weren't gentlemen.

They didn't fight fair; they used mustard gas. Lately, however, everybody seems to be using gas, which has, of course, made gas respectable. Viewing the takeover wars from the vantage point of a forward artillery observer, Salomon Brothers partner Ira Harris comments: "It isn't the Louis Wolfsons who are doing it today. It's the establishment doing it to itself."

What establishment c.e.o.'s [chief executive officers] are doing is sidestepping unreceptive managements and boards of directors and making offers directly to the shareholders they want to acquire.[2]

This new form of acquisiton has been increasing since 1974. In addition, the takeovers involve bigger targets. At the same time the premiums paid for the stock are growing. "The average premium in the ten $100-million-plus contests last year was more than 80 percent. In a few cases, the raider paid more than double the market value."[3] The target firm often sues the raider when the tender offer is made. However, "A raider has to be prepared for a lot more than lawsuits. Despite the new respectability of hostile offers, he will probably have to weather a barrage of name-calling orchestrated by public-relations specialists. 'You shouldn't be in this game if you have old-fashioned gentlemen on your board,' says Hill and Knowlton's Cheney. 'They don't like to be subpoenaed at garden parties.'"[4]

Another overview of the early stages of the current wave of acquisition activity focused on the tactics used. The terminology employed is quite revealing. Thus,

> Defensive fights like the one Microdot is waging are making it more difficult and costly to take over companies that do not want to be taken over. . . . In fact the fights are getting more vicious all the time. . . . It is important for the aggressor that he strike with great power and confidence. . . . It is also important to strike with vigor so that stockholders won't be encouraged to hold out for a high price. . . . And the successful defender is often at least as ruthless as his attacker. . . . The stakes are huge in these battles, and, not surprisingly, as fast as defenders of the *status quo* set up obstacles to takeovers, the attackers find ways around them.[5]

This description is captured in a picture accompanying the article. It shows Rudolph Eberstadt Jr., president of Microdot, which was then subject to a takeover attempt by General Cable, with a threatening countenance and a raised, clenched fist.

One of the earlier contests in the current merger wave was set off when United Technologies Corp. announced that it planned to acquire Babcock and Wilcox Co. One article stated that,

> Since Mar. 29, when United Technologies Corp. announced that it planned to acquire Babcock and Wilcox, the two companies have been fighting a high-stakes takeover war. The pace is now accelerating.

With "the blood in the water," as one observer puts it, other companies—most notably J. Ray McDermott and Co.—and arbitrageurs are jumping into the fray, driving the price of B & W's stock up to about $44 a share from $35, roughly $2 a share above UTC's original offer totaling $512 million.

In response to the observation that Gray (Chairman of United Technologies) would back off since the stock price of Babcock and Wilcox had moved above his $42-a-share offer, another Wall Street takeover expert cautioned, "Gray also has a reputation for liking deals that get done. He finishes what he starts." Further, "If McDermott attempts a tender offer, its hefty cash position of roughly $450 million would make it a formidable opponent in any bidding war for B & W."[6]

Another of the early takeover contests saw Herbert Siegel of Chris-Craft warning William Piper Jr., of Piper Aircraft, of a forthcoming tender offer for Piper's common stock. "When he broke the news to Bill Piper, Herb Siegel, at forty, was already a veteran of corporate warfare." From there came "one of the most prolonged, intricate, and delicately shaded corporate battles of all time.... the contestants have spent seven years in the courts."[7]

In early 1978 Sun, the giant oil company, made a tender offer for Becton, Dickinson & Co., a hospital supply firm. One article reported:

While Wall Street is still reeling from the boldness of the move, it now appears that Sun Co.'s lightning raid on the Rutherford (N.J.) hospital supply firm of Becton, Dickinson & Co. two weeks ago will bog down in the courts, or even in Congress. In a particularly competitive acquisition atmosphere, Sun, the normally staid oil giant, has managed to pull off the most aggressive takeover maneuver yet—suddenly emerging with 34% of BD's stock, bought from 33 institutions and individuals in private transactions that took place off the floor of the stock exchange.

If Sun gets away with the B D shares, other corporations with an eye for a takeover may try the same tactic. Says one observer: "No company with institutional holders will be safe."[8]

An article on Kennecott's acquisition of part of Curtiss-Wright bore the title "Winner In A Close Decision." It went on to note, "When they finally got around to signing a peace treaty last week, Thomas D. Barrow, 56, chairman of Kennecott, and T. Roland Berner, 70, head of Curtiss-Wright, elected to do so separately. The animosity engendered by two years of corporate battling was so great that they refused to appear in the same room." Further, "Each company gave up the stock that had made it the largest shareholder in the other. Each promised to refrain from going after the other for ten years. And each claimed victory." The conflict began when, "Target of a Curtiss-Wright proxy war two years ago, Kennecott faced another possible onslaught this spring when an agreement staying Curtiss-Wright's hand would have run out. Last November, when Barrow sprang a tender offer for control of Curtiss, he really was engaging in a preemptive strike." Finally, Berner of Curtiss-Wright accepted an acquisition by Kennecott as inevitable. "He recognized that Kennecott, nearly six times Curtiss-Wright's size, could outmuscle it."[9]

The unsuccessful attempt by Mobil to acquire Marathon Oil was reported in an article entitled "Clash of the Titans." The article began, "With stunning swiftness, the $6.5 billion battle between Mobil Corp. and U.S. Steel for control over Marathon Oil turned nasty last week. Mobil, still frustrated and angry over its defeat by DuPont earlier this year in the struggle to take over Conoco, seemed on the brink of losing again. Then Mobil went on the offensive with a daring ploy. The oil company announced that it intended to buy up to 25% of its bidding rival, U.S. Steel. Said one banker involved in the dealing: 'They have tried to put a gun on the head of U.S. Steel.'" Executives at U.S. Steel denounced the move by Mobil as "a very reckless action aimed solely at coercing U.S. Steel to abandon its acquisition of Marathon." As a result, "Mobil is now viewed by many in the financial community as a reckless predator that is willing to spend extravagant sums and stop at almost nothing to acquire another oil company."[10] The article went on to note, "Mobil's bid for Marathon seemed doomed almost from the start. The company suffered defeat after defeat in a series of legal battles fought on several fronts." The last sentence quoted an industry analyst who said, "Mobil is like the shark in *Jaws*. You never know where its going to pop up."[11]

After Edgar Bronfman of Seagram was bitterly rebuffed in his attempt to acquire St. Joe Minerals, his success in getting a minority position in DuPont-Conoco was evidently an important personal victory for Mr. Bronfman. After Bronfman's offer to buy St. Joe fell through, he was reportedly "methodically shopping for the right acquisition in a painstaking process." In doing so, Bronfman stated, "We're trying to be sensible, careful, and exciting all at the same time."[12] The article went on to note that, "He wants to avoid getting carried away by the excitement of bidding for a company he seeks. 'One of the big mistakes always made in business is that people's egos start to interfere with their judgement' he says. 'I don't permit myself to do that.'"[13] Keeping one's ego out of business decisions is no easy feat, for Edgar Bronfman or anyone else, as the article goes on to suggest. Having just sold Texas Pacific to Sun for $2.3 billion and a share in subsequent profits, Edgar Bronfman called his brother Charles on the phone to explain the deal. "Before Edgar passed word of the deal to his brother on the phone, Charles jokingly asked, 'What are you going to do now, buy Iran?' Edgar replied, 'No, but you're close.' Once the impact of the sale sank in, Charles recalls, 'I woke up all of a sudden and realized, hey, we've just doubled the assets of the company. Why, it was just like sending a small kid into a toy store with a hundred bucks.'"[14]

The complexity and intensity of recent takeovers is reflected in an article about the struggle initiated with the tender offer by Dome, on May 5, for 20 percent of Conoco's stock. The story emerged in "the aftermath of a war that fascinated the entire country for weeks. Companies with household names— DuPont, Mobil, and Seagram—were waging combat with sums of money that would make convincing defense budgets in many countries."[15] The article noted that the financial advisors to Seagram, Goldman Sachs, have an aversion to unfriendly takeovers and "if the guns began to roar, Goldman Sachs would excuse itself from the battle."[16] This was only the beginning of the battle for Conoco. According to another article a "prominent banker called it a 'feeding frenzy'. . . . Three giant companies—DuPont, Seagram and Mobil—were battling for control of Conoco, Inc., the nation's ninth largest oil concern, and the bidding was fast approaching the $8 billion level." In preparing for the battle, "the hunters and their prey had stocked up war chests of bank credits worth more than $25 billion—enough to buy Detroit's Big Three automakers with $10 billion to spare—and many analysts predicted that the marauders were preparing for a long-term merger binge of unprecedented proportions." According to Larry Goldstein of the Petroleum Industry Research Foundation, "Having had that first taste of blood, it is hard to believe they will pull back."[17]

In reporting the attempt by LTV to acquire Grumman, one article carried the title "LTV Mounts an Aggressive Bid for the Aircraft Maker." The article disclosed a letter from Paul Thayer, chairman of LTV, to John Bierworth, chairman of Grumman, noting that Thayer's proposal for a meeting between the two to discuss a combination had been rejected. Instead, Grumman elected to fight the bid and, "The battle has erupted on several fronts."[18] According to another article, "From day one, Grumman's management apparently decided to wage all-out corporate war on the widest possible front."[19] On the other side, "'We are in this for the duration' promises Paul Thayer, chairman of LTV who was in Washington to drum up support for the offer."[20]

A book review by Alice Priest described Sun Co.'s attempted takeover of Becton, Dickinson and Co. in 1978. "Sun's blitzkrieg on Becton Dickinson, orchestrated by investment banker Salomon Bros. and choreographed by legal expert Martin Lipton of Wachtel, Lipton, Rosen and Katz, was described as a 'brilliantly designed lightning strike.'"[21] The review concludes "that the war games of mergers and acquisitions are a mock battleground for *capos, consiglieres,* and soldiers eager to make their mark. As such, some form of the game will go on as long as there are corporations to play."[22]

It is obvious that mergers involve a lot more than a calculated drive for superior efficiency. Even the words used to describe these acquisitions are revealing—winner and loser, blood, war, peace treaty, and so on. Further, the names and often the pictures of the executives involved in these acquisitions appear in periodicals with captions describing the parties as winners or losers, as tough or hesitant. Such extensive publicity, good or bad, is seldom accorded the business executive who has increased the efficiency of his company, has supported process and product innovation, or has made significant inroads in foreign markets. It is evident that the personal element plays a major role in merger decisions in U.S. business. The drive to build an empire, the drive for power, comes through as a key factor. One of Wall Street's leading merger makers, Felix Rohatyn, observed, "There's too much macho involved. This has become show biz."[23] The former Cornell University economics professor Alfred Kahn in assessing recent merger activity stated,

> I am not an expert on the motivations of managers; but I have read enough of the literature to be aware that they may well be interested in the prestige, the public exposure and influence, and the higher remuneration that seems to go with their working for larger rather than smaller companies. To the extent that this is true, and to the extent that they are not subject to effective control by the stockholders, we have a powerful private motive for managers to engage in empire-building mergers and acquisitions.[24]

The current merger movement has revealed the importance of the desire for power in generating mergers. It has also revealed some important costs imposed on the economic system by the unchecked drive for power through mergers. Some of the costs of agglomerate and conglomerate mergers were discussed in the last chapter. However, other costs have recently been uncovered by the increasing inability of U.S. companies to compete with their foreign counterparts during the past ten to fifteen years. These other problems seem directly linked to merger activity. It took the exceptionally high degree of merger activity in the 1960s and again in the late 1970s and early 1980s to link these problems with merger activity. It is now evident, however, that mergers are both a cause and a symptom.

The preoccupation of U.S. business with growth and short-term financial considerations is the most basic problem. This preoccupation is encouraged by and manifested in mergers. Mergers provide the surest means for a business executive to achieve rapid growth of his company, establish a reputation for making a major financial deal, and leave a mark on the company. Thus, while mergers themselves satisfy a basic drive of business executives—the drive for power—they also provide a made-to-order mechanism for chalking up short-term growth and financial results.

Preoccupation with short-term results is reflected by the fact that U.S. businesses are increasingly run by executives with a finance or legal background rather than a technical or marketing background. Robert Hayes and William J. Abernathy reported that as of the mid 1970s, 33 percent of the presidents of the 100 top U.S. corporations had finance and legal backgrounds. This represented a 45 percent increase since around 1950.[25] Under the circumstances, it is hardly surprising that increasing emphasis is placed on financial and legal maneuvers with short-term objectives or that increased emphasis is placed on mergers. Nor is it surprising that so many of these mergers go sour after a few years. Unfortunately, long-run planning and operational considerations, including process and product innovation that yield increased productivity and a higher standard of living, suffer as a result.

The emphasis on short-term financial results is also reflected in the current business school curricula, particularly the Master of Business Administration (MBA) programs. One article on education in our business schools quoted professor of business Lee Seidler (New York University) as saying, "It may be that some of the basic tools we've been teaching in business schools for 20 years are inordinately biased toward the short term, the sure payoff." C. Jackson Grayson, chairman of the American Productivity Center is reported to have said, "American management has for 20 years coasted off the great research and development gains made during World War II, and constantly rewarded executives from marketing, financial and legal sides of the business while it ignored the production men."[26] In another article it was reported that, "Business school deans and placement officers claim that corporate recruiters provide little incentive for students to emphasize the operations end of the MBA curriculum. Very few companies recruit MBAs into line jobs. Those that do pay the fledgling line managers far less than their colleagues in entry-level staff positions."[27] Mergers are an important manifestation of this attitude. They are probably a significant factor in our shrinking productivity.

Foreign businesses have taken note of the growing penchant for short-term financial manipulations in U.S. business and business schools. While Japanese companies continue to send their young executives to U.S. business schools, the purpose is no longer to learn U.S. management skills. Indeed, the Japanese are critical of MBA programs that teach management strictly by the numbers for short-terms goals. Instead they come to make contacts, polish their English, and to more fully understand their Western competitors.[28] A European businessman remarked that U.S. companies seem "more interested in buying other companies than they are in selling products."[29]

Ironically, another manifestation of the preoccupation with short-term results is a new strategy that has come into vogue. Companies have attracted investors' attention recently by selling some of their assets. Management has discovered that this can sometimes make their stockholders richer overnight. For example, when Esmark and Seagram sold their oil properties in 1980, the selling price for each was higher than the market value of the company only a few months before the sale. Similarly, when American Can announced its intention to sell its paper and forest-products business in April 1981, analysts expected these operations to sell for around $1 billion. This would be equal to about $50 per share of American Can, which was selling for about $30 per share shortly before the announcment. Similar spin-offs include the sale of Safeguard Business Systems by Safeguard Industries (1980), Mesa Royalty Trust by Mesa Petroleum (1979), Valero Energy by Coastal (1980), San Juan Basin Royalty and Permian Basin Royalty of Southland Royalty (1980), and GEO International by Peabody International (1981). In these cases, the value of the stock rose by an average of 50 percent between the date of announcement and the date of spin-off, which was about six months on average.[30]

Such results have raised two disturbing questions. The first is whether the stock markets are indeed as efficient as popularly believed. Do stock prices reflect all of the available information about a company, or is that basic belief a fallacy? The other, emphasized in the preceding chapter, is whether a diversified company actually can allocate capital efficiently. Are highly profitable operations carrying losers? Whatever the answers, the buying and selling of companies is made-to-order for a business strategy bent on short-term financial results.

Focusing on short-term financial factors, especially mergers, carries significant costs. The long-run costs are reflected in our declining productivity and lack of competitiveness with foreign companies. There are some immediate costs as well. Particularly obvious among the short-term costs is the waste of talent of many top business executives. Their time is devoted to masterminding acquisition campaigns rather than to designing and building better products. Another cost is the entire industry of exorbitantly expensive deal makers which has sprung up. These are the financial intermediaries that put together the acquisition packages. They include well-known financial companies (Morgan Stanley, Salomon Brothers, Lazard Freres, Goldman Sachs, Shearson Loeb Rhoades, First Boston) and hundreds of smaller consulting firms. Their match-making fees are impressive. The financial intermediaries for the thirty-six largest mergers in 1981 earned a total of $144.6 million in fees. The DuPont-Conoco merger alone generated fees of about $30 million to financial intermediaries.[31]

The urge to merge has become so strong that the financial intermediaries sometimes go to companies and propose possible deals without waiting to be asked. The idea for the merger of American Express and Shearson did not originate with either partner first. The idea came from Salim Lewis of a small arbitrage firm. He took his proposal to the chairman of American Express, an old friend, and then to Shearson's chief. Lewis sold his idea and pocketed $3.5 million.[32] There is, of course, an incentive to dream up or support big mergers, since the fees are directly associated with the size of the deal. For example, Merrill Lynch and Co. recently decided to become more actively involved in the burgeoning merger business. In doing so, an official of the company, J.C. Mendel, observed that, "Our market will be industrial corporations with $100 million to $1 billion."[33]

The increasing number of mergers put together in this fashion raises at least two issues. First, the prospects for attaining either synergy or operational efficiency are very remote when the originators of the merger plans are Wall Street financiers. The training, talent, and objectives of the deal makers will serve to assure only that two firms get merged, and no more. Second, it seems reasonable to suspect that this activity represents a huge waste of talent and resources.

Defending against takeover generates significant costs as well. While financial intermediaries are receiving huge sums for putting together merger deals, law firms and other financial intermediaries are receiving equally large sums for defending companies from being taken over. Furthermore, just as executive talent in U.S. corporations is being spent on the acquisition trail rather than on business operations, other business executives are devoting their time and energy to avoid being acquired, even making business decisions to avoid the possibility. An example of the costs is provided by First Boston, the investment banking firm, which charged Pullman $1,500 per man-hour to defend it from being acquired and received a total fee of $6 million.[34] When Seagram moved to acquire Conoco, Conoco opened merger negotiations with Cities Service to thwart Seagram—the combined firm would simply be too big for Seagram to acquire. But Seagram persisted, and Cities Service broke off the merger talks. Then Conoco turned to DuPont, which was to serve as a "white knight" and acquire that firm instead of Seagram. The importance today of defending your company against acquisition was brought home harshly to Sanford Sigoloff, president of Daylin Inc. After Sigoloff brought Daylin from the verge of bankruptcy, Daylin was acquired by W.R. Grace for $140 million in 1978. In retrospect, Sigoloff recognized that he was too slow in moving from offense to defense—"in moving from a posture of ensuring his company's mere survival to one of assertive growth. . . . Had he moved faster he might have made it harder for prospective acquirers to swallow the company."[35]

After Mobil Oil made a $5.1 billion bid for Marathon Oil, one article carried the title, "Marathon Oil Executives Sharply Criticized for not Building Better Takeover Defenses."[36] Shortly thereafter, Marathon worked out an agreement whereby U.S. steel would acquire it and thus rescue it from Mobil. As a countermove, Mobil announced its intention to purchase 25 percent of U.S. Steel. In a further effort to defend itself, Marathon brought an antitrust suit against Mobil in Cleveland federal court. Marathon called in the investment banking firm, First Boston, along with a law firm to prepare the defense. In addition, Marathon hired a public relations expert with Hill and Knowlton to direct a media campaign. Other defensive options considered by Marathon were: 1) to buy back its own shares with a $5 billion line of bank credit that could be used for this, 2) to issue new stock to buyers unlikely to sell to Mobil, and 3) to buy another company so they would be too large to acquire easily.

It is not only the corporate giants who are involved in attack and counterattack strategies. For example, in 1981 Ryder System, the truck-leasing firm, purchased 4.9 percent of Frank B. Hall & Co., an insurance broker, and announced plans for further purchases. To thwart this takeover attempt, Frank B. Hall moved to acquire Jartran Inc. Since Jartran is also a truck-leasing firm, Ryder's acquisition of a combined Hall and Jartran would likely face an antitrust suit because Ryder's acquisition would then be a horizontal one.[37] When Whittaker Corp. announced a successful tender offer for 49 percent of Brunswick

Corp.'s stock, Brunswick suggested that it might sell its profitable medical supplies division to discourage Whittaker. Because Whittaker has operations in medical products (as well as railroad car manufacturing, hydraulic-power equipment, and pleasure boats), the medical supplies division of Brunswick was the main attraction for the takeover.[38]

In addition to the huge legal and financial costs, the waste of executive talent, the concoction of private antitrust suits, and the scramble for mergers purely out of expediency to thwart takeover, there is yet another cost of takeover defense. More and more executives are seeking "golden parachutes," that is, financial insurance for themselves against unfriendly takeover. For example, Weterau Inc., a St. Louis food company that is fighting a takeover attempt, will provide large cash payments to sixteen of its executives (including $1.25 million to its chairman) if the company is subject to an unfriendly takeover.[39] Conoco's board of directors guaranteed the salaries of nine of its top officers through mid 1984. Ralph Bailey, the chairman of Conoco, was guaranteed annual pay of $637,716 until 1989.[40] Before Whittaker Corp.'s attempted takeover of Brunswick, Brunswick's chairman and president were guaranteed their salaries through 1983 and 1986 respectively.[41] William Agee, who initiated the Bendix, Martin–Marietta, United Technologies, and Allied Corp. acquisition debacle, opened his $4 million golden parachute upon leaving Bendix in early 1983. The costs of financial insurance for executives are modest in comparison to many of the direct costs of today's takeover activity, but they are another indication that, in one way or another, mergers are taking the attention of U.S. business executives away from running the business.

So far, my attention has been directed at some of the direct, short-term costs of the current genre of merger activity. Other, more subtle costs are also becoming apparent. They illustrate the fundamental and insidious effects of unchecked merger activity on our economic system. One such cost is the high proportion (roughly 70 percent) of mergers that prove unsuccessful. Such mergers more and more often are showing up as spin-offs. The other cost, which is even more subtle and difficult to document, is the bureaucratization of U.S. business. Bureaucracy all too frequently brings with it a stifling influence on independent, innovative activity by individuals.

One reflection of unsuccessful merger activity in the United States is the substantial increase in spin-offs of formerly acquired units. The spin-off strategy, which is intended to dump acquired units that probably served some short-term financial objective but could not be operated efficiently by the acquirer, is called *asset redeployment* in today's business jargon.

A good example of this strategy is provided by ITT, the conglomerate firm fashioned through mergers during the 1960s by Harold Geneen. An article entitled "The De-Geneening of ITT" noted that the world's biggest conglomerate had bogged down by the mid 1970s. The blame for the lagging performance is attributed to Geneen: "'Harold Geneen was an absolute disaster as an operating manager,' complains one particularly critical analyst. 'You have only to look at the record—he could acquire companies but not manage them. And his further fault was that he couldn't recognize this.' Most analysts cheer the de-Geneening now in progress." It is important to add, however, that the analysts and investors who enabled Geneen to achieve his remarkable financial results through mergers in the 1960s failed to recognize this either. The objective at ITT today, under Rand Araskog, is to make ITT a leaner, more profitable company. The approach is a massive divestiture program that, according to one analyst, will be "the biggest sell-off of assets in corporate history."[42] More than forty companies and other assets have already been sold for over $1 billion. In January 1982, Rayonier, a forest-products company with about $1 billion in sales, was up for sale. Rayonier had been acquired earlier by Geneen. Other major sales expected by analysts include Continental Baking (Wonder Bread and Hostess Twinkies), Sheraton Hotels, Pennsylvania Glass Sand, Eason Oil, and Carbon Industries, all of which were acquired by ITT within the past fifteen years. Particularly unfortunate is that while many of these companies were profitable at the time of acquisition, they are now being sold off because they are operating in the red.

ITT is not an isolated case. There are many other examples of mergers gone sour. In 1977, Exxon Corp. set up Exxon Enterprises to make an acquisition that would add at least $1 billion to Exxon's revenues. In 1979, this objective was met with the acquisition of Reliance Electronics Co. for $1.2 billion. This established electrical-equipment manufacturer was supposed to produce a product envisioned by Exxon which was to be a device that would substantially raise the efficiency of electric motors. The project, including the acquisition, had the support of two major outside consultants. Exxon paid a $600 million premium over market to buy Reliance Electronics. The product never materialized and Reliance has proven to be a failure in other respects as well.[43]

According to one article, RCA, now an electronics and communications conglomerate with 1980 sales of $8 billion, suffered losses of $109.3 million in the third-quarter of 1981. In a revealing comment the new chairman of RCA, Thornton Bradshaw, was quoted as saying, "What I have been doing is spending a lot of time finding out what kind of a company this is so that we can decide where we are going to go." The article also noted that, "Many of RCA's current woes stem from some hasty and shortsighted acquisitions that were made during the 1960s and '70s when the firm, like many other big American Corporations, tried to boost earnings by diversifying into fields far outside its traditional lines of business."[44] These acquisitions included Random House, Hertz, and CIT Financial. Random House was sold in 1980 and Wall Street experts believe that Bradshaw is likely to sell off either or both Hertz and CIT Financial as well.

Mergers of the corporate giants are not the only ones that are going sour. Smaller companies have the same sort of experience. In the late 1960s General Foods acquired Burger Chef Systems Inc., the fast-food business. Burger Chef's earnings have since been modest; General Foods closed many outlets and took a $72.2 million pretax write-off on Burger Chef in 1972. In 1981, General Foods agreed to sell Burger Chef to Hardee's Food Systems Inc. for $44 million. In explaining the sale, Irwin Engleman, senior vice-president for finance, stated, "Even though it's fixed up, it isn't in our strategic interest to continue to bet on that business."[45] H.G. Parks Inc. (Parks Sausages) was sold to Norin, a conglomerate, for $5 million in March 1977. Almost immediately sales lagged and production costs rose. In July 1980, Canellus Acquisition Co., another conglomerate, acquired Norin. Also in 1980, Parks showed its first loss—$300,000. Then, in November 1980, Canellus sold Parks to the management of the sausage company. By late 1981, Parks' sales were rising and the company was once again making money.[46]

Banquet Foods Corp. suffered a fate similar to that of H.G. Parks Inc. In 1970, RCA acquired Banquet Foods, a poultry processor and frozen-foods supplier then called F.M. Stamper Co., for about $140 million. Subsequently, profits of Banquet dropped severely. In 1980, RCA sold Banquet for about $50 million. It was acquired by ConAgra, an agribusiness company with expertise in the chicken business; earnings have since improved markedly.[47] Pennwalt is another conglomerate that is "busy undoing some past mistakes" brought on from twenty-three years of direction by an acquisition-minded chairman.[48]

AM International, the former Addressograph-Multigraph Corp. (AM), was rapidly changed from a manufacturer of old-fashioned duplicators and addressing machines to a high technology company in the mid 1970s. The strategist was Roy Ash, a wunderkind of conglomeration at Litton Industries during the 1960s. In 1981, AM lost $245 million and its equity dropped to $14 million (compared to $232 million in 1980). The company's problems are traced to Ash's leadership, which began in 1976. Reportedly, Ash plunged it into high technology areas through the purchase of a dozen young companies. Furthermore, he did not devote much effort to maintaining the health of profitable older businesses and gave little attention to the hiring and firing of managers so as to match managerial skillls with the business operations of the companies. As a result, only a few years later, Ash was removed from the company and Richard Black, the new chairman at AM, found tremendous operating inefficiency in some units. In early 1982, he was planning to sell twelve of AM's business units, which accounted for about 25 percent of revenues in 1981. However, before completing the repair job, Black resigned claiming the company was in far worse condition than he had been led to believe. By April of 1982, bankruptcy proceedings seemed likely.[49]

In January 1982, CBS Inc. announced that it was selling Fawcett Books to Random House. CBS had acquired Fawcett in 1976, when Fawcett was the third-ranked publisher in the country. It is now ranked number six. Industry experts attribute the decline of Fawcett to "CBS managers educated at business schools like Harvard. 'Fawcett and Popular were ruined by Harvard MBAs' said Patrick O'Connor, editorial director of Pinnacle Books and a Fawcett alumnus. 'Book publishing is a unique business, it can't be done with case studies.'" The reason for dumping Fawcett given by the CBS/Publishing Group President Peter Derow was that, "Mass market paperback book publishing does not fit into our long-range plan."[50]

The remarkable lack of success of corporate mergers is starting to gain recognition by some long-time observers of U.S. business. Arthur Burck has spent the last twenty-five years as a consultant who puts together acquisitions. In an interview, Mr. Burck expressed his opinion about many acquisitions.

> Takeovers by the corporate giants have damaged a great many companies. The acquisitions have weakened or destroyed countless thousands of small and medium-sized businesses that were star performers when they were independent.
>
> Look at the wave of divestitures. In the past 15 years there have been thousands of divestitures of acquired companies. The buyer realizes that he simply got stuck. From my own experience I would say that perhaps 95% of the merger proposals that are explored never materialize, and among the 5% that do go through, a high percentage, perhaps seven out of ten, are so-so or bad deals.

In addition, Burck contends that, "Buying a company is an art not a science. Big companies normally process a possible acquisition through a bureaucracy of people who are essentially pencil pushers." But he also sees problems when outside advice is sought from Wall Street. "When the giants seek outside advice, they often get it from Wall Street where the adviser may only be interested in the huge fees flowing from the conclusion of a deal. Wall Street has an additional incentive to promote takeovers: the desire to serve customers who can make a large profit by selling their stockholdings."[51]

In another interview, Peter Drucker, who is widely known for his popular books on U.S. business management, attributes many of today's mergers to inflation. In the article, which carried the title "Why Some Mergers Work and Many More Don't," Mr. Drucker argued that good business judgment does not prevail. Businessmen are "like the German farmers buying three grand pianos during inflation. They couldn't play the pianos, but they believed the pianos would maintain their value."[52] Although this may partly explain today's merger activity, it does not explain that of the 1960s. I think the more important explanation was provided by Robert Pitofsky, an FTC Commissioner until 1980, when he said, "I am persuaded there are often no significant efficiencies. Sometimes it is simply empire-building."[53]

Another indirect and even more subtle cost of high levels of merger activity appears to be emerging. Mergers create large bureaucracies. Bureaucratization may bring with it a decline in innovation and individual initiative. Some commentaries on the recent merger activity support this thesis. One article on Peter Grace, head of the conglomerate W.R. Grace, notes, "'He is a trader,' says one W. R. Grace executive. 'He likes to buy and sell companies.'" Unfortunately, "Some of the small businessmen who have sold their operations to him were unable to adjust easily to this managerial style and to what retired Chairman Felix Larkin calls the 'institutional management' to which they were suddenly exposed."[54] Another article quoted William C. Norris, chairman of Control Data Corp., as saying, "Most large companies create a corporate bureaucracy that avoids risks wherever possible. The emphasis today is on immediate payoffs [and] in this environment, development of new products and services takes a back seat." It was noted that the legal and finance backgrounds "created a managerial outlook ill-suited to bold ventures with new products or costly modernization of plants to gain a leg up on competitors."[55]

In another article, the director of policy planning at the FTC observed that, "An ever larger portion of our economic activity is focused on rearranging industrial assets rather than increasing their size." The same article reported that a major study of corporate successes and failures by McKinsey and Co. concluded "that the most successful ones were more single-industry than conglomerate enterprises." The study also "found that one firm required 223 different committees to approve a new idea before it would be put into production—and few were." This article also said that the "urge to merge contributes to a growing and measurable decline in American innovation. U.S. companies in 1979, for example, spent more for acquisitions than for research and development."[56]

One article sought to determine what companies would buy the losers being spun off by large corporations. The answer was smaller firms. They do not have the layers of bureaucracy which often result in inefficiency by stifling quick decision making and individual initiative. The article concluded that, "Large companies with tremendous overhead and burdensome bureaucracies simply are not built to manage small businesses. An entrepreneur can make quick decisions, intuitively respond to changing market pressures, fire staff, and ignore Wall Street's need for ever-increasing quarterly profits."[57]

The acquisition of Houston Oil and Minerals Corp. by the giant conglomerate Tenneco Inc., in late 1980, resulted in the departure of many of Houston Oil's highly skilled people—geologists, geophysicists, and engineers. The reason given by one of the geologists is "that Tenneco is really limited as to what it can do. It's a huge conglomerate. You have a hierarchy and a chain of command. And no matter how Tenneco tries to change things, you're still stuck with a system that can be terribly frustrating and impersonal."[58]

Concern about the effects of bureaucratization in general was noted several years ago in an article entitled "The Breakdown of U.S. Innovation." The article argued that, "At the same time, the increasing concentration of products into larger and fewer companies also works against innnovation. Radical new ideas tend to bog down in big-company bureaucracy. This is why major innovations—from the diesel locomotive to Xerography and the Polaroid camera—often come from outside an established industry." The article also argued that the short-term financial orientation of business managers is partly responsible for weakening innovation in large companies. The problem is, "Within a growing number of companies such changes and pressures have led to a reappraisal of corporate goals and the emergence of what one top research scientist dubs 'the MBA syndrome,' a supercautious, no risk management less willing to gamble on anything short of a sure thing."[59]

More recently, Arthur Burck focused on the bureaucratization problem. In response to the question as to whether companies can recover if they are spun off after a sour merger, he said, "It's a long road. A company loses its momentum. Key people have left. Employee morale and efficiency have eroded. When workers become part of a sprawling, faceless bureaucracy, the identity with *their* company is lost. Productivity suffers. Ill-advised mergers have damaged an entire generation of incipient growth companies."[60]

In closing these observations on the costs of recent merger activity, I want to mention especially one subject. Proponents of the current wave of corporate takeovers contend that mergers are healthy for the economy—that mergers purge business of bad management. This argument appears to be a substitute for the synergy argument used by proponents of the conglomerate-merger wave in the 1960s; because synergy proved fallacious, they have come up with a new justification. Like the synergy argument, however, this new argument is wrong. As I described in the last chapter, systematic research in the United States and England reveals that acquired firms are typically average performers in their industries before the acquisition. If management were bad, one would expect that the acquired firms would be poor performers before the acquisition. One recent study focused on corporate takeovers—precisely those which are supposed to get rid of bad management. Walter Kissinger, head of the Allen Group, an auto-parts maker, commissioned a study on this subject by outside consultants. The study results led Kissinger to conclude that raiders go after "healthy not unproductive companies . . . and that the successful raider is left with a hostile, unmotivated management."[61] Similarly, an article by Neal Pearce noted:

> It's not weak or poorly managed firms that corporate giants seek to swallow. Rather, they are looking for profitable, conservatively run companies with a depressed market price for their strong stock, balance sheets and market positions. The sad fact, says Marquette University professor Peter Marchetti, is that good management can easily lead to extinction in a world dominated by "conglomerates for whom capital in the abstract is everything."[62]

The staunchest supporters of merger activity must have some doubt about mergers after the takeover imbroglio initiated by Bendix, and ultimately involving Martin-Marietta, United Technologies, and Allied Corp. After millions of dollars were spent along with untold man-hours by top executives of these firms, no meaningful merger was consummated. The only winners were the law firms and investment bankers who got their fee.

Only fifteen years after the peak of the tremendous conglomerate merger movement of the 1960s a new record for merger activity is being established. Never before have such remarkable levels of merger activity come so close together. I believe this reflects the recent penchant of U.S. business for attaining short-run financial goals. Mergers are especially well-suited for attaining such goals. Combine this with the fact that mergers are a perfect outlet for the drive for power by businesspeople and you have the ingredients for unrelenting merger activity that imposes fundamental long-run costs.

Notes

1. The acquisition activity in 1981 included the following companies: DuPont and Conoco ($7.2 bil.), Seagram and Conoco ($2.6 bil.), Flour and St. Joe Minerals ($2.3 bil.), Standard Oil of Ohio and Kennecott ($1.8 bil.), American Express and Shearson Loeb Rhoades ($1.0 bil.), Nabisco and Standard Brands ($.8 bil.), Occidental Petroleum and Iowa Beef Processors ($.8 bil.), Penn Central and GK Technologies ($.7 bil.), TCF Holdings and Twentieth Century-Fox Films ($.7 bil.), Sears Roebuck and Dean Witter Reynolds ($.6 bil.), Philbro and Salomon Brothers ($.6 bil.), Allegheny International and Sunbeam ($.5 bil.), Caterpillar Tractor and Solar Turbines International ($.5 bil.), and General Foods and Oscar Mayer ($.5 bil.). Information comes from *Fortune,* Sarah Bartlett (January 25, 1982), pp. 37-40, © 1982, Time Inc. All rights reserved.

2. *Fortune,* A.F. Ehrbar (May 8, 1978), p. 91, © 1978, Time Inc. All rights reserved. Reprinted with permission.

3. Ibid., p. 91.

4. Ibid., p. 93.

5. *Forbes* (February 1, 1976), pp. 25-27. Reprinted with permission.

6. *Business Week* (June 6, 1977), pp. 25 and 26. Reprinted with permission.

7. *Fortune,* Walter Guzzardi, Jr., (April 1976), p. 90 is the source of these data, © 1976, Time Inc. All rights reserved.

8. *Business Week* (February 13, 1978), p. 190. Reprinted with permission.

9. *Fortune* (February 23, 1981), p. 15, © 1981, Time Inc. All rights reserved. Reprinted with permission.

10. *Time* (December 21, 1981), p. 62. Reprinted with permission.

11. Ibid., p. 63.

12. *Fortune,* Louis Kraar (May 18, 1981), p. 57, © 1981, Time Inc. All rights reserved. Reprinted with permission.

13. Ibid., p. 58.

14. Ibid., p. 59.

15. *Fortune,* Lee Smith (September 7, 1981), p. 58 is the source of these data, © 1981, Time Inc. All rights reserved. Reprinted with permission.

16. Ibid., p. 60.

17. *Newsweek* (July 27, 1981), p. 50, © 1981 by Newsweek Inc. All rights reserved. Reprinted by permission.

18. *Barrons* (October 5, 1981), p. 10.

19. *Barrons* (November 2, 1981), p. 7.

20. *Business Week* (October 12, 1981), p. 46.

21. *Business Week* (November 23, 1981), p. 17. Reprinted with permission.

22. Ibid., p. 25.

23. *Time* (August 3, 1981), p. 44.

24. Alfred E. Kahn, "The New Merger Wave," (National Economic Research Associates, 1981), p. 4.

25. Robert Hayes and William J. Abernathy, "Managing Our Way to Economic Decline," *Harvard Business Review* (July/August 1980), pp. 67-77.

26. *Time* (May 4, 1981), pp. 60 and 61. Reprinted with permission.

27. *Business Week* (December 21, 1981), p. 73. Reprinted with permission.

28. *Business Week* (October 19, 1981), pp. 135 and 136.

29. *New York Times* (October 18, 1981).

30. *Fortune,* Mary Greenebaum (June 15, 1981), pp. 243 and 244, is the source of these data, © 1981, Time Inc. All rights reserved.

31. *Fortune,* Sarah Bartlett (January 25, 1982), p. 36, © 1982, Time Inc. All rights reserved.

32. Ibid.

33. *Business Week* (October 19, 1981), p. 119.

34. *Newsweek* (July 27, 1981), p. 52, is the source of these data, © 1981 by Newsweek Inc. All rights reserved. Reprinted by permission.

35. *Fortune,* John Quirt (May 7, 1979), p. 141, © 1979, Time Inc. All rights reserved.

36. *Wall Street Journal* (November 17, 1981).

37. *Wall Street Journal* (October 21, 1981).

38. *Wall Street Journal* (February 8, 1982).

39. *Wall Street Journal* (September 22, 1981).

40. *Time* (July 20, 1981), p. 49.

41. *Wall Street Journal* (February 1, 1982).

42. *Fortune,* Geoffrey Colvin (January 11, 1982), pp. 34 and 35, © 1982, Time Inc. All rights reserved. Reprinted with permission.

43. *Fortune,* Lewis Beman (October 19, 1981), p. 68, © 1981, Time Inc. All rights reserved.

44. *Time* (January 18, 1982), p. 49. Reprinted with permission.

45. *Wall Street Journal* (December 10, 1981).

46. *New York Times* (December 20, 1981).

47. *Wall Street Journal* (February 8, 1982).

48. *Business Week* (February 22, 1982), p. 76.

49. *Business Week* (January 25, 1982), p. 62.

50. *Washington Post* (February 7, 1982).

51. *Fortune,* Edward Meadows (October 19, 1981), p. 223, © 1981, Time Inc. All rights reserved.

52. *Forbes* (January 18, 1982), p. 34. Reprinted with permission.

53. *Washington Post* (July 19, 1981). Reprinted with permission.

54. *Business Week* (October 5, 1981), p. 86. Reprinted with permission.

55. *Washington Post* (January 17, 1982). Reprinted with permission.

56. *Washington Post*, Mark Green (May 10, 1981). Reprinted with permission.

57. *Fortune*, Peter W. Bernstein (January 26, 1981), p. 60, © 1981, Time Inc. All rights reserved.

58. *Wall Street Journal* (February 9, 1982).

59. *Business Week* (February 16, 1976), p. 56.

60. *Fortune,* Edward Meadows, (October 19, 1981), p. 223, © 1981, Time Inc. All rights reserved.

61. *Forbes* (August 7, 1978), p. 31.

62. *Washington Post* (December 27, 1981). Reprinted with permission.

14 Let Power Beget Power: A Proposed Blueprint for Monolithic Capitalism

The U.S. economy is in the throes of sweeping change. Agglomerate and conglomerate mergers are reshaping the financial and industrial structure of the country. Economic resources are being consolidated as independent businesses are pulled into huge private bureaucracies. Distinctions between industries are being blurred and conglomerate firms are becoming a substitute for the market in allocating resources. This weakens the market system's remarkably efficient and timely allocation of resources. Much of the transformation is taking place as the result of business executives' personal desire for power over people and events. No benefits to society from this transformation are apparent.

What, if anything, can or should be done about this state of affairs? One approach is to do nothing in the short run and to impose central planning in the long run when the concentration of economic power reaches a point where it is no longer acceptable to U.S. citizens. Some well-known economists appear to be waiting with anticipation for the call for more direct government involvement in the economy. This approach has received widespread public attention in the popular books of John Kenneth Galbraith and warrants careful examination.

Over the past quarter of a century the eminent Harvard economist John Kenneth Galbraith has published numerous popular books that have reviewed the state of and changes in various U.S. institutions as they relate to the performance of the economy. In essence, Galbraith concludes that the modern U.S. economy has endured such far-reaching institutional changes in such diverse areas as technology, advertising, national defense, business organization, government, and education that the economy does not and cannot operate as a free-enterprise, competitive system in the traditional sense. In his words, "the market is dead." It should be added, Galbraith thinks it should not be resurrected. For this and other reasons, Galbraith concludes that antitrust policy, our primary tool for maintaining competition and pluralism in the marketplace, is a "charade."

Galbraith does not believe, however, that increasing concentration of economic power can be ignored. Rather than staying the emergence of economic power, he proposes that it be accepted and nurtured because it results from the imperatives of modern technology. This power, he believes, should be kept in check through government controls and planning. The wisdom of this position would seem assured, given the stature and eloquence of its author. Moreover, if the large audiences that Galbraith's books have attracted are any indication, his views have wide influence. But I think we must look further.

The call for central planning by respectable, nonradical commentators became increasingly common in the mid 1970's. In the late 1970's, more and more economists were questioning the value of the antitrust laws. Galbraith has become part of the conventional wisdom. This disturbs me for reasons I hope to make clear in this chapter and the next.

The key to Galbraith's blueprint for the future of the U.S. economy is the notion of *technological imperatives*. This notion, which has its intellectual foundation in Joseph Schumpeter's work, is that modern technology requires giant firms with monopoly positions in order to foster the innovation and invention that will keep the system technologically progressive. According to this notion, only these firms can gather together the diversity of talent, bear the risks of research and development, and overcome the uncertainty of marketing in developing and producing technologically sophisticated products. As Schumpeter said earlier,

> ... the large scale establishment or unit of control must be accepted as a necessary evil inseparable from the economic progress which it is prevented from sabotaging by the forces inherent in its productive apparatus. What we have got to accept is that it has come to be the most powerful engine of that progress and in particular of the long-run expansion of total output.[1]

Galbraith tells us that, "The imperatives of technology and organization, not the images of ideology, are what determine the shape of economic society."[2] Advanced technology requires large size and planning in areas of research and development, production, marketing, and pricing. This technological imperative spells the end of competitive capitalism. The technostructure has evolved within the large corporation to serve this planning purpose. Galbraith's technostructure is the army of highly trained specialists (technocrats) gathered within the giant corporation. In Galbraith's view, the corporation and its technostructure have become an autonomous institution outside of traditional controls in society. He believes that because of the separation of ownership from management, illustrated by Berle and Means, and Larner (chapter 5), it is free of control by stockholders. As a result of internal financing, it is free from the influence of the capital markets. By virtue of its monopoly power, its prices are not subject to the fluctuations caused by the forces of supply and demand. Through mass advertising, the giant corporation is freed from the whims of the consumer—rather than bowing to consumer sovereignty, it manipulates consumer demand to its purposes.

All of this is inevitable in Galbraith's blueprint for the future. It is simply the result of the technological imperatives of modern industrial society. If this scenario is correct, as Galbraith contends, then competitive capitalism as a regulator of business behavior is dead. Since the antitrust laws are specifically designed to preserve the self-regulating features of the marketplace, these laws have, according to Galbraith, become irrelevant. Except as an ideological symbol of free-market capitalism, they have been largely ineffective. To the extent the antitrust laws have worked at all, they have been discriminatory; they have had little effect on giant corporations while preventing small companies from achieving the power of large companies. Galbraith assures us that there is no reason to mourn the demise of competitive capitalism and the passing of the anti-trust laws, because a natural mechanism has evolved to regulate the market-place—Galbraith's concept of *countervailing power*.

Countervailing power is power that develops in response to an existing (original) source of power. The emergence of unions in those industries with giant firms holding monopoly power is given as a primary example of its development. Galbraith believes that in most of the industrial sector competition is nonexistent; thus competitors do not hold private economic power in check. Countervailing power serves this role. He regards it as a self-generating force that offsets bastions of economic power.[3] This view implies letting what I call the rule *let power beget power* reign free and all will be fine with capitalism. However in my opinion, the consistency of this rule with a democratic, pluralistic society is highly questionable (a matter which is confronted in the next chapter).

Galbraith recognizes the need for some kind of social control over private economic power in the United States. Thus he observes that countervailing power, even though supposedly self-generating, provides inadequate and incomplete control, particularly during periods of inflation. Galbraith hints at the type of social control over business power that will become necessary during periods of ineffective countervailing power. He notes that during periods of "an excess of demand . . . the self-regulating mechanism based on countervailing power ceases to be effective. . . . What under all conditions of deflationary pressure, is an admirable device for countering the power of buyers of labor becomes a device for accelerating and perpetuating inflation."[4] Further, "It is inflation, not deflation or depression, that will cause captialism to be modified by extensive centralized decision. . . . There is no doubt that inflationary tensions are capable of producing a major revision in the character and constitution of American capitalism."[5]

Though expressed in subtle and guarded fashion, Galbraith seems to be heralding the drift toward this time of "major revision in the character and constitution of American capitalism." Thus, he urges that we let power beget power and nurture the development of countervailing power, in spite of his prediction that inflationary periods are capable of producing major revisions in capitalism under this rule. Similar subtle hints appear in *The New Industrial State*. For example, Galbraith states that, "Once it is agreed that the individual is subject to management in any case . . . the case for leaving him free from (say) government interference evaporates."[6]

If we were to adopt the rule let power beget power, the road to monolithic capitalism would be direct and certain. The innate desire for power beats strongly in the hearts of labor leaders and politicians as well as corporate leaders. To nurture the development of private economic power, or even to allow its development unhindered, is to assure that the government will intercede in the future.

This is not a call of alarm to those who prefer private rather than government enterprise in this country. Though Galbraith is cautious and vague about the role of government in his blueprint for the future of U.S. capitalism, he has added to the intellectual foundation for those who do favor government planning and control of the economic system. Recently, the call for government intervention has been heard, and the source has not been simply from a socialist fringe. Ralph Nader, for example, attracted public and congressional attention in the 1970s when he suggested that the 700 largest corporations in the United States obtain federal charters. A former leading U.S. senator and a candidate for the presidency of the United States, the late Hubert Humphrey, cosponsored the Humphrey-Javits bill formally known as *The Balanced Growth and Economic Planning Act of 1975*. The legislation was a joint product of the senate sponsors and the Initiative Committee for National Economic Planning whose coordinator was Myron Sharpe, editor of *Challenge Magazine*. The legislation proposed bureaucratic machinery for planning, though the precise intent and method of implementation was not clarified.

The intellectual influence in political circles provided by Galbraith is illustrated by a newspaper article. "[Canadian Prime Minister] Trudeau has read Galbraith's books, including *Economics and the Public Purpose*, which argues for the acceptance of socialism as the only alternative to the 'retarded development of the market system.'" When asked about Galbraith's influence, Trudeau reportedly said, "I'm not as wise and as experienced as Galbraith, but there's no doubt that his thinking has permeated my thought and that of a lot of other people."[7]

The idea of central planning received support from noted intellectual figures in the 1970s. For example, Robert Heilbroner seems pessimistic about central planning, relating its effect to the decline and fall of the Roman Empire, but views it as inevitable in the long run.[8] Robert Leckachman, on the other hand, is optimistic about the benefits of central planning but is concerned that economists lack the vision to call for its implementation immediately.[9] George Lodge, in another of the mid-1970s books on planning, contends that the old business and political values of competition, property rights, limited government, and individualism are ideas of the past. They are being replaced by the need for bigness in business, bigness in government (for the increasing task of planning), and by the individual's desire for belonging to a group or community.[10] The evidence reviewed in this book indicates that Lodge was unaware of the research showing increased bigness in business is not necessary for the sake of efficiency or technological progress. Further, the results of the presidential and congressional elections of 1980 show that he erred seriously in assuming that the philosophy of the people toward big government, private property, and individualism had suddenly and dramatically changed after more than two hundred years.

Others seem to have been attracted by the prospect that, with advances in such techniques as input-output analysis and the availability of the computer, it would be feasible to guide the production of private industry. A noted proponent of some form of national economic planning is economist Wassily Leontief, who received the Nobel prize for his development of input-output analysis. This is a system for describing the interdependency of the branches of an economy in terms of their inputs and outputs. Because of the essential role of input-output analysis under any regime of central planning, Leontief's interest is understandable. Some of his ideas were expressed in a *New York Times* article, "For a National Economic Planning Board".[11] Other noted intellectuals expressed their support for national economic planning by signing the statement of the Initiative Committee for National Economic Planning. These include John Kenneth Galbraith, Chester Bowles, Leon Keyserling, Gunnar Myrdal, Robert R. Nathan, and Arthur Schlesinger Jr. It is clear that the call for central economic planning has credible and influential allies. At the moment, they are a minority.

Galbraith has asked us to believe that competitive capitalism is dead and that the antitrust laws are a charade. Our economy must evolve into one of monolithic capitalism, he says, because to halt this evolution would be tantamount to halting technological progress. It is the natural course of events arising from the demands of modern technology. According to this line of reasoning, only giant firms with at least some monopoly power can assure the nation's technological progress. Thus, whether this is the only blueprint for the future of the U.S. economy depends heavily on whether technological imperatives do, in fact, require the emergence of monolithic capitalism.

To support his position on technological imperatives, Galbraith relies on anecdotal evidence. For example, in chapter 2 of *The New Industrial State* entitled "The Imperatives of Technology," Galbraith relies almost entirely on one anecdote to support his position. The tremendous cost of engineering, styling, and gearing up for production of the Mustang by the Ford Motor Co. is described in order to illustrate the necessity of corporate giantism because of modern technology. Similar anecdotes illustrate other points throughout the book. Such anecdotal evidence is often interesting and instructive, but generalizing from a sample of one or two is extremely risky.

My task here is to confront the technological imperatives argument with general evidence from statistical studies conducted by numerous scholars in the United States and abroad. I will also examine the claim that the antitrust laws are nothing but a charade.

Shortly after the appearance of Galbraith's *New Industrial State,* the Senate Select Committee on Small Business held hearings on the issues raised by Galbraith. On June 29, 1967, Galbraith along with Walter Adams, Willard Mueller,

and Donald Turner presented written and oral testimony to the committee. All
three of these scholars took strong exception to Galbraith's technological imperatives argument, citing both anecdotal evidence and more general evidence.
There is now even more evidence at odds with Galbraith's position.

For the sake of brevity, I will focus only on the general evidence relevant
to the issue of technological imperatives. Furthermore, because of the very large
number of systematic analyses that have been done on this subject, I will rely
on two major summaries of the research.

In the introduction of their survey article, Morton Kamien and Nancy
Schwartz cite the intellectual impetus for research in this area.

> Arguments about which institutional arrangements are most conducive
> to innovative activity begin with the Schumpeterian defenses of mo-
> nopoly power and bigness. A wide range of empirical interpretations of
> the Schumpeterian hypothesis has led to a diversity of tests.[12]

Galbraith has, of course, carried on the Schumpeterian tradition and attracted even wider attention. What does the evidence reveal? Kamien and
Schwartz report that, "Empirical studies over the last 10 years have typically
shown that while there may be certain advantages of size in exploring the fruits
of R&D, it is more efficiently done in small to medium size firms than in large
ones."[13] For example, Edwin Mansfield found that among major firms in
chemicals, petroleum, and steel, the number of significant inventions per dollar
of research and development (R&D) spending was lower in the largest firms than
in the small and medium-size firms. A.C. Cooper reported that it would cost
a large firm three times as much as a small firm to develop a given product.
Daniel Hamberg found that large industrial labs tend to produce mainly minor
inventions. Jewkes, Sawers, and Stillerman concluded that large research labs
of industrial corporations are not responsible for the bulk of significant inventions. In short, smaller firms produce more with a given dollar expenditure on
R&D than large firms.

The evidence clearly shows that large firms are less efficient in R&D activity, but do large firms put more effort into innovational activity, or spend more
in relation to their size? After reviewing the evidence from numerous studies,
Kamien and Schwartz concluded "there is hardly any support for the hypothesis
that the intensity of innovational effort increases with firm size."[14] For example, F.M. Scherer found that R&D employment increased faster than firm
size among smaller firms but more slowly among larger firms, and may even fall
among the largest firms in some industries. Dennis Mueller's analysis revealed
a negative relationship between firm size and research intensity. In a study of
Belgian firms, Louis Phlips found that research intensity increased with firm
size up to a firm size of about 7,000 employees and decreased thereafter. A
study of research intensity and firm size in France by W.S. Adams showed no
relationship at all between firm size and R&D intensity.

The evidence examined so far provides no basis for expecting firm size in itself to yield either more R&D or more efficient R&D expenditures. There remains another dimension of the Schumpeter-Galbraith position. In addition to proclaiming the necessity of very large firms to foster technological development, they also claimed that firms must have monopoly positions to assure technological progress. After reviewing the empirical evidence on the relationship between R&D activity and concentration (a measure of monopoly power), Kamien and Schwartz state, "In reviewing the diverse findings on research efforts and concentration, we find little consensus. In most instances, it has been difficult to discern a statistical relationship between these variables." Regarding the relationship between concentration and R&D results, Kamien and Schwartz conclude that, "The inconclusiveness of studies on concentration and innovational effort is reinforced by the studies [on concentration and innovation results]."[15]

Summing up their extensive survey, Kamien and Schwartz observe that the hypotheses that large size and monopoly power are essential for technological progress have been "supported by anecdotes by their originators, [and] were extremely vague regarding definitions of firm size, monopoly power, and inventive activity." Further, "A commonly tested hypothesis is that R&D activity increases more than proportionately with firm size. The bulk of empirical findings do not support it." In addition, they conclude that, "Little support has been found for the standard hypothesis that R&D activity increases with monopoly power."[16]

Kamien and Schwartz are not alone in their assessment of the evidence. In what is already becoming a classic graduate-level textbook and reference manual in the field of industrial organization, F.M. Scherer summarizes and assesses much of the evidence that concerns us here. He concludes that:

> What we find from analyzing the qualitative and quantitative evidence is a kind of threshold effect. A little bit of bigness—up to sales levels of $250 to $400 million at 1978 price levels—is good for invention and innovation. But beyond the threshold further bigness adds little or nothing, and it carries the danger of diminishing the effectiveness of inventive and innovative performance.[17]

Regarding the relationship between concentration (monopoly power) and innovation, Scherer reaches the same general conclusion as Kamien and Schwartz: "market concentration has a favorable impact on technological innovation in certain situations. How much concentration is advantageous remains to be determined." Concentration beyond some moderate level "appears on average to be unnecessary for, and perhaps even detrimental to, the vigorous exploitation of opportunities for technical advance."[18]

The careful research of many scholars without question demolishes the technological imperatives argument. The anecdotes provided by proponents of this argument are interesting and entertaining, but they are misleading.

Besides the notion of technological imperatives, another argument—that of scale economies—is sometimes used to show the need for larger firms. *Scale economies* is jargon for efficiencies arising from firm size. Though Galbraith did not emphasize this issue, other proponents of large firm size and mergers have. They argue that the imperatives of operational efficiency require more concentrated (monopolistic) industries with fewer firms if the firms are to operate efficiently. This argument is used most frequently as a justification for mergers, which is the fastest way to attain large size and monopoly power. Like the argument for technological imperatives, the argument for scale economies imperatives is generally fallacious. There simply is no evidence that mergers generally result in increased operational efficiency. Scherer concludes;

> With few exceptions, the minimum optimal plant scale revealed in studies of American manufacturing industries has been small relative to industry size. . . . We conclude then that economies of scale do not in the vast majority of instances necessitate high national concentration levels for U.S. manufacturing industries.[19]

A similar conclusion is reached by Douglas Greer in his new textbook, which is rapidly becoming the standard industrial organization text in undergraduate instruction. Greer concludes that "economies of scale appear to pose no more than a moderate barrier to entry for the majority of United States manufacturing industries, and they 'warrant' no more than moderate concentration."[20]

The technological imperatives and scale economies imperatives are most often justified with examples from manufacturing industries, as Galbraith did. In the manufacturing sector, which requires large physical plants and advanced machinery and techniques, such arguments should have the most merit. On the basis of studies of manufacturing, which I have just reviewed, the arguments simply cannot be justified by the facts. These arguments are much weaker when applied to other sectors of the economy such as the service sector or agriculture. In addition, the manufacturing sector accounts for a decreasing share of economic activity in the United States. Between 1960 and 1980, the percentage of national income accounted for by the manufacturing sector declined from about 30 to 26 percent. A legitimate case for corporate giantism and monopoly power cannot be made on the basis of available evidence on scale economies, and giantism and monopoly are not required for technological progress.

Next I will examine the proposition that the antitrust laws are a charade. Some form of antitrust law may be the only tool for preventing the consolidation of economic resources. I have suggested that the innate desire for power results in the continuous effort to increase and consolidate power whether in business or politics; consequently, the consolidation of private economic power, whether of the original or countervailing variety, is indeed a self-generating process. If the effort to increase private economic power is not or cannot be actively checked, monolithic capitalism will replace competitive capitalism.

Political and military power have been consciously held in check in the United States. This is reflected in our governmental system of checks and balances. The antitrust laws are supposed to serve the same function in the economy. The question of whether they are a charade is thus a vital one.

Unfortunately, the effectiveness of the antitrust laws cannot be systematically subjected to the kind of statistical testing that disproves the technological imperatives hypothesis. Consequently, I will focus on patterns of merger activity, which I believe provide a fairly strong indication that the antitrust laws, if enforced vigorously, do significantly affect merger activity. First, you will recall the massive consolidation of businesses around the turn of the century. After the Sherman Antitrust Act of 1890 was vigorously enforced beginning in 1904 under President Theodore Roosevelt, the horizontal-merger movement came to an end. The United States has not experienced horizontal mergers on such a scale in the eighty years since the Sherman Act was put to work.

Perhaps more precisely demonstrable was the effect of the 1950 Celler-Kefauver amendment to section 7 of the Clayton Act. As I noted earlier, the judicial interpretation of that act took a hard line against horizontal mergers, including those which might not create a monopoly and violate the Sherman Act. Horizontal mergers, which accounted for almost 40 percent of all mergers in the industrial sector between 1948 and 1951, accounted for only 4 percent by 1968. A similar pattern prevailed in banking. Could these patterns of merger activity be the result of pure chance? Perhaps. No valid statistical tests can be conducted to prove or disprove the propostion. Nevertheless, I doubt seriously if business people would unilaterally alter their behavior so quickly and permanently. The possibility is so remote that I believe the antitrust laws have been quite effective.

A bit of anecdotal evidence, which must admittedly be viewed with caution, suggests that other (nonmerger) forms of anticompetitive behavior have at least been influenced in form if not substance by the antitrust laws. The conspiracy among manufacturers of heavy electrical equipment (described in chapter 4) would never have been shrouded in such secrecy (clandestine meetings, the sophisticated formula to allocate business among conspirators) purely by choice. It must have been a conscious attempt to avoid detection of a gross violation of the antitrust laws. Of course we have no idea how many price conspiracies, or other types of illegal business behavior, have been avoided because of the risk of being caught. The publicity of prosecution may be more of a deterrent than the actual penalties.

There is no systematic scholarly evidence on the effectiveness of the antitrust laws, nor can there be. The evidence of history is, I believe, sufficient to support the conclusion that antitrust policy has not been a charade. We need not sit back and live with the consequences of the drive for power, which provides a self-generating process leading to monolithic capitalism and ultimately central planning. It has already been shown that modern technology does not require monolithic capitalism, and we now see that antitrust laws can be used to stop the move into monolithic capitalism. An alternative blueprint for the future of U.S. capitalism is feasible.

Aside from the sheer lack of supporting evidence, Galbraith's blueprint for the future contains an extremely serious error of omission. Specifically, what are the sociopolitical implications of Galbraith's scenario for the future? A country's economic system is not independent of its sociopolitical system. The two systems have what economists call a simultaneous relationship—they determine one another. Their interdependence arises from the philosophical outlook of the country's people. Basic institutions must be consistent with one another, therefore certain kinds of economic systems are incompatible with certain kinds of political systems.

The Galbraith scenario for the future of the economic system under the rule let power beget power is one of monolithic capitalism balanced by government power and controls. This scenario is inconsistent both with political democracy and with the social composition and philosophical disposition of the people. It is, therefore, no surprise that Galbraith does not explore this subject. He does hint at it, but he remains circumspect and does not pursue it. For example, Galbraith notes that, "For most of man's history, as philosophers of such diverse views as Marx and Alfred Marshall have agreed, political interest and conflict have originated in economic interest and economic conflict."[21] Further he observes, "The two questions most asked about an economic system are whether it serves man's physical needs and whether it is consistent with his liberty. . . . The prospects for liberty involve far more interesting questions."[22] In a somewhat narrower context, Galbraith contends that, "The relationship between society at large and an organization must be consistent with the relation of the organization to the individual. There must be consistency in the goals of the society, the organization and the individual. . . . As always in social matters, we have a deeply interconnected matrix."[23] Finally he asks, "To what extent does a society draw strength from pluralism of economic interest which, in turn, sustains pluralism of political discussion and social thought?"[24] This is a provocative and fundamental question, but the author made no attempt to answer it.

Galbraith has correctly identified and described developments that hamper the functioning of the market system in this country. However, I am convinced that his solution to these problems of competitive capitalism is not born of economic necessity. Furthermore, realization of the Galbraith scenario will have economic and sociopolitical consequences that are not acceptable to most U.S. citizens.

Notes

1. Joseph A. Schumpeter, *Capitalism, Socialism and Democracy*, 3rd ed. (New York: Harper and Row, 1950), p. 106.

2. John Kenneth Galbraith, *The New Industrial State* (Boston: Houghton Mifflin, 1967), p. 7.

3. John Kenneth Galbraith, *American Capitalism: The Concept of Countervailing Power* (Boston: Houghton Mifflin, 1952).

4. Ibid., pp. 190 and 191.

5. Ibid., pp. 200 and 201.

6. Galbraith, *The New Industrial State*, p. 217.

7. *Washington Post* (June 3, 1976). Reprinted with permission.

8. Robert Heilbroner, *Business Civilization in Decline* (New York: W.W. Norton, 1976).

9. Robert Leckachman, *Economists at Bay* (New York: McGraw-Hill, 1976).

10. George Lodge, *The New American Ideology* (New York: Knopf, 1975).

11. *New York Times* (March 14, 1974).

12. Morton Kamien and Nancy Schwartz, "Market Structure and Innovation: A Survey," *Journal of Economic Literature* (March 1975), p. 3. Reprinted with permission.

13. Ibid., p. 9.

14. Ibid., p. 18.

15. Ibid., pp. 22 and 23.

16. Ibid., p. 32.

17. Frederick M. Scherer, *Industrial Market Structure and Economic Performance*, 2nd ed. (Chicago: Rand McNally, 1980), p. 422.

18. Ibid., pp. 436 and 437.

19. Ibid., pp. 94 and 95.

20. Douglas F. Greer, *Industrial Organization and Public Policy* (New York: Macmillan, 1980), p. 185.

21. Galbraith, *The New Industrial State*, p. 322.

22. Ibid., pp. 396 and 397.

23. Ibid., p. 159.

24. Ibid., p. 323.

15 Let Power Beget Power: A Catch

There is a serious catch to implementing the rule let power beget power. A country's economic and sociopolitical systems have an intimate, causal relationship. That this relationship could be ignored in any proposal for a basic change in the economic system is striking for three reasons. First, the possibility that the economic and sociopolitical systems are interdependent is obvious and intuitively appealing. Second, those scholars who have considered the economic system along with one or more dimensions of the sociopolitical system invariably observe a strong interdependence between these systems. Third, the apparent nature and source of the interdependence suggest that any basic change to the economic system, such as that embodied in a rule of let power beget power, will affect far more than the economic system.

The source and essence of the connection between the economic and sociopolitical systems lies in the human element—the cultural values and philosophical disposition of the people who make up a society. The cultural values and philosophy of the people in the United States are rooted in a pluralistic society with a strong belief in individualism and freedom of action. This basic philosophy has led to an economic system that is free of extensive government planning, and to a relatively fragmented political process. The inconsistency of our cultural values with intensive government controls and planning has been noted by Henry Wallich, a former economics professor at Yale, member of the Council of Economic Advisors, and presently a member of the Federal Reserve Board of Governors. Wallich wrote:

> For the United States, the salient facts of the matter seem to be that neither our political processes nor the general condition of the country favor effective public planning. Compared to the highly structured and closely knit world of Japan, ours is wide open. As contrasted with the principle of consent in Japan, our public decision-making proceeds by competition and confrontation. It is a familiar dictum, of course, that politics is the art of compromise. But compromise, in the American framework, often comes only after bruising battles, and it need not carry any further than the point where one side manages to get 51 percent of the vote. The winner takes all; the loser's consent is not solicited.
>
> This, I submit, is a process that makes effective public planning difficult.[1]

A related observation was made by the Harvard professor Richard Musgrave. "The tight and continuing powers needed for the efficient conduct of global planning cannot be reconciled with the variety and obduracy of a democratic process."[2]

At the heart of this social philosophy is the distrust of concentration of power, of any kind. The distrust of power has a lengthy heritage. In the early eighteenth century, the French political philosopher Baron de Montesquieu advocated the separation of powers in government as a means of checking the abuse of unlimited power. This approach to the control of political power was directly translated into practice with the founding of the United States government. In the late 1930s, President Franklin D. Roosevelt expressed concern with mounting private economic power as he called for an investigation which took place in the form of the Temporary National Economic Committee (TNEC). He stated that, "The liberty of a democracy is not safe if the people tolerate the growth of private power to a point where it becomes stronger than their democratic state itself. That, in its essence, is fascism, ownership of government by an individual, by a group, or by any other controlling private power."[3] A similar message, though from a different perspective, has been delivered by Irving S. Shapiro. Shapiro is a leading U.S. business executive who was chairman of the DuPont Co. during the 1970s and was head of the Business Roundtable—a prestigious organization of major U.S. industrial firms—from 1976 to 1978. In response to a question regarding the burden of government regulation on business, Mr. Shapiro said, "Obviously, there are fields in which regulation is a necessity, and only government can do it. On the other hand, government has no self-restraint. Once it has power, it tends to exercise its maximum power without reservation. That's the heart of the problem."[4]

The institutions in a society derive their shapes and roles from the cultural values and philosophical outlook of the people. Indeed, each of the major institutions in our society reflects these values—particularly the aversion to concentrated power and the desire to preserve individual freedom and choice. To illustrate this point, I will briefly discuss the structure of major institutions in our society—government, business, military, educational, and cultural. Although other institutions might be added to this list, and some on my list might be subdivided, these institutions provide a representative basis for examining the structure of our institutions.

A system of checks and balances was designed into the basic structure of our federal government. This was accomplished by the establishment of three distinct branches of government—executive, legislative, and judicial—each with its own power and the power to check the actions of the other branches. At the same time, various powers were reserved for the individual states so that the people would retain control over decisions on local matters. Furthermore, most citizens have the right and freedom to participate in government at the local, state, and national levels both through voting and direct involvement.

Business in the United States has always been largely free of direct government control. The business structure reflects a good deal of fragmentation and dispersion of economic power. Relatively few industries are dominated by a single firm; no firms have the kind of immense control over economic resources that comes from having dominant positions in several sectors (for example, manufacturing and financial) of the economy. There is tremendous diversity in the types and sizes of businesses in this country. This diversity not only contributes to the dispersion of economic power but also provides a wide range of opportunity and choice in employment for the people. Each person is free to work in the bureaucracy of large corporations, to work for a small business, or to operate his own business. Society has consciously encouraged the freedom from government control and dispersion of power that characterizes the U.S. economy by choosing to rely on a capitalist, free-market system to provide goods and services. Congress has taken additonal steps to help maintain a reasonable dispersion of economic power by passing several antitrust laws.

The military establishment in the United States is structured so that power over the armed forces is dispersed. A civilian president is the commander-in-chief of the armed forces. The Congress controls appropriations for military expenditure. Even within the military, power is fragmented. The various services (Army, Navy, Air Force, and Marines) have been set up with separate bureaucratic structures. Competition among the services in this country has naturally been strong and is encouraged by the system that requires each of the services to go before Congress annually to vie for its share of the public funds allocated for national defense.

The educational establishment, particularly in the area of higher learning, exhibits a remarkable degree of diversity of control. As a consequence, there is little chance that the government, business, military, or an educational organization could exercise a high degree of control over higher education. There are literally thousands of colleges and universities in the country. Some are private, some are public schools run by individual states, and some have religious affiliation. The standard four-year colleges and universities, along with junior colleges and local community colleges, afford an impressive range of educational opportunities and choices to both the young and old. Even within educational institutions, control and decision making are dispersed. The various departments compete for funds and students, and they make their own hiring decisions. Teachers determine the content and reading material for their courses.

An equally notable diversity is found in our cultural institutions. Not only do we find a wide range of cultural activities—the symphony, theater, art, and so forth—we find many different sources of support. Some are sponsored by colleges and universities, some by federal, state, or local governments, and some are privately supported. The fragmented structure accommodates a wide range of ability and talent. Furthermore, this structure also permits and encourages the freedom of individual expression that might be stifled by highly centralized cultural institutions.

There is an apparent consistency in the structure of the major institutions in our society. The aversion to concentration of power and the attachment to individual freedom are fundamental elements of the societal makeup. This common denominator of cultural values and philosophical disposition underlie all the institutions in our society. It creates a fundamental though abstract interdependency among the institutions.

These institutions are interrelated in a practical, functional sense as well. Each performs a function in society, and each relies on and supports one or more of the other institutions. The government provides the society with national defense, police protection, highways, and aid to the elderly and needy. In doing so, the government directly interacts with other institutions in the society. It purchases goods and services from and provides funds to the educational establishment, and it supports and oversees the military establishment. Business provides society with the goods and services people need and want. It provides employment and income for many people and is a major source of technological progress that yields a higher material standard of living. In addition, business provides the often specialized goods and services required by the government and the military, and it provides financial support to the educational and cultural establishments. The essential function of the military establishment is to provide the unique service of national defense. Even with this highly specialized role, the military establishment interrelates with other institutions in society. It purchases goods and services from business, it provides employment and income for hundreds of thousands of people, it provides educational opportunities within the educational system as well as within the military establishment, and it supports research in both the business and educational establishments.

The educational establishment, of course, educates the people of the society. It also provides the government, military, and business with educated and technically trained individuals. Although this relationship to other institutions in society would appear to be laudable because it provides educated leaders for government and a highly skilled work force, it has been the subject of derision. For example Galbraith, echoing the earlier criticism by Thorstein Veblen,[5] has characterized the educational establishment as a pawn of big business. Galbraith has suggested that, because of the preeminent position of business in society, higher education is dictated and controlled by the needs of business. Though I agree that the business and educational establishments are interdependent—that is a basic point of this chapter—this view of the relationship is a bit extreme. In a sense the argument is valid—for people to earn a living in a society they need to acquire relevant skills. In an advanced society, the relevant skills may include computer programming and accounting. That students tend to specialize in education that enables them to earn a better living is neither surprising nor reprehensible. In any event, a student is not required to specialize in such areas unless he or she decides to do so. A student may major in philosophy, art, or music. Even if the student chooses to specialize in an area that is likely to provide more career opportunities, most institutions of higher learning require their students to take courses in the arts, social sciences, and philosophy.

Cultural institutions provide a myriad of forms of entertainment, fulfill-ment, and inspiration. They also provide employment and income to many people, they support the educational system, they receive support from govern-ment and business, and some are part of the business community.

Casual observation and common sense suggest that the economic and sociopolitical systems in a society are highly interdependent. Both philosophical and practical considerations suggest that this is so. In addition, noted scholars in various fields have pondered these matters and reached this conclusion.

Robert Heilbroner is a noted proponent of planning in the U.S. economy. Even so, he is pessimistic and worried about the results. In an article discussing the prospect for planning, Heilbroner expressed concern over the possible noneconomic consequences of central planning. "It would be foolish to deny that planning carries great risks, including that of a grave constriction of freedom as the consequence of a reckless proliferation of controls."[6] Nevertheless, Heilbroner concluded that these risks must be taken. The interdependence of the economic and sociopolitical systems Heilbroner observed will make any move to central economic planning far more costly than economic considera-tions alone indicate.

In a carefully detached, nonideological analysis of the prospects for central planning in various countries, Jan Tinbergen, a Nobel prize winner in economics, implied a connection between the nature of a society's economic system and its political system. Tinbergen observed that the controversy between communist and noncommunist countries focuses around both the political and economic systems and that a key element in this controversy is planning. According to Tinbergen, "The West considers the most important aspect to be the political system, that is, in Western terms, the conflict is between parliamentary democ-racy and totalitarianism. The East formulates as the most important aspect the *socioeconomic* system; it considers itself to be socialist and the others capitalist. Intimately connected with this contrast is the degree of planning applied."[7] He also suggested that the degree of economic planning acceptable in a country will depend on the "social welfare function" of the society. This is the economist's jargon for what I have been calling the cultural values and philosophical disposi-tion of the people. In this regard, Tinbergen argues that, "An example of the difference in priorities given to the elements of well-being is the weight attached to various types of freedom. Some Western countries or groups inside these countries reject some types of intervention because of an *a priori* very high weight assigned to consumer sovereignty."[8] Of course, this weight attached to consumer sovereignty is the importance accorded the freedom of the individual in the marketplace.

Another economist who has taken note of the interrelationship between the economic system and other institutions in society is Charles Kindleberger. Kindleberger focused on economics and politics and he noted that "Karl Marx was persuaded that any separation of economics from politics is idle. . . . It is not necessary to go far along the path trod by Marx, however, to reach the conclusion that politics and economics are intimately connected not only in techniques of analysis, but also in subject matter."[9]

The great economist Joseph Schumpeter made several directly relevant observations. In reflecting on the connection between the cultural values and the philosophical dispostion of the people and the nature of their economic system he argued that:

> Capitalism does not merely mean that the housewife may influence production by her choice between peas and beans; or that the youngster may choose whether he wants to work in a factory or on a farm; or that plant managers have some voice in deciding what and how to produce: it means a scheme of values, an attitude toward life, a civilization.[10]

Schumpeter also considered the consequences of a change from capitalism to socialism, which he defined as the situation where "the means of production are controlled, and the decisions on how and what to produce and who is to get what, are made by public authority instead of by privately-owned and privately-managed firms." If an economy should move into socialism Schumpeter noted "it is hardly possible to visualize a socialist society in this sense without a huge bureaucratic apparatus that manages the productive and distributive process and in turn may or may not be controlled by organs of political democracy much as we have today."[11] I have not considered the extreme case of central planning embodied in socialism, but any significant move toward central planning should logically be expected to have some of the consequences for the sociopolitical system envisioned by Schumpeter. The sociopolitical system cannot be ignored when discussing fundamental changes to the economic system.

In addition to economists, sociologists and historians have explored the relationship between the economic and sociopolitical systems. The sociologists Talcott Parsons and Neil Smelser devoted an entire book to an analysis of the relationship between the economy and the rest of society. Though the primary purpose of the authors was to integrate the theory of economics and sociology, they also xamined the interrelationship of the economic and sociopolitical systems. In fact, they made reference to each dimension of the interrelationship that I proposed at the beginning of this chapter. First, there is a general statement of this interrelationship and the observation that change in one institution will influence the other institutions of the society.

> Social interaction is the process by which the "behaviour" or change of state of members in a social system influences a) the state of the system and b) each other's states and relations. Every concrete act thus originates in a unit (member and has effects on the state of the system

and its other component units. Hence these units constitute a system in the scientific sense that a change of state of any one will effect changes in the states of one or more others and thus of the system as a whole.[12]

Second, the authors noted the practical functional interdependence of the institutions in a society and again suggested that changes in one will affect the others.

The whole society is in one sense part of the economy, in that all of the units, individual and collective, *participate in* the economy. Thus households, universities, hospitals, units of government, churches, etc., are *in* the economy. But no concrete unit participates *only* in the economy.

Thus the consequences of actions by any one unit can be traced through the system; ultimately these consequences "feed back" to the units initiating the change. All this is implied by the notion of interdependence. In this most general sense we propose to treat the economy as a social system.[13]

Finally, the importance of the cultural values and philosophical disposition of the people is cited as a key factor in the interrelationship of institutions. According to Parsons and Smelser these values not only provide consistency across institutions; they determine the basic structure of these institutions in the first place.

The integrative sub-system which provides cohesion of the society relates the cultural value-patterns to the motivational structures of individual actors in order that the larger social system can function without undue internal conflict and other failures of co-ordination. These processes maintain the institutionalization of the value patterns which define the main structural outline of the society in the first instance.[14]

The noted historian Charles Beard explored the relationship between economics and politics by studying both the abstract thinking of political philosophers and the historical relationship between economics and government. He found that the relationship between economics and government was a consistent theme among philosophers. Thus, Beard quoted Daniel Webster who argued that, "The freest government, if it could exist, would not be long acceptable, if the tendency of the laws were to create a rapid accumulation of property in few hands and to render the great mass of the population dependent and penniless. In such a case, the popular power must break in upon the rights of property, or else the influence of property must limit and control the exercise of popular power."[15] This, of course supports the idea that the economics and sociopolitical systems are interdependent, but it also emphasizes my concern about the implications of a passive policy toward the drive for power in the economic arena.

Having found an interrelationship between the economic and sociopolitical system in the abstract form in political philosophy, Beard sought to determine whether this relationship actually existed. Thus he stated, "we should inquire whether there has been in fact a close relation between the structure of the state and the economic composition of society."[16] He concluded that there has been "a transformation in the functions of government, particularly in those which call for wholesale intervention in economic operations. No doubt the nature and course of economy had been more or less shaped and directed by the state from early times."[17] In more general terms, Beard concluded that, "If historical experience is any guide, drastic changes in economy will find expressions in politics; and, on the other hand, changes in the functions of government will be followed by repercussions in economy."[18]

Will and Ariel Durant wrote prodigiously on history. In one of their smaller works, they looked at the connection between economics and other institutions in society from a historical perspective:

> Political forms, religious institutions, cultural creations, are all rooted in economic reality. So the Industrial Revolution brought with it democracy, feminism, birth control, socialism, the decline of religion, the loosening of morals, the liberation of literature from dependence upon aristocratic patronage, the replacement of romanticism by realism in fiction—and the economic interpretation of history.[19]

The Industrial Revolution was essentially an economic revolution, but it also profoundly affected other institutions in society. This historical example of the connection between economics and other institutions is especially relevant here. It is not just a statement of economic determinism. The Durants go on to say that while the economic system affects other institutions, values and form of government in turn affect the economic system—the relationship is a simultaneous one. Thus, they state,

> Since practical ability differs from person to person, the majority of such abilities, in nearly all societies, is gathered in a minority of men. The concentration of wealth is a natural result of this concentration of ability, and regularly recurs in history. The rate of concentration varies (other factors being equal) with the economic freedom permitted by morals and the laws. Despotism may for a time retard the concentration; democracy, allowing the most liberty, accelerates it.[20]

This particular observation by the Durants highlights another argument I have made. We have a democratic system; if we are to maintain an economic system largely free of government planning and controls, we must adopt a policy that checks the inherent drive for power in business that results in the concentration of economic resources. If we fail to do this, the result will likely be, as Webster observed, that "the popular power must break in upon the rights of property."

The logic and common sense of the argument that economic and sociopolitical systems are interdependent are compelling. Further, noted scholars in economics, sociology, philosophy, and history have reached a similar conclusion. This conclusion has some very practical consequences. The economic system and other institutions in the United States have a consistent foundation, a common denominator. The structure of these institutions springs from a common set of cultural values and the philosophical disposition of the people. These values, which include at their center an aversion to concentrated power of any kind, are consistent with our pluralistic society, democratic process, competitive capitalism, and individual freedom. If we implement (by conscious planning or benign neglect) the kinds of proposals for change in the economic system embodied in a rule of let power beget power, in which the growth of private economic power is allowed to develop, we must be prepared to accept fundamental changes in our other institutions.

The nature of such changes, in my judgement, would be unacceptable to most U.S. citizens. If the concentration of private economic resources were perceived to increase substantially, the philosophical aversion to concentration of power would cause the people to demand that their government bring this power under control. Such a scenario is not improbable—the tendency toward increasing concentration of economic resources is, as Webster observed, inherent in an essentially free-market, democratic system. Furthemore, the desire for power by businesspeople assures that, unless checked, concentration of resources will take place. Consequently, it is essential that an alternative to the rule let power beget power be sought to solve some problems of our economic system, particularly the problems arising from unchecked merger activity that leads directly to the concentration of economic resources. The key to an effective alternative solution is to control the drive for power by U.S. business.

The application of substantial economic controls or planning is sure to lead, in time, to a vastly expanded demand for economists. Implementation of the Galbraith scenario could require armies of economists to do the job. Central planning could be the boon to the economics profession that fault-type automobile insurance has been to the legal profession—an expensive, inefficient system of insurance that has created a huge job market and handsome incomes for many attorneys. In addition, since a Galbraithian scenario involves an expansion of government economic planning it will be accompanied by all of the bureaucratic trappings—some economists will become super czars and many others may become economic czars, or assistant czars, or at least deputy assistant czars. In spite of such a prospect, however, I must propose an alternative.

Notes

1. Henry Wallich, paper presented at the annual meeting of the American Economic Association (December 29, 1975), p. 4.

2. Richard A. Musgrave, "National Economic Planning: The U.S. Case," *American Economic Review* (February 1977), p. 50.

3. Franklin D. Roosevelt, Message to Congress (April 29, 1938).

4. *Washington Post* (February 8, 1981).

5. Thorstein Veblen, *Higher Learning in America* (1918).

6. *New York Times* (January 25, 1976).

7. Jan Tinbergen, *Central Planning* (New Haven, Conn.: Yale University Press, 1964), p. 74.

8. Ibid., p. 77.

9. Charles P. Kindleberger, *Power and Money* (New York: Basic Books, Inc., 1970), p. 15.

10. Joseph A. Schumpeter, *Capitalism, Socialism and Democracy,* 3rd ed. (New York: Harper and Row, 1950), p. 419.

11. Ibid.

12. Talcott Parsons and Neil J. Smelser, *Economy and Society* (New York: The Free Press, 1956), p. 9.

13. Ibid., pp. 14 and 15.

14. Ibid., p. 48.

15. Charles A. Beard, *The Economic Basis of Politics* (New York: Knopf, 1945), p. 23.

16. Ibid., p. 29.

17. Ibid., p. 71.

18. Ibid., p. 112.

19. Will and Ariel Durant, *The Lessons of History* (New York: Simon and Schuster, 1968), p. 52.

20. Ibid., p. 55.

16 An Alternative Blueprint for U.S. Capitalism

The technological imperatives argument is without substance, as I showed in chapter 14. That is, to assure technological progress it is not necessary to encourage the centralization of private economic power and abandon the free-market system. It is thus feasible to adopt an alternative to the rule let power beget power—an alternative to government controls and central planning. This alternative is based on the position that uninhibited merger activity and the evolution of monolithic capitalism carry tremendous costs to the economic and sociopolitical systems. These costs are not necessary and they can be avoided.

My alternative blueprint provides a means of stemming the consolidation of economic resources. This objective is probably more difficult to achieve than a Galbraithian scenario, because the innate desire for power in humans does indeed make consolidation of economic power a self-generating process. Galbraith's solution is a passive one, at least until the consolidation of economic power causes public outcry for government planning and control. My solution requires direct, positive action to stem the trend that Galbraith correctly observes. Because the U.S. legislative process tends to be reactive, anticipatory or preventive legislation is difficult to achieve. Meanwhile, the self-generating process of power consolidation in the economy continues.

My approach to dealing with some of the problems outlined earlier in this book is centered on a new antitrust law to complement, not replace, existing antitrust laws. This is certainly not a radical proposal; we have had antitrust laws in this country since 1890. Nevertheless, before presenting the proposal, it is important to note the current debate in academic and political circles regarding the value and role of antitrust policy.

In spite of the call for central planning during the mid 1970s and the attack on antitrust more recently, antitrust policy has a history of both academic and political support. The current takeover activity involving such well-known partners (willing and unwilling) as American Express and Shearson Loeb Rhoades, Prudential and Bache, Nabisco and Standard Brands, Sohio and Kennecott, DuPont and Conoco, and Bendix, Martin Marietta, United Technologies, and Allied Corp. has attracted attention and concern. In response to mergers such as these, Congressman Peter Rodino (D–N.J.) called in 1981 for congressional hearings on antitrust policy; antitrust policy has also attracted other political interest in recent years. The conglomerate-merger frenzy in the 1960s resulted in the establishment of a task force under the Johnson administration.

The task force proposed (the Neal Report, 1968) a Concentrated Industries Act under which the leading firms in some concentrated industries would be reorganized (broken up). The late Senator Philip Hart (D-Mich.) introduced the Industrial Reorganization Act in 1972 and again in 1973, which would require the reorganization of firms in industries exhibiting little or no competition. William S. Comanor, while director of the Bureau of Economics at the FTC, indicated in 1980 that he supported a proposal to deal with conglomerate mergers by restraining the external growth of very large firms. A previous director of the Bureau of Economics at the FTC, F.M. Scherer, presented testimony before Congress supporting a program of divestiture in the petroleum industry.

In addition, revitalizing the antitrust laws has had considerable academic support during the past decade. Willard F. Mueller, one of the leading academic experts on mergers in the country and the director of the Bureau of Economics at the FTC during the 1960s, called for new antitrust laws in congressional testimony, speeches, and academic papers. The late John Blair, who spent most of his career as an economist studying the structure of U.S. industries, supported a major reorganization of concentrated industries and a stringent antimerger policy. The late Corwin Edwards, who called widespread attention in the profession to the adverse effects of large conglomerate firms in a 1955 article, supported various proposals to curb merger activity and to reorganize concentrated industries.

Among younger economists, Dennis C. Mueller stands out because of the significant theoretical and empirical research he has conducted on conglomerate mergers. Mueller has proposed a "new, tough antimerger law."[1] Alfred Kahn, the Cornell University professor who led the drive for airline deregulation as chairman of the Civil Aeronautics Board in the Carter administration, has called for a more stringent policy toward mergers. Many other scholars support much stronger antitrust laws for mergers. The takeover mania of the early 1980s has even raised doubts among some of the deal makers. Both Felix Rohatyn, one of Wall Street's leading merger makers, and Arthur Burck, merger consultant, have recently questioned the desirability of the current wave of takeovers.

Although a vigorous antitrust policy toward conglomerate mergers has a good deal of support, others oppose such a policy. For example, William Baxter, President Reagan's appointee as the Attorney General for Antitrust at the Justice Department, thinks the antitrust laws often inhibit efficiency by preventing companies from doing what they would like to do. In order to reduce the inhibiting features of our antitrust laws, Baxter intends to enter ongoing private antitrust cases (those brought by one company against another, which accounted for 97 percent of the civil antitrust suits filed in 1980) on the side of the defendants; throw out the Justice Department merger guidelines and replace them with new guidelines that will give far more latitude to acquisition makers; and give a sweeping go-ahead to vertical and conglomerate mergers.[2]

The new merger guidelines were issued in mid 1982. Mr. Baxter's view of U.S. industry is summed up in a *Wall Street Journal* article: "He believes big businesses are 'very valuable things' because they tend to be the most efficient."[3]

A string of recent court decisions appears to reflect recent disenchantment with the antitrust laws. One indicator of the changing attitude is provided by the Federal Trade Commission. The commission dismissed its staff's attempt to reverse DuPont Co.'s rapid extension of capacity to produce titanium dioxide—a strategy that might lead to monopoly in that product. One article reported that, "Explaining the unanimous decision, Commissioner David A. Clanton wrote that 'the essence of the competitive process is to induce firms to become more efficient and to pass the benefits of the efficiency along to consumers. That process would be ill-served by using antitrust to block hard, aggressive competition that is solidly based on efficiencies and growth opportunities even if monopoly is a possible result.'"[4]

Some economists who believe that antitrust policy is important also believe that significant changes are needed to streamline the application and reduce the cost of administering these laws. F.M. Scherer and H.M. Mann, both of whom headed the Bureau of Economics at the Federal Trade Commission during the 1970s, have called for changes. This viewpoint is given impetus by extremely costly antitrust proceedings such as those against IBM and AT&T. In January 1982, the Justice Department ended its suit against AT&T with an out-of-court settlement requiring the company to spin-off twenty-two local operating companies and allowing it to maintain its long-distance services as well as enter data processing and communications for the first time. This case lasted for seven years, cost the company an estimated $360 million, and cost the government $15 million. On the same day the government settled with AT&T, the Justice Department dropped its suit against IBM. The department's effort to break up IBM had lasted thirteen years. After the actual trial began in 1975, over 66 million pages of documents were filed in connection with the government's case and the dozen or more antitrust actions brought by private companies in the wake of the government's case. This and other antitrust actions do suggest the need for streamlining the process and they provide a rallying point for opponents of the antitrust laws.

Opponents of an antitrust policy directed at conglomerate mergers argue that large firm size and mergers lead to economic efficiency and that competition in an industry is not related to the number of firms. The evidence from research does not support this view, as shown in chapter 14. Instead, views such as this are often supported by the assumptions and beliefs emanating from the University of Chicago school of economics. In essence, those of the Chicago-school persuasion hold that all business decisions are profit motivated. Thus, any business behavior, including mergers, is assumed to result in efficiency or monopoly. If monopoly and monopoly profits are not the likely results of a particular business action, then efficiency must be—in which case, mergers should not be questioned or subjected to government interference.

I have shown that business executives are very likely motivated by power at least as much as by profits. Further, a great deal of research evidence shows no indication of efficiency gains from conglomerate or agglomerate mergers. This suggests either that continuing to hang on to the strict assumption of profit maximization is foolish, or that business executives generally make poor decisions. I believe that the latter explanation is false. However, it must surely be difficult to let go of the profit-maximization assumption because it provides a practically ironclad microeconomic model in terms of its logic. Unfortunately, the theory may often be irrelevant. Ironically, application of this theory that holds free enterprise and laissez-faire capitalism as an idol will support the march into monolithic capitalism. In our society with its philosophical disposition, the trend toward monolithic capitalism will call forth direct and pervasive government intervention in the marketplace.

Existing antitrust laws are designed primarily to constrain mergers and other business behaviors aimed at increasing profits by way of monopoly. Once it is recognized that the desire for personal power is a primary motivator of businessmen, the large body of evidence showing that mergers generally do not result in higher efficiency begins to make sense—many of the mergers are primarily motivated by neither efficiency nor profits. Consequently, antitrust legislation that would sharply curtail merger activity would neither stifle invention and innovation nor reduce economic efficiency. The opposite would more likely be true. To preserve competitive capitalism and the pluralistic sociopolitical system that is consistent with it, the power drive of businessmen must be constrained. I propose constraints along the following lines:

A.   No company, regardless of size, would be allowed to acquire or merge with more than one other company during a single calendar year.

B.   No company, regardless of size, that is among the top quarter of the number of firms in an industry or accounts for 20 percent or more of industry sales would be allowed to acquire a firm that is among the top quarter of the number of firms in another industry or accounts for 20 percent or more of its industry's sales. (For example, a top maker of hair tonic could not acquire a top maker of toothpaste.)

Point A is the essential feature of this proposal. Point B is intended to prevent firms that occupy leading positions in one industry from expanding into another industry by acquiring one of the leading positions. Several studies, including one of my own, suggest that industry leaders enjoy extra profits from a form of monopoly that I call *inherent product differentiation*. Industry leaders earn higher profits because their product is perceived to be better and because of the name recognition that accrues to industry leaders. Businessmen themselves apparently believe in the benefits associated with being top in an industry.

This is suggested by statements of businessmen, frequently found in business periodicals, that they plan to expand into some industry but only if they can acquire a leading market share. The purpose of point B is to nurture the erosion of whatever monopoly power exists in an industry. Allowing a firm that is already among the leaders in one industry to enter another industry only by acquiring a nonleader holds out the prospect that the new entrant will erode the position of the industry leaders. This might create a more competitive industry. At least this way, the new entrant would have to prove itself and earn its way to the top.

The benefits of implementing this antitrust proposal, or a similar one, are numerous. Essentially, implementation would be a major step toward eliminating or reducing many of the problems of competitive capitalism. The imagination, creativity, and energy of U.S. business executives could focus on business operations, rather than on short-run gains from financial deals. Mergers would no longer be the overriding concern of corporate executives. This would almost certainly increase productivity in U.S. industry and would probably stimulate technological progress, both of which would provide long-run benefits to all. Such a policy would stem the tide of compulsive diversification which has no apparent public benefits but appears to have important costs. Whatever mergers and acquisitions are made under this policy would be made carefully and thoughtfully. Mergers would more likely yield real economic benefits. Finally, and most fundamental of all, this policy would help to maintain sufficient dispersion of control over economic resources so that any call for central economic planning and controls would probably be a weak one. The key to achieving these benefits is that the drive for power by businessmen be constrained. My proposal provides a method for constraint.

This proposal for a new antitrust law has several attractive features. First, I believe it would effectively solve many of the problems outlined earlier. Second, the proposal is realistic and feasible because it neither focuses on large firm size in itself nor requires divestiture. Third, it is simple, so that the government's cost of administration would be very low, and the direct cost of compliance by business would be nonexistent. Finally, the proposal is anticipatory and preventive in nature, thereby avoiding the tremendous cost to society of permitting the unconstrained drive for power to carry us into monolithic capitalism and afterwards trying to readjust the system.

Even though the policy I recommend does not require dissolution, it does interfere with the right to purchase and sell private property. The concept of private property is highly complex in philosophy and law. I cannot even attempt to deal with the subject in detail here. However, a brief justification is needed for a policy which will infringe on private property rights. The justification is based simply on legal precedent.

When, as a society, we have determined that the sale or use of one person's private property demonstrably harms others, we have restricted the use of that private property. The ban on the use of firearms in most communities is one example. More directly relevant are laws that ban the sale or purchase of private property, such as laws prohibiting the sale of alcoholic beverages and tobacco to minors; drugs such as heroin, cocaine, and marijuana; pornographic literature; fireworks; and one company to another if the two are significant competitors (horizontal mergers). The key to such infringement on our right as private citizens to purchase and sell property is that the costs to society are greater than the benefits to individuals, including the benefit of freedom.

To infringe on the use of private property, including its purchase and sale, is not novel. Nevertheless, in a free society any infringement on private property must be done with great care and sensitivity. It must be done only when we believe that the cost to society of one's free use of their property is greater than the cost of infringing on our freedom. Uninhibited merger activity is now more costly to society than the restriction I have proposed. Agglomerate and conglomerate mergers provide few, if any apparent economic benefits. The costs, however, are numerous and significant.

I believe that proposals for new antitrust laws have failed to obtain support because they center on a program of divestiture or dissolution—a blatant attack on existing private property. Such a policy may be justifiable on grounds of economic theory and evidence. However, because the institution of private property in this country is fundamental, the burden of proof to support such a policy is so great that such a policy is probably not generally feasible.

My choice of excluding divestiture as an element in a new antitrust law is not simply bowing to expediency. Dissolution may not even be necessary to preserve and invigorate competitive capitalism and to assure the dispersion of control over economic resources. Existing antitrust laws would constrain anticompetitive profit-motivated behavior, and my proposal would constrain the power drive.

My position rests on the observation that overall (aggregate) economic concentration in banking and the nonfinancial sector of the economy has risen only slightly over the last twenty years. That overall concentration has not risen much recently is quite remarkable in view of the tremendous number of mergers that have taken place in this country over the past twenty years. This is remarkable because mergers contribute to increasing aggregate concentration. It is apparent that dynamic forces are at work in the system. So far, they have offset the concentrating effect of conglomerate mergers. Schumpeter maintained that there is a "perennial gale of creative destruction," by which the positions of leading firms are continually eroded as new technology and new firms emerge to take their place.[5] Some form of this "gale of creative destruction" is at work. Its most pronounced effect seems to be in the development of new technology around which entire new industries develop. The new firms help to keep economic power reasonably dispersed. The role of this creative destruction where Schumpeter expected it—in eroding monopoly positions within existing industries—is less apparent, however.

The premise that sharply curtailed merger activity would help maintain the dispersion of economic power, or control over economic resources, is not idle speculation. This idea has empirical support. For example, a study of mergers and concentration in the United States by J.J. McGowan and another study by L. Hannah and J.A. Kay in the United Kingdom indicate that overall economic concentration would actually fall in the absence of mergers.[6]

In any event, it would be a mistake to assume that this balance, with mergers increasing concentration and other forces decreasing concentration, can be counted on as mergers reach ever higher levels like those we are witnessing today. If the U.S. economy should go through periods of technological stagnation or move into a less dynamic stage, as some believe it is doing now, the inherent tendency producing the dispersion of economic power will not be sufficient to offset the inherent tendency of business to increase power through mergers. A policy designed to constrain the power drive of businessmen should lead to a general dispersion of power gradually and may lead to the erosion of positions of monopoly power in individual industries. Because this sort of policy would not require such a direct assault on private property as in dissolution, the policy is considerably more feasible.

Opposing the sort of antitrust law proposed here would be short-sighted on the part of U.S. business. Opposition will, over the long run, set the stage and provide the ammunition for proponents of government planning and controls in the economy. Remember that the antitrust laws are a unique and unobtrusive form of regulation. These laws do not dictate what business should produce, how it should produce, where it should sell its product, what price it should charge, or what profit it should make. The antitrust laws establish the rules of business activity and the antitrust agencies serve as referees, not participants. Within the boundaries of these rules, business can pursue its objectives, be they power or profits, aggresively and without interference. The same cannot be said of a system that relies on government planning and controls. To turn economic planning and controls over to government bureaucrats, no matter how noble the objective in the beginning, would be to create a powerful, self-perpetuating governmental apparatus that would at some point directly impinge on basic business decisions and ultimately on our individual freedom. The desire for power would assure such an outcome.

The key role of power was noted by Oliver Wendell Holmes, Jr., who observed, "The only prize cared for by the powerful is power. The prize of the general is not a bigger tent, but command."[7] The implications of such power vested in government were suggested by James Madison, "I believe there are many more instances of the abridgement of the freedom of the people by gradual and silent encroachments of those in power than by violent and sudden usurpations."[8] A similar warning was issued by Justice Louis Brandeis in *Olmstead v. United States* (1928):

> Experience should teach us to be most on our guard to protect liberty when the Government's purposes are beneficient. Men born to freedom are naturally alert to repel invasion of their liberty by evil-minded rulers. The greatest dangers to liberty lurk in insidious encroachment by men of zeal, well-meaning but without understanding.

One very practical implication of government involvement in the marketplace has been voiced by Ralph Nader. This leading critic of the automobile industry once remarked, "If there is one thing worse than GM producing cars, it would be the U.S. government producing them."

Thus, a seemingly perverse position for U.S. business—support for new antitrust laws—would, over the long run, serve the best interest of business and of society at large. Given the alternative, the choice is clear. Constrain the drive for power in business now, and preserve competitive capitalism and a free society over the long run.

Notes

1. Dennis C. Mueller, "Do We Want a New, Tough Antimerger Law?", *Antitrust Bulletin* (Winter 1979), pp. 807-36.

2. *Business Week* (June 8, 1981).

3. *Wall Street Journal* (July 8, 1981).

4. *Business Week* (December 15, 1980), p. 58.

5. Joseph A. Schumpeter, *Capitalism, Socialism and Democracy,* 3rd ed. (New York: Harper and Row, 1950), p. 97.

6. J.J. McGowan, "The Effect of Alternative Antimerger Policies on the Size Distribution of Firms," *Yale Economic Essays* (Fall 1965), pp. 465-71, and L. Hanna and J.A. Kay, *Concentration in Modern Industry* (London: Macmillan, 1977).

7. Oliver Wendell Holmes, Jr., *Law and the Court* (1913).

8. James Madison in a speech at the Virginia Convention (June 1788).

17 Conclusion

This book has warned of the serious long-run implications of corporate mergers for both the economic and sociopolitical systems. It was emphasized that the profound effects of mergers become apparent only over long periods of time. As a consequence, mergers and antitrust policy arouse little popular concern and rarely make headlines. It is thus ironic that as this book was being written, the highest level of merger activity in the nation's history took place. Mergers and antitrust policy made headlines during 1981 and 1982. Anyone who read the newspapers or general magazines watched corporate-takeover dramas, such as DuPont and Conoco, or Bendix, Martin-Marietta, United Technologies and Allied Corp., unfold. The Justice Department, which is responsible for enforcing antitrust policy, was in the news because of its concerted effort to soften antitrust enforcement toward mergers under President Reagan's administration. Formal announcements from the Justice Department indicated that mergers which previously would have been challenged by the department would henceforth be ignored. Justice Department suits against AT&T and IBM were dropped in January 1982.

The traditional explanation by economists for mergers, as with all business behavior, is that they are motivated by expected profits. However, the evidence on conglomerate and agglomerate mergers provides no indication whatsoever that these mergers yield the increased efficiency and thus profits that proponents of uninhibited merger activity would have us believe. I have proposed that a more plausible explanation is that mergers are a manifestation of the desire for power and empire building by U.S. business executives.

The desire for power by individuals is strong and pervasive. Power has been a major theme in the works of many great philosophers for over two thousand years. Further, a major school of psychology stemming from Alfred Adler is founded on the notion that the drive for power is the basic motivating force in individuals. The power motive underlying corporate mergers has for years been hidden behind the assumption of profit maximization and much unsupported rhetoric about the efficiency achieved from mergers. I believe, however, that the merger wave of the late 1970s and early 1980s points convincingly to the role of power as a cause of mergers. Surely the evidence is clear about one thing—conglomerate and agglomerate mergers in this country since 1960 have in general provided no gains in economic efficiency.

The desire for power provides a strong impetus for mergers. In recent years, the penchant for mergers has been complemented by the business community's preoccupation with short-term financial results. Mergers are made to order for this purpose. For example, the stock price and earnings per share of a company can be greatly influenced by merger or even a merger announcement. Unfortunately, the practical results of uninhibited merger activity and the preoccupation with short-term financial results are costing this country dearly. Many large conglomerates and agglomerates have difficulty in allocating resources among their various operations simply because of the practical problem of determining just exactly which operations are most profitable. This does not bode well for the economy's ability to allocate scarce resources efficiently. Thousands of efficient, well-managed, and innovative companies disappear annually. Many of the large acquiring companies are illogical and inefficient rather than systematically integrated businesses. The result is that often within a few years the acquired companies are sold off after the acquiring company has proven incapable of operating them effectively. The original management and key employees frequently depart and profits and efficiency deteriorate under the control of the conglomerate. Because of the preeminent role of short-term financial considerations, more and more large corporations are headed by finance experts and lawyers rather than operations people. Therefore, fundamental long-run business considerations such as operational efficiency and research and development receive little attention—a fact noted by foreign businesses in explaining the inability of many U.S. corporations to compete with their foreign counterparts.

The U.S. economy is undergoing fundamental changes as the desire for power by business executives is played out through mergers. The economy will move inexorably from its present state of competitive capitalism into monolithic capitalism—a system dominated by very large conglomerate and agglomerate corporations and operated by a bureaucratized work force. Resources will be allocated by cumbersome, bureaucratic institutions that may bear an unfortunate similarity to the caricature of inefficiency in government. The change is slow, but this makes its consequences no less significant. It simply makes it more difficult to recognize and to inspire remedial public policy.

Some observers have contended that the requirements of modern technology, so-called technological imperatives, necessitate the replacement of many smaller companies with corporate giants. According to this line of argument, only the corporate giants with few, if any, competitors can conduct the research and development, and provide the innovation to assure that our economy remains technologically progressive. Proponents of this view recognize that an increase in the concentration of private economic power will require a means of holding this power in check. That role would fall upon our federal government. It would require increased government oversight and control of business activity. Such a scenario is not inevitable in order for the United States to remain technologically progressive because the technological imperatives argument is wrong. It does not accord with the facts. Indeed, the evidence suggests just the opposite. Smaller and medium-size firms provide the best environment for research and development. This is most fortunate because otherwise we would be facing a very difficult trade-off—to assure technological progress we would have to sacrifice competitive capitalism and freedom.

The basic institutions in our society are interdependent—a fact conveniently ignored by those who favor monolithic capitalism with attendant government controls and planning. The institutions in our society help shape and are in turn shaped themselves by the cultural values and philosophical disposition of the people. In this country, the social disposition includes a strong aversion to concentration of power in any of our institutions—in the government, military, business, and education. It also includes a strong belief in freedom and individualism. Presently, the structure of our basic institutions reflects this philosophy and at the same time these institutions support and nurture the philosophy. If we permit our economic system to undergo fundamental changes away from competitive capitalism toward monolithic capitalism and cope with this change by vesting more power over private business decisions in the federal government, then we will be embarking on a course of profound change in our entire sociopolitical system. Since there is no substance to the view that our economic system must evolve into monolithic capitalism to assure technological progress, we do not have to accept fundamental changes in our economic system as inevitable.

In order to avoid sweeping change in the U.S. economic and sociopolitical systems, direct action must be taken. If nothing is done, the country will continue its drift into monolithic capitalism, followed by increased government controls and planning. To avert this from happening, it is essential to check the drive for power by businesspeople so far as it is manifested in mergers. Proposing a policy to check business behavior is surely not radical. When, in the late nineteenth and early twentieth centuries, the desire for profits by businessmen resulted in a massive merger movement aimed at monopolizing many basic industries, the drive for monopoly profits was checked by congressional passage of several antitrust laws. Today, the desire for power is responsible for mergers (largely beyond the scope of the antitrust laws) that will have highly adverse effects on the economic and sociopolitical systems. Therefore, I propose that the drive for power through mergers be checked in the same manner that the drive for monopoly profits through mergers was checked earlier. A new antitrust law that would drastically curtail merger activity should be passed. The law proposed in this book does not call for breaking up existing corporations. I do not believe that will be necessary to halt the drift into monolithic capitalism.

Businesspeople are usually staunch opponents of the antitrust laws and certainly any new law that would restrict their activity. However, opposition to the sort of law proposed here would be a short-sighted strategy and a tragic mistake. If something is not done to stem mergers in this country and get the attention of businessmen back on business, we may all pay a very high price in the future.

Index

Adams, Walter, 125
Adler, Alfred, 54–56, 151; on conscious, ego, and desire for power, 54–55; on constraint of power, 55–56; and individual psychology, 54; on power drive in adults, 55; on power drive in children, 55; on power drive in infancy, 55
Agglomerate: definition of, 82. *See also* Conglomerate mergers
Aggregate concentration: effect of mergers on, 62
American Tobacco Co., 70–71, 76
Antitrust laws: Clayton Act, 75, 76–78; critics of, 122–123, 144–145; Federal Trade Commission Act, 75, 77; origin of, 75–76, 153; purpose of, 77–78; and private property, 147–148; proposal for new, 3, 146–147, 153; Sherman Act, 75–78; success of, 78, 129; support for new, 143–144; weakness of, 78–79. *See also* Antitrust policy
Antitrust policy, 151; as constraint on profit drive, 16–17, 59; and failure to constrain power drive, 17; intent of, 16; and power motive, 3; and profit motive, 3; weak enforcement of, 16. *See also* Antitrust laws
Automobile industry: development of, 23, 67–69

Bacon, Francis: on power, 47
Banking: conglomerate mergers in, 96–97
Baumol, William J., 40
Beard, Charles, 139–140. *See also* Sociopolitical system
Berle, Adolph, 35, 51, 122
Blaugh, Mark, 33
Brandeis, Justice Louis: on government and freedom, 150
Buchwald, Art: on conglomerate mergers, 92–93

Burck, Arthur, 95–96, 115, 117, 144
Burke, James, 96
Burns, Arthur, 7

Capitalism: resource allocation under, 11
Central planning, 124–125, 130, 153; implications of, 149
Clark, J.M., 98
Collusion. *See* OPEC; Electrical conspiracy
Competitive capitalism, 1, 3–4, 37, 97; euthanasia of, 9
Conglomerate firms: mergers by, 82–87; questions about, 91–93; research on, 93–97
Conglomerate mergers: and Art Buchwald, 92–93; in banking, 96–97; costs of, 97–101, 108–118, 152; definition of, 2; desire for power and result of, 2–3, 81–82; examples of, 82–87; and impotence of antitrust laws, 78–79; motives for, 90, 151; and private property, 147–148; and profit maximization, 2, 59, 81–82; research on, 95–97; and Rube Goldberg, 87–88; speculative results of, 90–91; and synergy, 89; trends in, 81
Curry, Timothy, 96

Durant, Ariel, 140. *See also* Sociopolitical system
Durant, Will, 140. *See also* Sociopolitical system

Edwards, Corwin, 99
Electrical conspiracy, 24–26, 129

Federal government: and similarities with private conglomerates, 85, 88, 152
Federal Reserve Board, 5, 7–8
Federal Trade Commission, 5, 77

Ford, Henry, 23, 67–68
Freud, Sigmund, 53–54; on id, ego,
    superego, and sex, 53–54; and
    psychoanalysis, 53
Friedman, Milton, 7

Galbraith, John Kenneth, 3, 121–126,
    130, 143; on antitrust laws, 122–
    123, 125; and countervailing
    power, 123; and economic power,
    121; on education, 136; and mar-
    ket competition, 121
Galton, Francis, 53
General Motors, 67–68
Goldberg, Rube, 87–88
Gordon, Robert, 36, 40
Greer, Douglas, 128

Hannah, L., 149
Heilbroner, Robert, 124, 137
Hierarchical theory of motivation, 56.
    See also Maslow, Abraham
Holmes, Oliver Wendell, Jr.: on power,
    149
Horizontal mergers, 81, 129; defini-
    tion of, 2, 62; effect of, 62–63;
    examples and costs of, 62–71; and
    profit maximization, 2, 82
Humphrey, Hubert, 124

Individual psychology, 54. See also
    Adler, Alfred
Inferiority complex, 54. See also
    Adler, Alfred; Overcompensation

Justice Department, 5, 76–77, 151;
    and electrical conspiracy, 25

Kahn, Alfred, 108
Kamien, Morton, 126–127
Kant, Immanuel: on power, 48
Katona, George, 29, 41; on business
    motives and power, 58
Kay, J.A., 149
Keynes, John Maynard, 6–7, 39; on
    decline of profit rates, 32–33

Kindleberger, Charles, 137. See also
    Sociopolitical system

Labor: monopoly power of, 8, 68–69
Larner, Robert, 35, 122
Leibenstein, Harvey, 40
Lekachman, Robert, 124
Leontief, Wassily, 125
Lewellen, Wilbur, 36
Lodge, George, 124

McClelland, David C.: on power, 57;
    on psychological motivation of
    businessmen, 57; on psychological
    motivation in economic develop-
    ment, 57
McGowan, J.J., 149
Machiavelli, Niccolo: on power,
    46–47
Macroeconomics, 1; influence of
    Keynes on, 6–7; problems and
    issues of, 5; in public policy, 8; in
    undergraduate education, 5
Madison, James: on government and
    freedom, 149–150
Marx, Karl: on decline of profit rates,
    31–32
Maslow, Abraham, 56–57; on Adler,
    57; hierarchical theory of motiva-
    tion of, 56
Means, Gardiner, 35, 51, 122
Meeks, G., 95
Mergers: dollar volume and number of,
    61, 151; costs of, 103, 107–118;
    effect of, 61; and effect on aggre-
    gate concentration, 62; fallacious
    arguments for, 71–72; in 1981,
    103; and private property, 147–
    148; recent examples of, 104–107;
    trends in, 81; by twenty largest
    banks and industrials, 61. See also
    Conglomerate mergers; Horizontal
    mergers
Microeconomics, 1, 11; definition of,
    12; implications from neglect of,
    8–9; macroeconomic effects of, 8;

neglect of, 5–6; origins of, 12; problems and issues of, 5–6; in undergraduate education, 5

Mitchell, Wesley C., 41; on human nature in economics, 41

Monetarism, 7–8

Monolithic capitalism: definition of, 1–3, 152; and economic performance, 9; Galbraith on, 9; implications of, 4, 9; and mergers, 2–3; and power motive, 3; and profit maximization, 146; sociopolitical effects of, 130, 133–141, 153

Monopoly: problems of, 14–16

Moody, John, 71

Mueller, Dennis C., 95, 144

Mueller, Willard, 125, 144

Musgrave, Richard, 134

Nader, Ralph, 124, 150

Nelson, Ralph, 71

Nietzsche, Friedrich: on power, 49

OPEC, 34, 62, 69; collusive behavior of, 15

Overcompensation, 54. See also Adler, Alfred; Inferiority complex

Parsons, Talcott, 138–139. See also Sociopolitical system

Pearce, Neal, 117

Petroleum industry: development of, 22, 65–67

Philosophy: power motive in, 45–51

Piper, Thomas, 96

Plato: on power, 46

Power motive: as alternative to profits, 39, 42; and antitrust policy, 17; and conglomerate mergers, 2, 59, 78–79, 151–152; constraint of, 56, 146–147, 153; costs of, 103, 108–118; definition of, 2; and government service, 42; implications of, 9; neglect of in economics, 39–40; in philosophy, 45–51; in psychology, 53–59; as revealed

by unfriendly takeovers, 103–118; sociopolitical effects of, 133–141

Profit motive, 1–2, 59, 62, 151; and antitrust policy, 17; benefits of, 19–24; and conglomerate mergers, 82, 101, 146; as convenient assumption, 39, 81–82; costs of, 24–26; 61–71; decline of, 29–37; effect of affluence on, 29–30; effect of manager control on, 35–36; as incentive to collude, 14–16; long-term decline of, 30–34; in microeconomics, 13, 19; operational convenience of, 58–59; no proof of, 59

Psychoanalysis, 53. See also Freud, Sigmund

Psychology: power motive in, 53–107; problems of research in, 59

Rhoades, Stephen A., 62

Ricardo, David: on decline of profit rates, 31

Rockefeller, John D., 66

Roosevelt, Franklin D., 134

Russell, Bertrand: on power, 2, 49–51, 56

Scale economies, 128

Scherer, F.M., 127–128, 144–145

Schopenhauer, Arthur: on power, 48–49

Schumpeter, Joseph, 148–149; on power, 41; on sociopolitical system, 138

Schwartz, Nancy, 126–127

Shapiro, Irving S., 134

Smelser, Neil, 138–139. See also Sociopolitical system

Smith, Adam, 12–13; on benefits of competition, 13–14; on decline of profit rates, 31; on division of labor, 20–21; on oligopoly, 14–15; on problems of monopoly, 14

Socialism: resource allocation under, 11–12

Sociopolitical system: and inter-
    dependence with economic system,
    133–141, 153; and monolithic
    capitalism, 141, 153
Sophists: on power, 45
Spin-offs, 109–110, 112–114
Spinoza, Baruch: on power, 47–
    48
Standard Oil, 66–67, 76
Steel industry: development of, 22–
    23, 63–65
Steiner, Peter O., 94–95
Synergy, 89–93, 95, 97; definition
    of, 81

Takeovers: costs of, 103, 108–118;
    examples of, 104–107
Technological imperatives, 3, 122,

    125–126, 128, 143, 152; evidence
    on, 125–128. *See also* Galbraith,
    John Kenneth
Tinbergen, Jan, 137. *See also* Socio-
    political system
Tobacco industry: development of,
    21, 69–71
Trusts: extent of, 71
Turner, Donald, 126

U.S. Steel Corp., 63–65

Volcker, Paul, 8

Wallich, Henry, 133
Weiss, Leonard, 62
Williamson, Oliver, 40
Wundt, Wilhem, 53

About the Author

Stephen A. Rhoades received the B.A. and M.A. in economics from The American University and the Ph.D. from the University of Maryland in 1971. The author was a staff economist at the Federal Trade Commission from 1965 to 1971 and is now a senior economist at the Federal Reserve Board where he has worked since 1971. His research has been primarily in the areas of industrial organization, antitrust, and banking as reflected in the eighty articles he has had published in various academic and professional journals. The author has lectured on a part-time basis at the University of Maryland and does so now at The George Washington University.